THE DREAM OF MAGNUS MAXIMUS

Arthur and the Matter of Britain
BOOK ONE

THE DREAM OF MAGNUS MAXIMUS

Arthur and the Matter of Britain

BOOK ONE

NIGEL COLLETT

First published in Great Britain in 2025 by
The Book Guild Ltd
Unit E2 Airfield Business Park,
Harrison Road, Market Harborough,
Leicestershire. LE16 7UL
Tel: 0116 2792299
www.bookguild.co.uk
Email: info@bookguild.co.uk

Copyright © 2025 Nigel Collett

The right of Nigel Collett to be identified as the author of this
work has been asserted by him in accordance with the
Copyright, Design and Patents Act 1988.

All rights reserved. No part of this publication may be
reproduced, transmitted, or stored in a retrieval system, in any form or by any means,
without permission in writing from the publisher, nor be otherwise circulated in
any form of binding or cover other than that in which it is published and without
a similar condition being imposed on the subsequent purchaser.

The manufacturer's authorised representative in the EU
for product safety is Authorised Rep Compliance Ltd,
71 Lower Baggot Street, Dublin D02 P593 Ireland (www.arccompliance.com)

This work is entirely fictitious and bears no resemblance to any persons living or dead.

Typeset in 12pt Adobe Jenson Pro

Printed and bound in Great Britain by CMP UK

ISBN 978 1835743 126

British Library Cataloguing in Publication Data.
A catalogue record for this book is available from the British Library.

In memory of my mother
Moyra Ellen Collett (1923–2017)

and my father
Albert William James Collett (1922–2023)

whose love of the past prompted the writing of this book

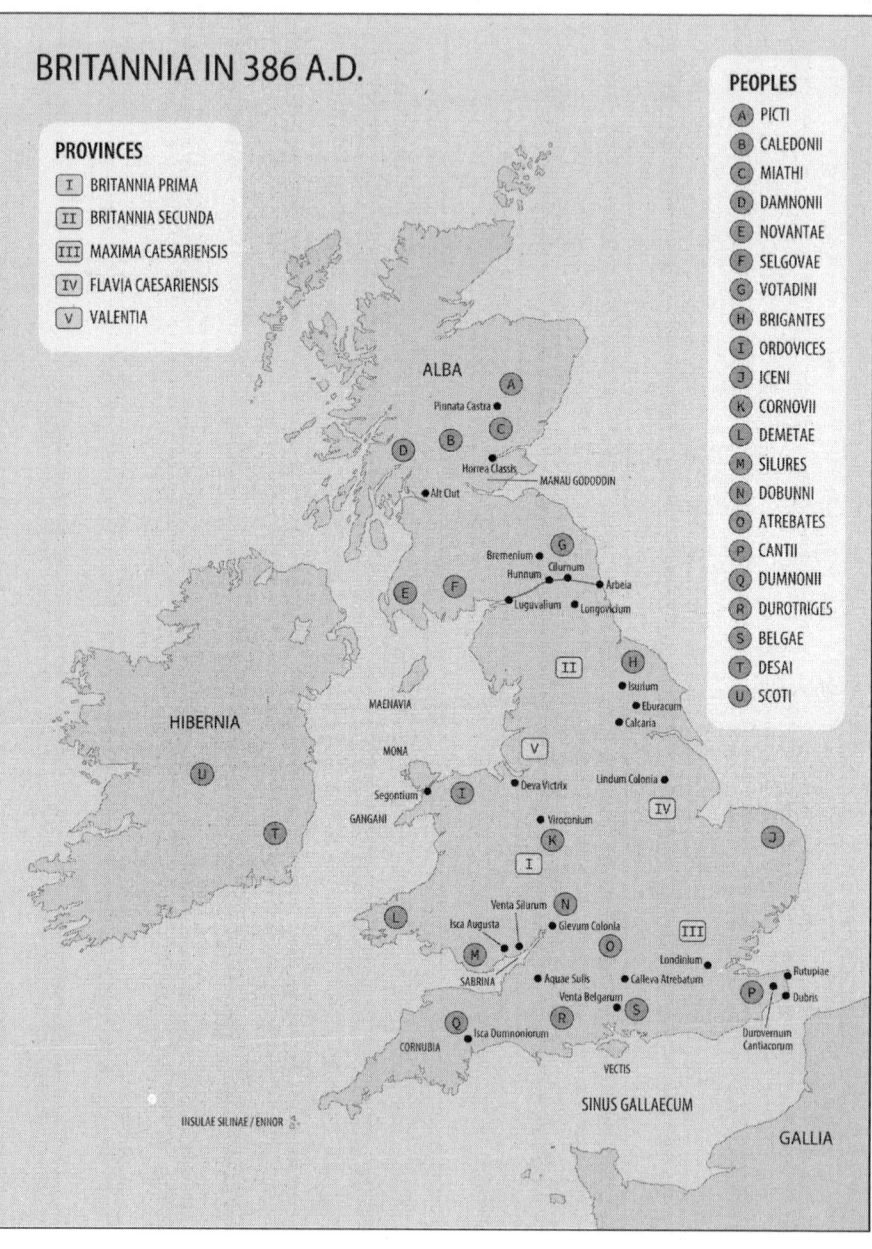

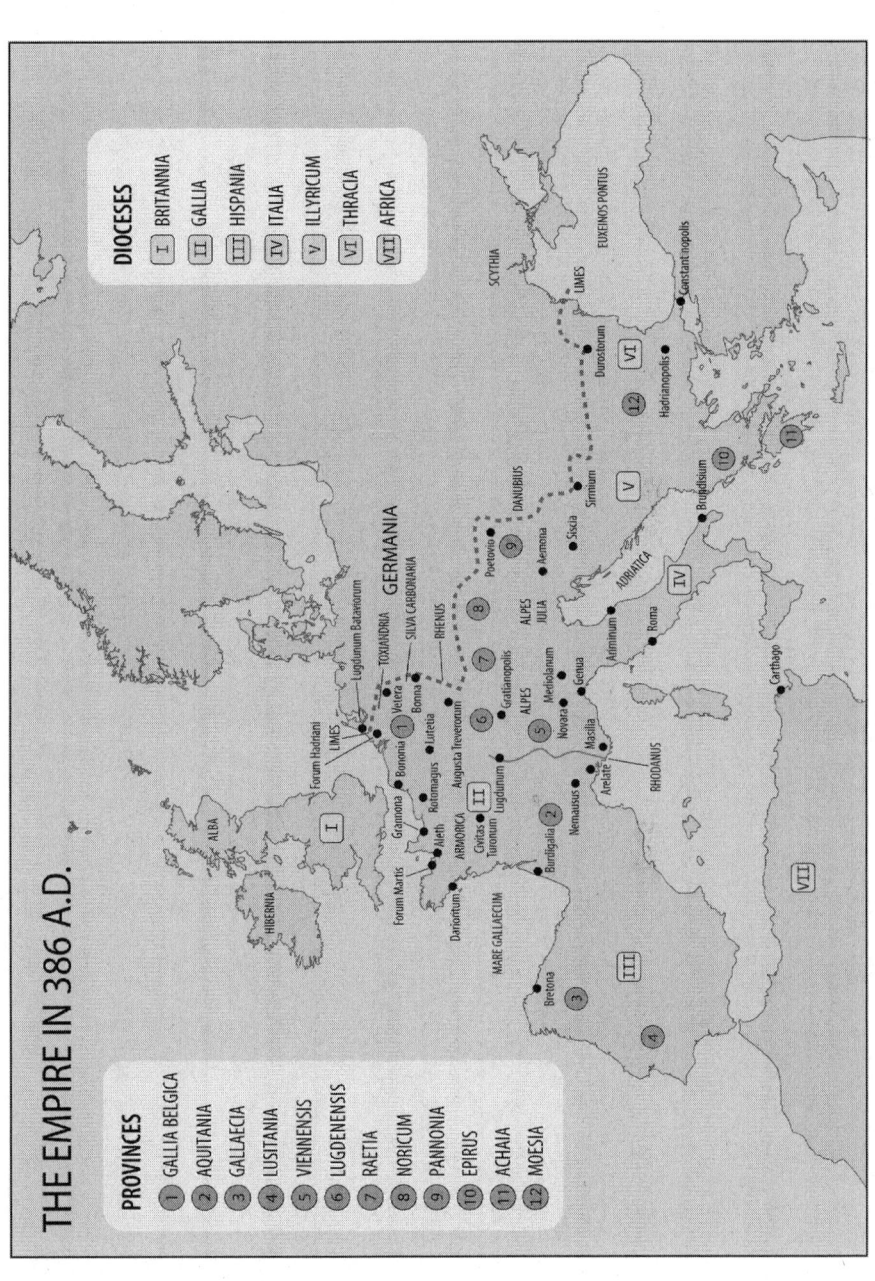

THE END AND THE BEGINNING

Arthur, leader of battles, is dead. He lies, quiet now, in his tomb at Glastonbury. His companions have long passed. Myrddin, Morgen, Cai, Bedwyr and the rest have played their part and have left the stage of this world for Avalon, or heaven, or wherever the different dreams of each have taken them.

All that was then is now lost. What was glorious has vanished into dust. Now, the story of how Arthur saved his people is nowhere remembered. His victories are neither recorded nor sung. His life's work is judged a myth, or at best a defeat.

And yet, Arthur's history still morphs and grows, the stuff of legend. The fame of his triumphs, once the glory of his nation, changes still, expanding year by year into the vastness of the Matter of Britain, where it grows brighter and more fantastical in each new iteration. Duke Arthur has long ago become King Arthur, even Emperor, and his warrior companions, knights of a table round.

Arthur's tale will never die, different for each generation though it may be. His fight for liberty and his leadership of resistance against foreign oppression inspire us still.

The Dream of Magnus Maximus

What is the real story of the man behind the legend? Who was he and what was he trying to do? Where does it begin? To answer all that, we must go back to the century before he was born and to the farthest outpost of the Roman Empire in the west, to Caernarvon, in Wales, to Segontium as it then was. The old world is fading and the new world is being born…

Chapter One

INCEPTION

The afternoon spring sun glistened on the glassy surface of the sea, reflected from waters which were so smooth that, as the oars dipped and lifted, dipped and lifted, only tiny flecks of foam marked their passage. Aft, as the small flotilla ploughed up the strait, its wake rippled out to lap the shores of the narrow channel. On the left loomed the dark mountains of mainland Britannia, on the right stretched the flat, green expanse of Mona, the Britons' sacred island of the west. It was the year of our Lord 383, although no one would have thought of it as that then, for to the Romans on board the ships it was the year of the consulships of the generals Flavius Merobaudes and Flavius Saturninus, or by their other system, 1,136 years *ab urbe condita*, from the founding of the city of Roma. What year the Britons considered it to be, the Romans had neither idea nor interest in knowing.

On the deck of the leading ship, the general Flavius Magnus Maximus stood tall and magnificent in his parade uniform. He was holding his scarlet-plumed helmet next to his gleaming breastplate while his sharp eyes watched the progress of his small fleet. Maximus was the most powerful military officer in Britannia, the *vir spectabilis dux britanniarum*, the admirable Duke of the British Provinces, commander of all the imperial forces in the north of the island. Standing beside him was the diminutive figure of his wife, Elen, the darkness of her plaited tresses visible under her bright red woollen shawl. Just behind them both stood two officers, the elder of whom was Promotus, the general's *princeps*, or chief of staff, a middle-aged soldier who now, as he always did, was wearing a concentrated and rather anxious frown. His junior colleague was Flavius Claudius Constantinus, the fresh-faced young *protector* who commanded the general's personal bodyguard, an officer upright in stance, imperturbable in expression and strong in body. All four were shaded from the bright sunshine by the small turret of the poop.

As their ship began to pass a long spit of sand that stretched out from the shore of the mainland, the *navarchus*, the squadron's commander, pointed out to his general the strip of shallows. A salt-and-sun-tanned officer with a much-scarred face, now near his retirement, he spoke with a degree of caution and exaggerated respect, for he had come to know the duke well enough on this short voyage from Deva Victrix to know his dislike of being interrupted in his thoughts. Maximus could be a boisterous and inspiring officer when in a good mood, but he was wont to visit his harsh ill temper on those around him when things were not going his way. Nevertheless, the *navarchus* knew that the duke had not been this far west in his area of command, so he had become confident in feeding him small gobbets of information as they sailed. The captain knew these seas better than most, having for many a long year patrolled them against the Scoti who sailed over from Hibernia to raid. On this occasion, Maximus took no exception to being addressed.

"It was from that piece of the mainland, admirable lord, over 300 years ago, that the governor Suetonius drove his legionaries across the water to put to the sword the rabble of prancing druids massed on the beach we are just passing. You will recall that our men had been brought up short by the spectacle of those ghastly, unkempt priests and their screaming women, all rattling their bones and imploring their gods to drown our boys in the sea. Suetonius, though, was more frightening to his men than the crones across the water, so the legion crossed, killed them all and burned their sacred groves."

"I know the story, *navarchus*," replied the duke, "but thank you for pointing out the place where Roma's gods proved once again invincible." Elen, who was British, shuddered. She could see in her mind's eye the massacre of her countrymen and she could smell the blood in the water. She looked away. She had another reason for revulsion at the memory of this massacre, for she was a newly born follower of the risen Christ, to whom the gods of both sides in that climactic struggle were anathema. Since her conversion, she had not ceased to deplore her husband's refusal to acknowledge her new faith and his insouciant adherence to the old. She was also in denial, for she had the gift, something that ran in her bloodline, but chimed not at all with her new faith. That she could see what she saw was, to her, now the work of the Devil.

Talk of Suetonius' great victory had the opposite effect on her soldier husband, who seemed buoyed up by the captain's tale. He took the scene of that successful slaughter as an auspicious start for a day in which he planned to unfold a scheme of such daring and risk that he had kept it secret even from his wife. He smiled self-contentedly.

Maximus was one of the most powerful men in Britannia, one whom it was politic not to offend and certainly sensible not to cross. He answered to no civilian official on the island, and owed respect, but not obedience, to the *vicarius*, the vicar who, in the system of administration then in place, ruled the diocese of Britannia. The duke's military superior, the *magister peditum*, the commander-in-chief in the west, was based far off in Gallia; as a result, Maximus exercised a great deal of independence in what he did. In addition, his office gave him the personal right to correspond with the emperor, whose court had, until recently, been at Augusta Treverorum in Gallia, but had now removed to Mediolanum in Italia. The troops of the other British command, the *comes litoris saxonici per Britannias*, the admirable Count of the Saxon Shore, who commanded the south and east coasts, were far fewer in number than his. Maximus governed the military area of the north, which, from the *vallum aelium*, the Wall built by the divine Hadrian, ran south as far as Deva Victrix. All of this gave him pre-eminence among the island's military officers.

The general turned to address his two subordinates. "How the army has changed," he said. "In Suetonius' day, just two legions would have had as many men as half the thirty-eight units I command, more if you count their auxiliaries." Promotus knew little of what he thought of as ancient history, so responded merely with a "Yes, my duke."

"I do not think they were better soldiers, or better led, duke," Constantine chipped in. "The army is perhaps better designed for what faces us nowadays." Constantine was a coming man, liked by the duke and clearly destined for greater things, which made him the subject of envy among the less talented. Speaking as freely as he did, he evidently irritated the senior, but duller, Promotus.

The ships rounded a bend in the channel and ahead of them on the hillside, dominating the coastline and silhouetted against the declining sun, emerged Segontium, Roma's westernmost bastion. In the clear air, they could see the sun glinting on the spear tips and armour of men on the battlements and towers of the fort. Forewarned of the coming of their commander, the garrison was awaiting them.

"There is the fort, Elen, and there we'll find your father, for those are his ships." Maximus pointed out to his wife the tops of a small forest of masts just visible behind the shoulder of land that ran down from the fort to the sea. "Your father has made good time," he added, and Elen could see that this had made her husband very happy. "Our plans begin well."

"It has been a very long time coming, this meeting, husband; we have not seen my father, or any of my family, since our wedding, and we have been halfway round the empire since then. I fear they will all have changed beyond recognition. As, my lord, have I, for I have both borne you four children and have been born again into the risen Lord."

"You are still as beautiful as the day I saw you in your father's hall in Isca," he replied, ignoring, as he usually did, her continual reminders of her newfound religion. He himself neither adhered to any faith, nor wished for one, although he had a superstitious, albeit very real, suspicion that the forces that controlled his destiny, whatever they were, were powerful and needed continual placating.

The compliment that he had given his wife was no mere flattery, for although short in height she was slender and gave no sign of the effects of all those childbirths. Her lustrous black hair, knotted in plaits around her head, was secured with gold pins in the old British style, and her deep, dark brown eyes shone like jewels when she laughed. She was still beautiful in a way that drew men's eyes, which made her husband proud of her, even if the Christian priests had softened her senses.

*

The flotilla rounded the point and entered the narrow estuary, dropping sails and then anchors alongside the motley collection of vessels tethered in the small bay. These were

British vessels from the southwest, ships that had carried a party of southerners to this out-of-the-way spot. Why he had summoned them there, none of them, nor any of Maximus' own party, as yet had any idea.

Chapter Two

THREE PRINCES OF DUMNONIA

Some of the ships the Romans saw moored in the harbour were fighting craft, as sleek as the Roman vessels that had brought the duke's party from Deva. The rest were cargo vessels, fatter in the beam, all differing in design and size, many with a ramshackle air, their canvas patched, their woodwork scarred and algae-covered, but they had made it up the west coast all the way from Dumnonia at Britannia's south-western tip and they were all clearly still very seaworthy. The men they had carried were now camped out under canvas on the open slope that was protected by a stone-built bastion which fronted the harbour.

Still on board the biggest of the warships were Elen's father, Eudaf Hen ap Caradog, Prince of the Dumnonii, and her two cousins, the brothers Conan and Gadeon ap Geraint. As Maximus' ship rounded the promontory, the brothers were already at the prow of their uncle's ship, eagerly watching for the arrival of the Romans. Of the two princes, Conan was the taller, nearly six feet in height and broad in the shoulder. Amongst his people he was considered a giant. His flaming ginger hair fell in locks and ringlets halfway down his thickly muscled back, and his arms were tattooed with circles and swirls of blue that set off the gold torcs twisted at his neck and wrists. He was a man impossible to miss or, once seen, to ignore. In his early forties now, he was in the prime of his powers. He had a good-humoured smile that was framed by his extravagant moustaches and gave a hint that here was a man who was happy with his lot in life. He had good reason to be: his open, sunny and uncomplicated way of dealing with everyone made him a prince almost universally admired and liked by his people. The Dumnonii were proud of the fact that he was a warrior renowned all along the western seaboard and a slaver feared by the Scoti, whom he and his men harried all along the coasts of Hibernia. When his uncle Dunaut, Prince of the Cornovii, had died some years back, Eudaf Hen had appointed Conan to rule the people of the island's farthest south-west tip in his stead. So, Conan was rich, a well-regarded, semi-independent ruler. He was happiest, though, not when ruling his lands, but when at sea, fighting his enemies.

Conan's brother, Gadeon, was so different in appearance and bearing that people who gossiped often doubted their common ancestry. The older of the two by a couple of years, he was darker, smaller and lither in build. Despite the fact that his was not the body of a warrior, his sharp, intelligent face and piercing eyes intimidated almost all he met. Since his childhood, he had known this and had used it to get his way. He had come to rely on his brain to make up for any deficiencies in his physique. Although he could never rival Conan as a warrior, his swift intellect always outfoxed his brother, as it did everyone else. Inevitably, he had found that this trait made him a prince unloved by the world, although one feared and respected, something with which he was content to live. He was also a man who carried a grudge and was most certainly not a man to be gainsaid or to upset without cause. He was his uncle's heir.

As the Roman ships dropped anchor, Conan called to his men on the shore to get ready, then sent for his uncle. The old man had been sleeping in the stern and joined them now at the prow. Prince Eudaf was small, wizened and showing his age. He hobbled from the arthritis that plagued his hips, and the damp at sea had made the passage this far up the coast a painful one. He was, however, inured to the pain, having spent a good deal of his life on the water. As was his custom, he was so ill-dressed that he could have passed for the lowliest of his subjects. It was almost as if he were trying to cover up the fact that he was rich, for so he was, as he and his people made a very good living from slaving and trade. His tribe was not at all fooled by his parsimony. He was congenitally mean and a rather sour old man (hence his nickname, *hen*), now at sixty-three years old more than ever ungenerous in the giving of gifts. He was respected due to his canny ability to lead his people to prosper but he was not much liked by many of them.

It was typical of Eudaf that he had never stopped lamenting the expense he had been put to for his daughter's wedding that had taken place over a decade before. In what he had come to feel was a moment of madness, he had spent a lot of money to provide a fit place for the ceremony, bringing in craftsmen from Venta Belgarum and Corinium to restore the ancient basilica of his capital, Isca Dumnoniorum. At the time, he had uncharacteristically expended a small fortune on a building he did not much like and that he didn't himself use. He did so partly for the love of his only daughter, Elen, but more so as a canny bet on the future prospects of his son-in-law, Magnus Maximus. He had judged that rightly, but the expense still rankled. He had hardly visited the basilica since then and it was already again falling into disrepair.

Eudaf Hen was ruler of one of the most important tribes on the fringes of Britannia. The Dumnonii had owed allegiance to Roma for over 300 years, since the day the divine Vespasian had brought the Second Legion to the tribe's lands and had built a fortress at Isca. Having seen what Vespasian had done to their neighbours, the Durotriges, who had unwisely resisted the Roman juggernaut only to see their hillforts reduced to slaughterhouses, the Dumnonii had bowed to the inevitable and submitted to Roma without a struggle. That had proved a very wise decision, for the Second Legion soon marched off to the north to fight other, less accommodating tribes. After that, the Dumnonii had been left pretty much to their own devices. They paid Roma an annual tribute and provided men for the army when called upon, but their lands remained free of garrison troops. They had kept their arms and their fleet of ships, which enabled them to make a good living by controlling trade from the continent up the west coast and from slaving in Hibernia. Roma had delegated to them much of the control of its far western seaboard for several hundred years and continued to treat the tribe and its rulers with respect. So, as they had watched other tribes across the rest of lowland Britannia destroyed or impoverished, their lands parcelled up into large imperial estates or sold off to enormously rich foreigners, the Dumnonii had prospered.

In one other area had they been left to their own devices. They had not been bothered by the growing number of imperial decrees enforcing changes in religion. In their territories, temples to the old gods stood and functioned unscathed. No rabid Christian partisan had dared to raise a hand to deface or destroy the shrines of the gods that the people believed to be the heart and sustenance of their tribe. Eudaf in particular looked with horror at the dissension and vandalism that were becoming common on the other side of the frontiers of his lands. Conan felt exactly the same.

Although Eudaf Hen and his nephews had come to Segontium at Maximus' summons, they did so without knowing his intentions. They had come in order to keep things the way they always had been.

*

A few months before this meeting, Eudaf had been sitting together with his nephews and retainers in his wooden hall on the hill outside Isca. This was where he preferred to live, just as his ancestors had done. A fire was blazing to keep the winter chill out of the hall, its smoke hanging in the rafters. Outside, the splatter of rain and the sound of the tree branches being tossed by heavy gusts of wind almost obscured the clatter of hooves and cries at the gate as a small group of horsemen rode up from the town and demanded admittance. The door to the hall was thrown open to discover two Roman military couriers, who strode in with squelching boots and saluted the prince. From a saturated leather satchel, one of them handed Eudaf a sealed despatch, the answer to which, he stated, they had been ordered to await by the next morning.

As the couriers were led away for refreshment and rest, Gadeon took the despatch from his uncle. He was the only member of the family able to read Latin, so he read it now to Eudaf, translating it as he went into their native Brythonic tongue.

"It is from Macsen Guledig," he revealed, "and he is in need of our help." Macsen Guledig was what the British called the Duke Magnus Maximus, *guledig* being the British term for a patriarch or a supreme military leader. "He wants you to meet him at Segontium in three months' time with as many ships and fighting men as you can muster. He says that he will explain all when you meet, uncle, but you must, he says, bring with you men enough to harry the Scoti in their homes in Hibernia over the summer fighting season. He also wants you to bring at least 500 men prepared to act as a garrison of the fort for the next year or even longer. He promises much gold and many slaves and says that his plans will benefit our people for generations to come. He asks us to reply that we can do this, and he looks forward to seeing his father-in-law in person there. You will see your daughter again, uncle, for he will be bringing her with him."

Eudaf was taken aback by this message. He had never been asked for anything like this before and did not understand its import. Astonished, he looked around him and found, by the looks on their faces, that everyone else was as astonished as he. The prince liked the sound of a golden, slave-filled future, but he was utterly dubious of big Roman schemes, which in his experience invariably involved a lot of killing and always involved unwanted imperial interference.

His nephew Conan, however, smelled an adventure and a lot of loot, and saw no need to overthink his response. "Uncle," he interjected, "we should send back our acceptance. Your son-in-law is offering us the chance to join some adventure that he says will make us rich. We'd be mad to deny him."

Gadeon was not so sure. "I counsel a little delay to let us consider this," he said. "We can't send the couriers back until tomorrow, when they will have rested, so we have time to think this through."

Eudaf nodded in agreement. "As in everything important, we must seek the direction of our gods. Let us consult them. Go now," he told one of the men around the hearth, "fetch Diviacus. Be quick."

Diviacus was Eudaf's druid, his conduit to the gods of the Dumnonii, the adviser he had trusted to guide him in every matter of importance he had ever faced. The druid had the power to both ascertain the future and, it was believed, to alter it. Eudaf relied on him utterly. The druid's access to the spirit world gave him great power in the tribe. Its people were in fear of him, though, and avoided his presence when they could, not least because his smell preceded his appearance. He gave off an odour that was a powerful and unattractive melange of the blood and innards of various kinds of dead animals and the pungent rot of fruit and vegetation. Even among men who did not bathe too frequently, his smeared robes and the chains of macabre items he wore around his neck and arms made him repugnant. He jangled and rustled as he moved, which gave good warning of his coming and so time to get out of his way. Everyone in the household was glad that Diviacus, by nature of his calling, lived alone with a slave in a round hut some way outside the palisade.

When the druid shuffled in, Eudaf informed him of the contents of the Roman message and sent him away to conduct his usual divinations. "See what you can see of the Roman's real purpose, Diviacus. Look for the profit in whatever scheme he is hatching for us and what dangers we might face if we accept his invitation," directed the prince. "I must send a reply tomorrow." The druid said nothing, inclined his wizened head and withdrew.

It was dusk by the time he returned; the rooks had started to settle and quarrel in the trees above the hall and the bats were flitting in and out of its rafters.

"My prince," began the druid, speaking slowly and deliberately, "I can see little to tell you of what Duke Magnus Maximus is seeking. He has not touched this piece of parchment himself, so I cannot read his mind. To divine his thoughts, I must get closer to the duke himself. However, our gods have shown me enough to allow me to say that the gold and slaves he promises you are there for you to take. There's more, though, to this scheme than the Roman is revealing now. I can feel something bigger, something new that may lead to a different future for our people. I can see already that the path to this future will involve many deaths and much loss for some of those involved. However, although the eventual outcome has been kept clouded from me, I do not think that this doom will be ours. Our gods look in favour on what it is that this Roman is offering us."

"So, we should go, uncle, and meet the duke, for there is fortune here for us to grasp," said Conan, leaping in once more. For him, the chance to enrich his tribe and himself was irresistible. His older brother, Gadeon, was, for once, of similar mind. "I am with Conan, uncle," he said. "It would do us ill to offend the most powerful Roman officer in the land. We have little to lose by going and we can assess whether there will be profit in what he offers us when we hear his full story. I say we go to Segontium and take with us the forces he has asked of us."

Eudaf did not need much persuading. In his younger days, he had been almost as daring in his enterprises as his nephew Conan was now. There was something else driving him, too, for in accepting a part in whatever this strange adventure turned out to be, he would, at last after so many years, meet his dearest daughter. He knew that he had little time left on this earth, and although he was far past campaigning himself, his nephews would do this for him. He reckoned he was still fit enough to journey to Segontium.

"So shall it be," he agreed. "Draft the reply, Gadeon, and, Conan, start tomorrow to get us ready to meet the duke in Segontium on the date he has set."

Chapter Three

SEGONTIUM

On the shore at Segontium, Eudaf's men ran to line one side of the path that ran up from the quay. They formed up in a ragged, un-military order, but though they may have had an unkempt appearance, nonetheless their weapons gleamed and their shields had been freshly painted to please the duke. They now bore not the device of their tribe but Maximus' insignia, five castles representing the provinces of Britannia. In front of his men stooped Eudaf, a short, bent figure dressed in a simple, tan-coloured tunic with a small circlet of gold on his brow.

On the other side of the path, behind the tribune commanding the cohort that garrisoned the fort, a guard of honour was being swiftly drawn up in two smart ranks under a dragon standard that flapped in the slight breeze. As Maximus handed Elen onto dry land, the trumpeters and horn blowers on the towers of the fort blasted out a welcome, the tribune and the garrison saluted and Eudaf Hen bowed as deeply as his joints would allow.

Maximus turned first to his father-in-law, who held out a gnarled hand. "It is good to see you again, Prince. It has been a very long time, and I and your daughter have been across half the world and back since then. We have much to talk about." The general pumped Eudaf's hand so forcefully that the old man staggered forwards a pace.

"You are welcome, my lord," Eudaf stuttered in his uncouth Latin, making a semblance of a smile in his toothless face. He had never much liked this haughty Roman and had often regretted giving him his daughter; he wasn't at all sure he'd like him, or whatever scheme he had cooked up, better now. He put that thought aside, for here was his daughter before him, and with much greater warmth than he had welcomed the general, and this time in his native British tongue, he greeted her, clasped her to his bosom and let her kiss his cheek. He was glad to see her again before the gods took him.

Maximus turned to the tribune, who introduced himself as Flavius Pulcher, welcomed the general to Segontium, then swaggeringly escorted him to inspect the garrison's guard of honour. The duke, who had been sizing up officers all his career, immediately took Pulcher's measure as a conceited, overbearing and not very bright commander, but one who kept his men in fine shape. Maximus could see that they were a soldierly looking lot of men. They were, he found as he inspected them, mostly Gauls, but there were a few Germans and men of other races in their ranks. The duke was pleased that they were in such good order, for he needed them for what he intended to do. Pulcher was clearly an old-fashioned sort of regimental officer, punctilious about standards, the sort of man the general appreciated.

Courtesy then required that Maximus go back across the path to shake the hands of each of Eudaf's men, hands that were all none too clean, but he was a soldier and their stench did not offend him in the slightest. They were a tough-looking bunch, which was just what he wanted.

The welcoming ceremony complete, they climbed the small town's main street up to the fort. The local populace had spilled out in front of their poor shops and hovels to be held back from the path behind the spears of the troops. They gawked unashamedly at the unusual sight of a real Roman general and his raven-haired British wife. Segontium was the principal town of the Ordovices tribe, but it was a poor place and had never been turned into one of the civilised capitals of the lowlands. The tribe had been almost destroyed by its resistance to the conquest over 300 years before and its numbers had not grown greatly since then. Their town was little more than a collection of low dwellings huddled around the fort; there was neither forum nor basilica, and there were no baths.

As they walked up the path, two figures detached themselves from the ranks of Eudaf's men and came up alongside Elen. Prince Conan took Elen's left arm in his, Gadeon her right. Elen had not needed to worry, she had no difficulty at all in recognising the princes. "Welcome, cousin," boomed Conan, "Dumnonos has brought you back to us at last. We are all really happy that you have come with the duke."

"No demon from hell has brought me here, brother, only the risen Lord, whom I serve, and who watches over this empire and all of us."

There was an explosion of laughter from Prince Gadeon. "Come, cousin," he jested, "I had heard that you had abandoned the ways of our tribe and our ancestors, but I hadn't thought to hear you so shrewish in condemning the ways of your people and your old life. Smile at being with us again and put your faith away for a while lest it spoil our happiness."

Elen was about to respond to this, but caught herself, for now, she knew, was not the time to give offence by preaching the faith. She broke into a smile that lit up her face, for she was genuinely glad to see her cousins after so long a time. They were both looking a bit older, of course, but she could see that they were still at the peak of their manhood, unlike her poor father, who had aged badly.

Reconciled and happy, at least for the moment, the three of them followed the general into the fort. They were to be there together for two days, so they would have plenty of time to catch up on each other's news. The tribune's quarters to which Maximus and Elen were escorted were comfortable, if plain, and included a small suite of heated rooms for bathing. With so many guests to accommodate, Pulcher had moved into the house of the inspector of the local silver and lead mines, an engineer who lived inside the fort. Pulcher had told the man to make himself scarce for the duration of the visit and had not invited him to that night's supper laid on by the garrison's cooks. As they ate, and as Elen's people discussed news of their family and of her homeland, Maximus ran through in his mind what he was about to tell them. He would not explain everything yet, only enough to set his plans in motion, but he needed their participation; without it, his path would be even more dangerous than he expected it to be. He would need them to have his back in Britannia and the west. He had great plans for the dynasty he was founding. Tonight, he would have to be at his most persuasive to carry them with him.

It was dark by the time the group rose from their couches. Maximus, his staff officer, the *protector domesticus* Promotus, and his bodyguard commander Constantine walked across the roadway to the fort's headquarters, leaving Elen to retire for the night. There, torches in wall sconces lit the hall. Already seated around a table were Eudaf and the two princes, Conan and Gadeon, with some of their principal nobles.

Placed on the table between them all was a large map of the diocese of Britannia, marked with its five provinces and the lands surrounding them. On one side of the table, facing the

British on the other, sat the Romans who had journeyed there with the duke. Next to the general sat Flavius Aurelianus, the prefect of the Twentieth Legion, the Valeria Victrix, which was based at Deva, the major garrison of the northwest. Aurelian was a battle-hardened veteran who bore the scars of wars and frontier skirmishes; he was one of Maximus' most senior and reliable officers. Despite the fact that he was a Briton, whose people were the principal family in the Atrebates' city of Calleva, further back in the prefect's line lay a cadet branch of the family of the heroic soldier emperor Aurelian, who had reigned a century before. Maximus had seen much proof over the years that the Twentieth's prefect was a man much in the mould of his renowned ancestor. Aurelian had sailed with his general in the second ship of the convoy and had slipped away from supper to be in the praetorium before the duke arrived. Leading the rest of the room, he rose now as Maximus entered to take his seat at the head of the table, Promotus at his elbow.

Before he could start, the duke was taken aback by the approach of an austere figure in long, tattered robes who had been seated next to Prince Eudaf. Bones hung on cords around his neck and wrists, his hair was long and matted and his feet were bare. The Romans stirred nervously, and the duke could not help flinching as the man held out long bony fingers towards him and seized his wrist. Maximus had met druids in his time and did not much like them, but he remembered this one as the druid he had seen at his wedding. He knew that his father-in-law travelled everywhere with this man and took no decision without seeking his counsel, so he gestured to his officers to be still. Diviacus looked into his eyes and Maximus felt that it was as if the druid were searching out his soul. There was an awkward pause, then the moment passed and Diviacus returned to the seat next to his prince. Searching out the Roman's soul was, of course, just what he had been doing.

Recovering, the duke began. "I thank you all for being here this day. It is good to see so many who are dear to me, my family, my friends and my allies. I welcome you to our enterprise. Together we shall serve the empire and do great deeds. Please, be seated."

The general spoke slowly, as his words needed translation for Prince Eudaf and for some of his men; Gadeon, who had excellent Latin, translated for them. "The times are perilous," went on the duke. "The empire's forces in the east are still battling the Gothi, for, as you all know, the frontier on the Danube was breached a few years back. The German tribes across the Rhine have watched our defeat six years ago at Hadrianopolis and have been stirred up by the death there of the eastern emperor of blessed memory, the divine Valens. Trouble will come nearer to us, I am sure, and I fear we shall soon face a call upon us for reinforcements for the frontier in Germania. We must make dispositions to be ready. You know that my responsibility is for Roma's frontier in the west and in the north of Britannia, and I intend that we strike to pacify the barbarians beyond our frontiers before they can strike at us and before we lose the means to do so."

There was a murmur of approval in the room, for the horror of Roma's defeat by the Gothi only six years before hung like a shadow over all those whose safety depended on the defence of the empire's borders. Those present knew from a lifetime of conflict that the threat to Britannia from Hibernia's Scoti and the Picti of the far north was ever present, and that now was a dangerous time. They had all fought against these peoples over many decades and knew that their enemies would take advantage, if they could, of any weakness they saw in the empire.

"Prince Eudaf," went on the duke, "you are most welcome here today, and I thank you for coming so far to meet me. Your people have, for over 300 years now, been faithful allies of Roma. Ever since your ancestors submitted to the divine Vespasian, your tribe has helped the empire when it called. Roma calls for your help now. Over the years, your people have helped control the western seas for us and have given us men for our armies. We need that help again now.

"Gentlemen," the duke continued, addressing now the whole room, "I intend to strike north this year, to so crush the tribes across the Wall that they will not think of troubling us again in a generation." Looking now at tribune Pulcher, he went on: "For this, I need troops, which are in short supply everywhere, and I must take them from the west, including from here, from Segontium," and here he nodded at the prefect of the Twentieth, "and from Deva and the rest of the western highlands. Yet I shall not leave these lands undefended, and I will tell you, now, how you will help to keep them safe."

Maximus' speech thus far was what the room had been expecting to hear, for the despatch that had summoned them had already warned them of the duke's need for men. "As I march north to crush the Picti, I shall take the commander and most of the Twentieth Legion. I shall leave the deputy prefect of the Twentieth in command of those troops left behind. From Deva, he will control the northwest. Prince Eudaf, I want your fleets to control the western seas for him and I want you to harry the Scoti in their homes in Hibernia. You will burn their ships, kill their men and stop them raiding us. You will take and sell as many slaves as you can, for let us all profit by the weakening of our enemies!"

The duke chuckled, for he was well aware that Prince Eudaf had a similar grasp to his of the opportunities offered by war.

"In addition," he went on, "for the time being and until we return, you will garrison Segontium, because, tribune Pulcher, you and your men will accompany me to the north. I need you and every spare man I can find." There was a ripple of surprise;

none had thought that the Roman cohort in Segontium would be moved, and the men of Dumnonia, whilst used to serving the empire at sea, had not, hitherto, been called upon to provide garrison service.

The torches threw shadows from the hall's pillars across the map and accentuated the features of the warriors around it. The darkness in the aisles seemed to hem the small group in closer. Maximus observed their faces closely; it was vital that they all understood what he needed and that he could see that they were with him. Shifting his gaze back to Prince Eudaf, he went on: "Prince, just west of here, on our side of the sea in the peninsula of the Ganganii, there are Scoti whom the slackness of our government has allowed to settle over many decades. They pose a threat to the garrison here, but there are too many of them now to eliminate easily, and certainly we cannot do that with the forces we have at our disposal. So, I want you to intimidate them, take their ships and stop them communicating with their kin in Hibernia. There must be no more immigration here.

"The Scoti are a problem we have brought upon ourselves," the duke continued. "We have allowed them to settle inside the empire. They must not be allowed to get out of hand any further, and I intend to deal with them. It is not just here that they have infiltrated our lands. In the southwest, in Demetia, the tribe of the Desi has been allowed to settle in such large numbers that we shall never be able to eradicate them. We must control them, though, and that will be the task of the Second Legion in Isca Augusta."

With this the duke had finished. Questions followed, but there were few, for he had been very clear, and he left logistic details to be covered by Promotus in his absence the next day.

In the meantime, however, Maximus had a deeper, more perilous business to conduct. Now, he moved to set in train his deeper plans.

Chapter Four

THE BREATH OF TREASON

"Prince Eudaf," the duke beckoned, "come with me. I have need to talk with you of some family matters. I have more to tell you. Let us go somewhere more private." Maximus led him and his two nephews out of the hall into one of the smaller rooms used as an office at its rear.

"Diviacus must hear what you say, too, lord. He is a seer of things of the future and without his divination we can do nothing. He will ascertain the direction of the gods on our behalf." Maximus nodded his assent and gestured to Promotus to permit the druid to enter, then asked his staff officer to leave.

When they were all settled in chairs around a small table, the duke began again. "I have brought you in private," he said, "to learn my true purpose and to outline the part that I shall give you, my family by marriage, in what I intend to do. Ours will be a most perilous enterprise, but one that will bring you and your descendants great glory. I have another purpose in marching north, one which only those of us in this room will know. Once I have dealt with the Picti, and once you, Eudaf, have dealt such a blow against the Scoti that they will never forget, I shall use my forces to cross the seas and march on Augusta Treverorum, the capital of the west."

A discernible shudder passed between the three British princes, who could not prevent themselves glancing at each other to see the reaction on each other's faces. What Maximus had said was high treason and even whispering it here could lead not only to their deaths, but also to the destruction of their family and even of Dumnonia itself. Roma already had three legitimate emperors, and not one of those would ever permit a failed usurper and his supporters to survive.

Maximus did not have to remind the princes that Augusta, now, as he had revealed, the duke's target, housed the chief part of the administration of the west. Power over Britannia, Gallia and Hispania was exercised there on behalf of the Emperor Gratian, elder son of the old emperor Valentinian. Gratian had ruled from there himself until very recently, when he had moved his throne to Mediolanum in Italia. His younger stepbrother, Valentinian II, who was still just a youth, was also at Mediolanum, nominally ruling Italia and Africa, although the little power that Gratian's ministers allowed him was wielded not by the boy emperor, but by his mother, the Dowager Empress Justina. The rest of the empire was in the hands of a third emperor, Theodosius, Maximus' old colleague in arms, who had replaced Valens, who had gone down with his army at Hadrianopolis, and ruled the east from Constantinopolis.

The princes knew enough history to remember that past usurpers from Britannia, and the last of these had aimed at the throne not so long ago, had all failed. They also knew that all of them and their adherents had perished miserably in the attempt.

"I shall take the throne of the west," went on Maximus, ignoring the visible unease he had created, "because it needs to be done for the safety of us all. Gratian is too weak to defend the empire. He is surrounded by effete counsellors and has been corrupted by his German entourage. He favours only his Alamanni auxiliaries. He gives them donatives of gold and silver that he refuses to his Romans. A mere six years after the barbarian Gothi destroyed two thirds of the army of the east at Hadrianopolis, Gratian fawns on his barbarians and even prances around in Gothic clothes."

Maximus was steadily increasing the force of his words, looking hard into the eyes of his audience as he did so. He emanated a confidence he didn't really have. Would they follow him? Could he trust them? He knew he had no choice if he was to succeed. He had to have allies he could trust to secure his British base.

"Gratian has ceased to be a Roman," he went on. "He is unfit to rule. The German tribes smell his weakness and he will never be able to hold the frontier on the Rhenus in the conflict that will come. If he fails, all is lost, for Valentinian is a mere boy in the hands of his mother. Without a strong soldier at its head, the empire in the west will slip into the same morass that has engulfed the east. If we do not act, none of us will survive the storm that will be unleashed from Germania." The general had worked himself up into a fury with the force of his words. He paused for them to sink in.

"Why should you join me in this enterprise?" he resumed. "It is because, Prince Eudaf, I shall make you the father-in-law of the emperor and the premier prince in Britannia. All here will bow to you and give you honour. Your heirs will inherit and pass on your glory, and you will die with riches to bestow upon your people, more than any prince possessed before you."

The duke could see in the flickering torchlight that, despite the fear his earlier words had aroused, his father-in-law's eyes had lit up at the notion of the status and the gold he was being promised. It had never escaped the general that Eudaf had married his daughter to him in the hope that one day he would reach the highest rank. Now he was offering the prince more than the fulfilment of his old, and until now, disappointed hopes.

"There is more," went on the duke. "I shall place you, Prince Conan, at my right hand, literally so, for as I march into Gallia, you will be my duke of the sea, my *mare dux*. I will place in your hands all the Roman fleets that are now on the coasts of Britannia, then later, when they are in our hands, those of Gallia as well. You shall rule the western seas from Armorica as far south as Hispania. For me, you will control and tax all trade and keep us safe from interference by any hostile fleet."

Maximus could see that Conan had already taken his bait. His face had lit up; the prince had never conceived such a path to fame, fighting and glory.

"Your role in this, Prince Gadeon, will be more difficult and complex. You will hold Britannia's princes together while we are away. You will persuade, flatter, bribe and coerce your fellow princes in the west to be loyal to me. I need your leadership in the diocesan council to keep Britannia loyal while Conan and I are at war. There is a huge amount at stake here. It is my intent that at last the chief families of this island will find a place in the imperial sun, just as have, in the past, those of Hispania, Pannonia and Africa. No more will it be possible for the empire to treat Britannia as some cast-off, peripheral province of no account in imperial affairs. The riches of patronage and power will be opened to its leaders. I am going to take Britannia with me and in turn it will be my rock, my fortress. For this, I need your help." Gadeon's face was unreadable, but he nodded in acknowledgement, which was, for the general, enough.

"You will need time to consider this, I know," Maximus concluded, "but I must have your answer tomorrow as I and Elen will leave for Deva on the day after. Come to me in the afternoon. May the gods guide your deliberations."

*

The meeting over, the princes walked back down through the town to their ships, while the duke went back to the tribune's quarters. Elen was awake and waiting for him in its small garden, swathed in a cloak against the chill of the spring night. "Shall we walk a little?" he asked her.

"Yes, husband, let us clear our heads before we sleep." Elen knew a campaign in the north was afoot, but she had not been made aware of the rest of her husband's scheme. She suspected, however, that there was more in what was happening than she had been told. She hoped that Maximus might divulge to her now whatever this was, but she knew better than to ask, and, in the event, he disappointed her and said nothing.

The couple mounted the staircase to the fort's perimeter wall, and, acknowledging the salute of the sentry, walked to the northernmost corner turret. The night was clear enough for the stars to light their way and the moon was rising. From the top of the tower, they could see the island of Mona across the water, dark, brooding, mysterious, still.

"This was a place sacred for generations to your people, Elen," the general said. "We must hold it and never let it go."

"Yes, husband, but we must make it sacred once again, and this time with the true faith. There is nothing but superstition and devilry there still. One day, the word of the risen God will be brought even to the ends of the earth in this island and make it truly holy."

This remark was so far off what was in Maximus' mind that he let it pass in silence into the still night air.

*

Back within the shelter of the wall guarding the harbour, inside the large tent that had been pitched for their use, Eudaf, his nephews and Diviacus sat cross-legged on skins placed on the floor around the central hearth. The prince called for cider. When they were alone, he opened the discussion. "There is no time for sleep yet. We must let Diviacus consult the gods tonight so that we can give an answer tomorrow."

Gadeon was the first to offer his thoughts. "By revealing his plans, uncle, the duke has placed us in deep peril, for whatever course we take may lead to our deaths. If we deny him, he will count us his enemies, and in-laws though we be, we may not leave this place alive. If we support him, we shall take a path that, if he is defeated, will lead almost certainly to our ruin."

"So it is death now or possible death later," said Conan laughing, "and we shall all, even you, brother, die one day."

"True," replied Gadeon, "but though we ourselves may die, we must ensure that our dynasty and our people are not extirpated by some vengeful emperor."

Eudaf looked at both his nephews. In the little time he knew he had left to him, he was happy to wager his life for the sake of gold and prestige. But the maintenance of their line had forever been the policy of his forebears, who had watched what had happened to their Durotriges neighbours and to other tribes like the Iceni and Brigantes who had stood in Roma's way. Their ruling lines had been eradicated, their lands divided and their way of life changed irrevocably. By bowing to the Roman yoke, his ancestors had kept their freedoms and their lands. They had kept the Romans at bay. He would not jeopardise that now.

"Let us see what the gods tell us." Eudaf turned to Diviacus. "Ask them, I pray, to give us guidance."

The druid made no reply, but instead placed in front of him the sacred bones he wore and some small sprigs of mistletoe from the pouch at his waist. He placed his hands upon these. His eyes clouded over and almost closed. He began to murmur and chant softly, uttering words that Eudaf and his son could not understand.

It seemed to them in the dim light of the tent, lit only by a few torches and the embers of the fire, that a shadow was slowly gathering above the druid, a shadow that rose and stretched towards the canopy. Imperceptibly, it took the shape of a dark figure. Antlers spread on either side of its head. A face slowly formed, its writhing cheek muscles and staring eyes formed by a myriad of creatures that ceaselessly but silently heaved and intertwined, then opened to form a mouth from which freezing mist exhaled. Dumnonus, for this was he, inclined his head towards them, then pointed in turn at each of the flinching mortals around the fire, his long, translucent fingers, accusing and terrifying. They heard the god sigh, enveloping them in his breath, and his face became a mask of such sorrow as they had never seen.

The tent was deathly quiet and very cold. For what seemed a very long time, none of them moved. Then the shadow was gone and Diviacus opened his eyes.

"When you join this Roman, my prince," Diviacus began, "which you will, for the game has already begun, your line will gain great power and huge wealth. Yet doing so will involve your people in treachery that will bring great suffering across the world. Today, I touched the hand of this Roman and looked into his eyes. I felt his life force. He is powerful but he is not to be trusted. Yet the gods have granted that he will win his throne, although maybe they have not given him long to enjoy it."

He pointed a bony finger at Gadeon and Conan. "I was shown that the seed of one of you, although I do not know which, will carry your dynasty forward to great power and for many generations. Remember, though, that back at Isca when Macsen's summons came, the gods showed me blood. That cannot be avoided. It will be shed. It is your and Macsen's fate."

"It is enough," cried Conan. "It is all to play for."

Gadeon took longer to respond, and when he did, he spoke more softly and, looking at Conan, with some sadness. "For the sake of our tribe, we shall need to make sure that one of us survives, whatever happens, and that means that if one of us is close to the duke, the other must be distant from him, for it is those close to him that will be most in danger. You, brother, are designated in his plan to be his right hand, so in what follows it must be I who must appear to distance myself, in order that if he loses, I shall not fall with you both." Gadeon's was an argument balancing logic and self-interest in equal measure, but that was always so with Gadeon, and though they did not much like it, his uncle and brother saw the sense of what he said.

"We shall tell Maximus so," concluded Eudaf. "Goodnight, get rest, we shall need clear minds tomorrow."

Chapter Five

THE BLOOD OF THE BULL

On the morrow, the princes did not see the duke again till almost the end of the afternoon, for he spent the day visiting the silver mine that was administered by the inspector who usually lived in the fort. This small, weaselly civil servant had been creaming profit from the imperial account for years, selling off surplus ingots and under-accounting for the ore mined by the slaves he managed. Although the duke was not his superior, who was a financial official in far-away Londinium, the inspector could not avoid a courtesy visit by such an eminent military officer. Just to make sure his visitor would pose no awkward questions, he presented the general with a carefully boxed set of some of his illegal ingots, something that Maximus, naturally, had expected. It was, in truth, the reason for his visit; he had no interest in the workings of a mine. The general was in a very good mood when he returned to the fort.

Prince Eudaf, his nephews and the druid were waiting for him in the headquarters. After bathing and scraping away the dust of the mine and changing into fresh clothes, Maximus walked over to the praetorium. He did not take Promotus with him this time. His *princeps* had only recently been posted in from headquarters in Gallia, and as yet Maximus did not know whether he could be trusted enough to make him party to what he intended. This was family business, he told Promotus. He did, though, take Constantine with him for protection; they were about to go unescorted outside the fort, and the duke was not a man who took personal risks. He knew Constantine well enough to know that he could trust him, although once in the back office of the headquarters, he posted him outside the door to stop anyone else overhearing what was said within.

"Prince Eudaf, princes, I am glad to see you so promptly," the duke began, ignoring Diviacus. "Have you an answer for me?"

"We have, lord," replied the prince, Gadeon translating into Latin on his uncle's behalf. "You have done us and our family great honour in asking for our support in your enterprise. That support is yours."

Maximus smiled, relaxing fully for the first time since he had set out in the ships from Deva. "I am very glad that you have chosen this path," he responded, "and I thank you."

Gadeon now saw the opportunity to say his piece. "I shall myself be most effective, lord, if I am seen, in the deliberations of the princes and the diocesan council, to stand separate from your enterprise, whilst always behind the scenes working to further it. I shall need your forbearance in listening to some, perhaps negative, things you will hear of me or of what I may say, but I promise that I shall be as much your man as will be my uncle and brother." Maximus immediately saw the point of this and nodded in agreement.

"There is now one thing we must do to seal our pact," the duke concluded. "We must all of us swear a most sacred oath to carry forward our enterprise. Come with me now, the arrangements have been made. This for once," he spoke here to Eudaf, "is not a matter for your druid."

Dusk had fallen by the time they emerged from the hall. At its door was waiting a figure in a dark robe that was covered with strange insignia. The man was wearing a strange, almost conical cap. The British princes had never seen such a costume; only the two Roman officers understood that this was a priest of Mithras, the soldiers' god. Maximus had brought the man with him, for he was one of the troops serving in the garrison at Deva. Such things may have been frowned upon by now in this Christian empire, but the army was a law unto itself. The priest and a similarly dressed acolyte led them out of the fort's eastern gate and down a narrow track that followed a small stream bed. In the deepening dusk, little was visible, but after a few minutes Eudaf and his nephews found themselves before a darkness opening into the ground. Eudaf was nervous about what was happening; this was no ritual he knew, these were not his gods. "What is this, lord?" he asked.

"It is the fort's old temple of Mithras, prince. It is, alas, no longer used, but still within its depths dwells the mystery of the god," replied the duke. "Down there, Mithras shall bind us as one as we make our solemn oath."

Leaving Constantine outside the entrance, again to keep watch, they followed the priest down muddy steps deep into the earth. The passage was low and unlit so that they had to feel their way as they descended by running their hands along walls slippery with water and the slime of centuries. At the bottom of the staircase, a passage led into a small antechamber, which opened into a low hall. Pillars ran down both sides of this, dividing its space into a nave and two side aisles. In the dim light, they could make out three altars at the far end of the nave, their carvings cast into sharp relief by the flickering candles mounted in old, rusty candelabra on each of the pillars. Both side aisles were sunk in darkness. Incense filled and thickened the still air. Everything bore the marks of neglect; dust lay everywhere. The paintings on the walls had been defaced with graffiti and Christian symbols. All the faces had been scratched out. As they got closer, they could see that even the altars were covered with the dirt from which they had, only today, been resurrected, for they had been buried face down and deliberately desecrated by the Christian zealots who had vandalised the temple.

Behind the altars, looming menacingly from the far wall, the figure of Mithras slashed the throat of the massive bull he was astride. The figure had been partially smashed out of the wall so that Mithras' face was gone, but his conical Phrygian cap left no doubt that this was still the soldiers' god, the guardian of the light. In front of the central altar stood a statue, taller than a man, half of whose lion head had also been smashed off. The wings of the figure and the serpent entwining it were still perfect, as was the horrible open maw of its mouth and the key and sceptre it held in its hands. In front of the winged figure was a deep pit.

As the princes hesitated at the door to this unearthly scene, they were startled by a shuffling and snuffling in one of the side aisles. From it, the acolyte led a white bullock to a place before the pit, where it swayed, stamping its feet and snorting drowsily. It had been doped with alcohol in the grain it had been fed and it stank of both this and of its own urine, which was puddling the floor.

Eudaf and his nephews were quiet now, even the loquacious Conan unable to speak, for they had never been in a place such as this, the shrine of a god very alien to them. Already slightly dizzy from the incense, they were afraid of the mystery they had entered, deeply in awe of the power of the divinity they feared was present here. Reluctantly, they followed the duke to the altars.

The priest began to pray in a language none of them knew. The duke opened his hands and prayed in Latin: "Mithras, bring your light to our enterprise and fend off the evil meted out to mankind by Ariman, the god of darkness. Bless this our compact and avenge any who break it." He leapt into the pit and fell to his knees before Mithras, beckoning the princes to follow him. Copying Maximus, the princes all raised their arms so that the priest could knot together their right hands. They knelt, bound together, gradually aware in the darkness of the pit that the stone slab upon which they were kneeling was the cover of a tomb.

The darkness inside the pit deepened as the acolyte brought the bullock staggering over them, its bloodshot, drunken eyes and slobbering jaws only inches above their heads. As they looked up with horror, the priest cut the beast's jugular with one swift movement of his sacrificial knife. The bullock lurched forward, bellowing, its blood pumping out over them, splattering onto the tomb below their knees. "Mithras is risen," chanted the priest and Maximus together, "the god is reborn, restorer of the eternal light."

As the beast bled out its lifeblood over them, the duke cried, "Swear now, say as I say.

"I swear," he bellowed, gripping tightly the hands of the princes, "on forfeit of my life, and that of my family and my heirs of every generation, that I shall be true to you three princes, your line and your people! Now swear, on your own lives, on the lives of your family and on the succession of your line, that you will be true to me, to my line, and to our enterprise. If you who have drunk Ariman's blood betray me, may Mithras take your soul to him in the darkness!"

Trembling, drenched in blood, they swore, one by one.

*

Up in the tribune's house in the fort, Elen heard the death bellows of the bullock and hid her head under the bedclothes, frightened by a magic in which she professed not to believe. When Maximus came to bed, having bathed again, she could still smell the blood which had covered him. She prayed to her God to protect her and her husband from the evil she knew he had done.

*

The next day, the duke's party took ship again for Deva, leaving Eudaf and his nephews to take over the garrison from the cohort, which would march within the week to join the field army gathering at Eboracum. The cohort had not left the fort for nearly a century and had been there so long that it had become known, even officially, after the name of the place, as the Segontienses. Many of the men had families in the town, many had been born there. They were soldiers, however, and loyal to the duke. They would go where they were told.

Thus it began. Flavius Magnus Maximus, Duke of the Britannias, with his wife Elen by his side, sailed forth out of the harbour to make real the dreams of power and glory that consumed him. They were dreams that would consume his entire world.

Chapter Six

JULIAN

The *vir clarissimus*, the most excellent, Sextus Rusticianus Julianus, *consularis*, consular governor of the province of Valentia, was bored, very bored, both with his life and with everything in Britannia. He was fed up with being so far from all that he cared about or had any interest for him. It had been over a year since he had been able to visit his big estate in Gallia or seen his wife, for she had opted to stay at home there rather than venture with him over the seas. He hadn't been in Roma for half a decade, not since his son had been elevated to the senate, and every now and then would bring to mind the glorious memory of that day. He himself had been the first of his family to make the senate, his son was the second, an elevation made thanks to the support of his friend and countryman, Quintus Aurelius Symmachus, and the usual liberal spreading of gold. Recalling both days brightened up the leaden skies that hung over his capital in Deva.

Correspondence from Symmachus, in fact all the letters from his friends in the informal but very influential literary circle of which he was proud to be a part, came infrequently to Deva. What letters did make it through the imperial post were often out of date or drenched in water. It seemed to Julian that the rain came down in sheets off the western sea almost every day in this blighted outpost. When letters arrived, none of his correspondents showed much interested in what was happening in Britannia. What they wrote about was what was going on in Gallia or Italia. He felt no longer able to contribute; his duty was making him culturally illiterate already.

To make matters worse, he had found since his arrival in Deva that he had far too little to occupy his mind and prevent his subsiding into disgruntlement. When he had been appointed Governor of Valentia, the fifth and least important British province that had been established only recently, in the late emperor Valentinian's day, he had been impressed with his own good fortune. He had even had the foolishness to think that the post was a good career move. To his chagrin, he quickly found that he had been woefully mistaken. Deva Victrix, the town which was to be his capital, turned out to be little more than an enormous army base. They were not under his control, and rather than his word, it was the word of the prefect of the Twentieth Legion that counted throughout the northwest. On top of this, he exercised jurisdiction over what was almost an empty space. To his north, the vast area running up to the Wall was under the military control of the *dux britanniarum*. To his west, he had jurisdiction over the northern half of the land mass that stuck out westwards towards Hibernia and ended at Segontium and Mona, but thanks to the efficient destruction wreaked upon the Ordovices by Suetonius' conquest 300 years before, there were scant few inhabitants there to administer.

Julian was surrounded all day by uncouth soldiers and he hated it. Unusually, and because the establishment of his province had been an administrative afterthought, his residence was right inside the enormous area of the Twentieth Legion's fort. However, and also unusually, the building was not a military one. Although it was surrounded on all four sides by barracks, it was itself a complex of ancient and peculiar design. It was about the only thing, Julian thought, that made governing Valentia tolerable. More of a palace than a house, the building was uniquely egg-shaped, its richly decorated walls curved in a most un-standard, convex fashion. It was very old, having been built to provide a residence for the great Julius Agricola, one of the early governors of Britannia and conqueror of its north. Agricola had been a man who demanded and deserved a suitable headquarters, so it had been built to an elaborate design with reception rooms, baths and courtyards, all beneath a vast roof. It was so large and had taken so long to build that, by the time it was finished, Agricola had gone back to Roma and would never see it completed. Subsequent British governors, like the current vicar of the British diocese, lived in Londinium. The palace at Deva had remained, something of a white elephant through what was now centuries, made use of by the legionary commander and any imperial official or senior officer passing through. So, when the province of Valentia was carved out of the other provinces some twenty years before, the building, with a heavy bout of redecorating, had proved to be a perfect residence for its governor.

It was lucky, Julian thought, that he had had the foresight when he heard of his posting to have his British agent purchase a big estate with a villa near Corinium, down in what was, at least for Britannia, the very fashionable province of Britannia Prima. He could scarcely bring himself to confess it, but he actually enjoyed being there. There were cultured folk on neighbouring estates, there was plentiful game to hunt, and the fact that so many of the island's rich had chosen to settle in the region meant that almost anything could be acquired in the market, or at worst could be easily imported. The villa wasn't exactly up to the standard of the one he owned at Baiae, but it was in a beautiful, wooded landscape and was balm to his frustrated soul. As a result, Julian spent as much time away from Deva as he could. Instead of doing his duty and putting up with what passed for conversation amongst his dull, uncivilised, military dinner guests, he absented himself to bustle about building a new suite of baths in his villa. He had just had up-to-date mosaics installed in its public rooms. He enjoyed pottering around the woods and fields of his land, which, to make him even happier there, was selling so much corn and wool to the military that it was turning a nice profit.

There were two issues, however, which the time he found on his hands had allowed him to turn over repeatedly in his mind until they had rankled into grievances that grew ever sorer as the empty months went by. The first of these was of lesser importance, but still stung. It was now clear to him that hardly anyone in his province wanted or needed to offer him a bribe. There was virtually nothing here out of which he could make enough money to repay what it had cost him to buy his post. People here would rather die, it seemed, than indulge in the expense of a lawsuit. Two years back, he had lavished presents on his friend, the emperor's favourite, Decimius Magnus Ausonius, and on those of the latter's circle at court. This had cost him a lot of money. He was bound to be out of pocket at the end of his governorship.

Julian's second grievance was that Valentia was about as far from the corridors of the western empire's centres of power as it was possible to get. His post offered a distinct lack of any possibility for further advancement when what he viewed as his exile was over. Valentia was the dead end that was blocking his advancement. The hitherto marked upward mobility of his family had stalled. He had succeeded in reaching a high position in society; both he and his son were now in the senate. He was now entitled to be called *clarissimus*, "the most respected". Yet the fact that he was no aristocrat, combined with the public knowledge that only in his lifetime had he become a great landowner, meant that he was in reality still an outsider. He desperately wanted in.

Over several generations before him, Julian's forebears had made a fortune from trade up the western seaboard. His grandfather and father had amassed a fleet of ships, offices and agencies that were now scattered as far north as the Rhenus and as far east as Roma itself. Wine, olives and luxury goods went north in their ships, while minerals, horses, wool and slaves returned with them southwards. The wealth that these round trips generated had brought the family lands and respectability. In turn, those had very slowly brought an association with the Gallic nobility, aristocrats who found to their dislike that they were now neighbours of business people, but to their pleasure that these people had enough money to make it worthwhile cultivating them. At last, in Julian's generation, the family had produced an offspring who had been sufficiently educated by *grammaticus* and *rhetor* to pass muster in polite society. Julian was the first of his family to fit comfortably into the world of the cultured and this had secured him entry to the Gallic circles of the imperial tutor Ausonius and his powerful friend, Symmachus. Manipulating these powerful relationships had brought Julian to Deva, with a tenure that was supposed to be for two years. How they must be laughing at him now.

If he was to advance his prospects further, he would need better help than they had given him, and that meant some form of imperial favour. He was in his late forties. He had little time left to get back in the race.

Duke Maximus, whilst staying in Deva's fortress on his trip through to Segontium, had been quick to smell Julian's discontent and had been sufficiently confident late one night after supper to deliberately drop a hint about his intentions, a hint broad enough for Julian to divine his thoughts. The governor had made it clear, although not in any words that might be quoted by any spy in his household, that he might very well be interested in working together with Maximus, whose own discontent Julian could feel under his brash surface. They had agreed to talk more deeply on Maximus' return.

*

The duke's small flotilla made swift passage from Segontium. Disembarked on Deva's quay, his party was whisked up to the fortress. Maximus settled Elen into the suite they had been allocated and, leaving her to investigate the luxury of the palace baths, he headed off to meet the governor. Julian received him in his private quarters, where, over supper, they reclined on couches placed around an apse that looked out over a huge mosaic of Neptune surrounded by sea creatures. The governor was pleased that this had not been carved up by any Christian zealot. He was a believer in the old religions, gods that had served his family well for generations. For reasons of their trade, they propitiated the gods of the sea, and the Neptune mosaic suited his taste perfectly.

Over the many courses of the meal, while the slaves hovered around, and before the wine mellowed them enough to be indiscreet, they made polite, if dull, conversation. "How were the farthest parts of my province, duke?" the governor asked. "I imagine you found it a particularly uncivilised place." Julian had, of course, never visited Segontium, or indeed very much of his province, and the only fort he had ever entered was the one he lived in now. The flabby weight that even his loose, silken tunic couldn't hide made journeys unpleasant for him and he was confined to carriages and litters when he travelled. The fact that this happened as little as possible made the slaves who had to carry him very happy.

"We enjoyed the visit, governor," Maximus replied, "but I think it unlikely that you'd have enjoyed the accommodation. I imagine you have no property west of Deva?"

"No, who would have?" responded the governor. "My nearest property is in the hills north-east of Corinium, where I have a small estate just outside the city." Julian was attempting to indicate polite modesty whilst at the same time boasting about the enormous country villa he had bought there. Maximus was well aware that his host owned many large estates that were worked by thousands of slaves across the empire. His property was truly vast; houses and lands in Gallia, Italia, Hispania and Africa, as well as large urban palaces in Roma and Constantinopolis, most of which he had never bothered to visit, but which helped make him rich and gave him great status. One of his villas in Calabria even had a horizon pool looking out over the ocean; he had relaxed in it once.

"I travel on to Eboracum tomorrow, governor, where I shall be collecting a force to march north across the Wall to deal with the Picti barbarians. As usual, they have been raiding both east and west along the coasts below the Wall and it is time for a bit of chastising."

"Show them what happens when you challenge the might of Roma, duke," replied the governor. The meal and pleasantries over, with a wave of his hand the governor dismissed the slaves and the pair drew closer to talk. The governor took the lead.

"I think, my good duke, that there were reasons of statecraft that took you to Segontium, not just the need to collect a few more soldiers. Would I be right in that thought?"

The duke looked his host in the eye. He had earlier made sure that he knew enough about Julian and the likelihood of his aspirations to surmise that he was a tool of which he could make use. If his plans were to succeed, he would need money, the sort of money that Julian could provide, not to mention the ships his company possessed. Warily, for neither could trust the other yet, they guided their conversation towards the treason that both knew was at stake here.

"I have a horrible fear that the young Emperor Gratian is not going to be capable of following in the footsteps of his father, the late, great and divine Valentinian." Maximus saw that this did not frighten the governor and decided to go further. "It is clear to me that we are in grave danger here in the west of suffering a catastrophe such as befell the eastern empire. I was there when the Gothi irrupted inside the frontier, and I saw the destruction that they wreaked. Gratian failed to come to the aid of his uncle, the divine Valens, when he lost his life resisting the Gothi at Hadrianopolis. It is disturbing that reports have reached me that Gratian now finds it amusing to dress like a Goth and to surround himself with Germans. He is not a soldier. It would be for the good of the empire, and particularly for the safety of your people in Gallia, were the young emperor to be retired and replaced by someone with the experience and strength of character to keep the barbarians at bay."

The governor was well aware that Maximus' claim that Gratian had failed to come to the aid of his uncle was an unfounded smear, but Maximus had indeed been in the theatre at the time, while Julian had been safe in Gallia, and it did not suit him now to gainsay his visitor.

"I am in sympathy with your view, duke, but such opinions are very dangerous, even in the uttering. There is little, I think, that a mere provincial governor can do to change any of this, and I am, in any case, due to leave this post this year. I have no current prospect of any further advancement."

"You would, I imagine, wish to make your family greater and to write your own name in the annals of Roma," responded the duke. "I might be able to offer you a way to do both, were you prepared to take a risk. What I have in mind would be a way for you to stay hidden, behind the scenes, undetected, and so able to evade any responsibility were things not to work out in our favour, but well placed to enjoy the public rewards if they did."

"Staying safe for as long as possible would be a good idea," the governor chuckled.

"Even my telling you my thoughts now, governor, would by itself place your future in the hands of the gods, and mine in yours. Do you wish me to proceed?" asked the duke.

"We have passed that point already," responded the governor. "Please go ahead."

Maximus did as he was bid. He outlined his plan to use his forthcoming campaign against the Picti to gather and harden a force with which he would first ensure the security of Britannia, then use to sail to the mouth of the Rhenus. There, the loyalty of the troops on the borders of Germania would be secured before the main thrust south to replace Gratian. He added the thought, which he knew would attract the governor, that, were circumstances to allow, he would later be able to move against the boy emperor Valentinian II and his mother, the Dowager Empress Justina. That would, of course, make him emperor of the whole west, with an imperial court at Augusta Treverorum and maybe later at Mediolanum. Roma itself, the fount of all patronage, would inevitably be in his hands.

Julian affected to look both shocked and impressed, but he could not have been surprised by the treason he had just heard. What other outcome could there be of a plot by the most powerful military officer in Britannia? He knew enough history to understand that what Maximus was proposing had happened all too often before. The size of the army in Britannia, maybe one tenth of the military strength of the whole empire, had often made it a tempting tool for an ambitious or aggrieved commander. Nearly a hundred years before, Carausius, the Count of the Saxon Shore, had styled himself Emperor of the North, and had held the west for seven years before going down to an assassin. Seventy years after that, so within living memory, the Gallic general Magnentius had also usurped the purple and had managed to hold the west for three years before losing it all and being forced to take his own life. The short-lived success of those two did not bode too well, but then they were not facing weak youths who had split the imperial thrones of the west, or an eastern empire under serious threat from Gothi and Persians. A *coup d'état*, or even two, should not be too difficult in the current circumstances. After that, all would be in the hands of the gods.

There was another thought in Julian's mind. News had rippled across the empire that Gratian had just rejected out of hand a petition from the senate, one led by the governor's friend and sponsor Symmachus, to restore the Altar of Victory in the *curia*, the senate House. Gratian, a Christian, had ordered the altar removed. The emperor had also overturned the edict of toleration that wise counsels had persuaded him to issue on his accession. He had intended then that every man should be able to exercise his own conscience in matters of religion. Immediately, he had found himself swimming against a strong tide of Christian extremism, one that would brook no coexistence with what its priests called paganism and idolatory. Egged on by his Christian advisers and browbeaten by the bishops and chaplains at his court, who told him that he was endangering not only his own soul but the well-being of his empire, Gratian had yielded, renouncing the edict of toleration. He had refused to take the title of *pontifex maximus*, the chief priest of the empire, one hitherto held by all emperors, and instead had promulgated laws defunding pagan temples and preventing sacrifices.

Back had come the bad days, when Christian mobs had torn down statues, razed or appropriated temple buildings and attacked and murdered pagan priests. Although no ripple of violence had as yet reached Valentia, there was once again news of riots and mob violence across the west, including in the chief cities of Britannia. More to the point for Julian, Gratian had stopped the appointment of pagans to key imperial posts. Now, if you wanted to get ahead in this world, you had to acknowledge the Christian god. The governor wanted to put the world back the way it had been, and that meant ridding the west of Gratian.

All these factors had been exercising Julian's mind long before Maximus turned up at his capital. He was ready not only to listen to the duke's plan, but to risk all by supporting it.

"May I ask what part a retired and not very significant provincial governor might play in any possible plan?" he ventured.

"In the short term I have need of money to pay the troops, when and if imperial funds are cut off, and later to bribe the troops on the Rhenus and in Gallia," answered Maximus. "I also need the support of, or at least a lack of opposition in, the imperial court in Mediolanum and in the senate in Roma. Your network of friends in the right places will help this. When we have secured the seats of power, I shall need good men to exercise it on my behalf. How, for example, would you feel about being made urban prefect of Roma?"

Julian felt that being urban prefect would suit him very well. He smiled for the first time. An agreement had been reached.

The two men did not shake hands. They had no need. Now both had the other in his power, either one could betray the other. They knew there was no going back. They bade each other goodnight and retired to restless and dream-wracked sleep.

Chapter Seven

EBORACUM

Before first light the next morning, the duke's convoy clattered out of Deva's east gate to begin its journey to Eboracum. Maximus left behind the deputy commander of the Twentieth, as he had promised, but left him few of the legion's troops; the majority came with him to join the core of his field army. In their place, he left orders to move in a force of tribal cavalry from the Cornovii, troopers who had been policing the central range of the western mountains. Their reassignment was as unusual as had been the move to Segontium of the men of Dumnonia; here was another element in Maximus' scheme of delegating to the British princes responsibility for the security of the west.

The presence of legionaries in and around the column meant that it was guaranteed secure passage across the spine of Britannia, which in any case had long been a land at peace. The duke rode with Constantine and his bodyguard close around him, whilst Elen was transported in a comfortable carriage that had some springing but metal-shod wheels and so made a relentless clatter on the roadstone. She had been given her own personal protection under the command of an officer named Gerontius, a gentle, happy Briton whose company she liked and who rode alongside her carriage from time to time to amuse her with conversation in their native tongue.

As they made their way slowly up the slopes of the hills that separated Deva from Eboracum, they camped at the end of each day in and around the abandoned fortresses that had been built to guard the road long before, during Roma's first conquest of the north. At first as they travelled, fields bordered their route. They passed plenty of country people working on this land, as well as in the brine pans from which the state extracted revenue. As they climbed higher, industry and agriculture gave way to moorland. There, through what was often driving rain, they travelled on through wildernesses of rock and sparse grass fit only for grazing sheep, some of which ended up in the column's cooking pots each night. Elen remained dry inside the coach; the rest had no other protection from the wet save for their thick and almost waterproof British cloaks, made of the wool of the ragged sheep they were eating as they went. At night, they slept inside leather marquees.

On the afternoon of the fifth day, they reached the small town of Calcaria, where limestone was quarried. Here was the first government staging post they had met on this journey, and this allowed Elen and the duke to sleep the night in a building, albeit a grubby and ill-furnished one.

*

As the column settled down for the night around the small *mansio*, Maximus walked through the camp accompanied only by his *protector*, Constantine. He wanted to get the feel of the men of the Twentieth, a legion he knew less well than his northern troops. The men were gathered about their campfires, finishing off their meals and drinking their issue of cheap, sour wine. Sentries were out in the gathering darkness, but there was no need here for further defensive measures, so the men could relax when not on watch. Maximus could hear the singing of the usual ribald, soldierly songs he had known from his youth. From around some fires came the rattle of dice. His men rose as he reached each group, to be seated again by a gesture from their general. With each he passed a few minutes, tasting a little of the mutton they were roasting, joshing the men about their bad cooking, checking how they responded to his jokes and questions. He was good at this sort of casual interaction and his men liked him for it. He found them sound and in good heart.

Before turning in to bed in the *mansio*, the duke climbed onto the fence that encircled the paddock where the column's horses were corralled, then sat to talk with Constantine, who stood respectfully below him. The commander of his bodyguard was a very handsome young officer, whose habitually imperturbable expression matched the seriousness with which he approached not only his military duties, but everything he did. He had come up the hard way in the army as a result of his diligence and bravery, which he coupled with an ability to act on his own initiative. Offspring of a long line of soldiers who had served in the legions and had fought the empire's wars on the Danubius, he had enlisted as a cavalryman in the Eleventh Claudia Legion at Durostorum in Moesia Secunda, the province of his birth. Due to his exemplary service, he had been transferred to a regiment of the *scholae*, the imperial guard of the eastern emperor Valens, where his ability had raised him swiftly to the rank of *primicerius*, the senior non-commissioned officer of his unit. In this role he had impressed so greatly that he had been given a commission as a junior officer, a *protector domesticus*. He was the first of his family to become an officer. In his new rank, Constantine had served close to the emperor and found himself increasingly trusted with tasks requiring intelligence and a quick wit. It was lucky for him that he had been detached on a mission to Duke Maximus at Durostorum when the Emperor Valens and most of his troops perished at Hadrianopolis at the hands of the Gothi. Had he been with the emperor, he would, almost certainly, not have survived.

Maximus had quickly taken to this young man. He liked his earnest, eager face and his evident desire to please, and he had made sure to include him among those he took with him to Britannia when he was posted there. The duke had watched him leading his men and approved of his strict enforcement of discipline. His soldiers were always perfectly turned out, sharp as buttons, yet cheerful with it. Constantine was no martinet and the standards he insisted on were those he more than met himself. He was a good commander of bodyguards, his men always carefully positioned in the right place to make sure that no one got close to his general without good cause.

"Constantine," commenced the duke, "what you doubtless heard at Segontium must have surprised you. What do you think of my project of keeping the empire safe?"

"Admirable lord, it is not for me to give an opinion on what you decide, merely to carry it out. If I may, though, with your esteemed permission, I shall say that it is my belief that whatever protects the empire is an imperative. As you know, lord, my people are from Moesia and many generations of our family have suffered at the hands of barbarians from across the Danubius. What happened at Hadrianopolis was a warning to us here. The price of our peace is perpetual vigilance and it is our job, the army's job, never to let down our guard."

"You have it exactly right, Constantine, and do you think your brother officers will think the same when they learn what I intend?"

Constantine thought a little before replying. He was no dissembler or idle flatterer, and if he had a fault in the eyes of his superiors, it was his candor, which at times ran beyond what some would have thought politic. "They will, I am sure of it. The times require leaders of strength to defend our frontiers. The army loves the kind of emperor that the divine Valentinian was, a man of strength who will not shrink from doing whatever it takes to keep the empire safe. They believe you are such a man, lord. They will follow you."

"I thank you, Constantine," replied the duke. "I am fortunate in having so close to me the services of such an honest man and such a good soldier. A word of caution, however, I must give, although in my sure estimation it is not needed in your case. What you heard in Segontium must remain deadly secret, as it could cost both our lives and the collapse of our plans were it to become public. The future of the empire, of Roma itself, depends upon your silence."

"You may rely upon my silence, lord."

"Then goodnight, Constantine, rest well until the morrow." The general went in to find Elen in the guest house, leaving Constantine not to rest, but, as was his duty, to perform his rounds and check upon the sentries who kept safe his duke and his wife.

*

The next day, sometime after the column had set off, Eboracum appeared in the distance. They were now in the duke's kingdom, for the city was the headquarters of his command and the base of Roman power in the north. Here, there was a *praeses*, a civilian governor, the *vir perfectissimus*, the most perfect, Flavius Eventinus. This governor was no pampered aristocrat, rather a member of the equestrian order and a professional bureaucrat. In this quarter, however, even with the power of his civilian office, a governor lived in the shadow of the army. Eventinus was a man of nervous disposition, whose main intention in life was not to make any mistake that would cost him his position, so he did what he could to offend no one. In Eboracum, this meant complying with whatever the duke had in hand. He made plain their relative positions this day by just happening to be riding out of the city when he met the duke's party as it arrived; in effect, he had come to greet Maximus on his return.

The governor rode with them as the column wound its way into Eboracum, passing through the cemetery to its west, with its monuments to the eminent citizens and prosperous merchants of a city that was, in Britannia, only second in size to Londinium. The civilian city lay to the west of the River Usa and possessed all the appurtenances of a flourishing Roman town: a forum, a basilica, baths, an amphitheatre, and rows of stalls and craftsmen's workshops. West of the river was also the governor's residence. Eventinus was lucky enough to inhabit one of the largest imperial palaces in the empire, in earlier years a mansion developed as a temporary home for the Emperor Septimius Severus and his court, and later refurbished for the Emperor Constantius. Eventinus rattled around in the vast and by now rather rundown palace like a pea in a pod; unlike Julian at Deva, he had not the funds to make the place more comfortable than the state's provision allowed.

Maximus graciously allowed Eventinus to take his leave at the edge of the city, where he and the column crossed the bridge to his headquarters in the vast fortress on the other side. Always a bustling garrison, it was now filled with troops gathering to march north. More were also billeted in the town, while those for whom there was no space inside the walls were housed in tents on the river meadows outside. There was a feeling of energy everywhere; the fort resounded with the noise of men being drilled, horses put through their paces and equipment being repaired. The fortress was throbbing with the heartbeat of an army preparing for war.

At the porch of the praetorium, Maximus was greeted by the tall and burly figure of his chief officer, the *praefectus* Andragathius, whom he had left holding command in the north while he was on tour. Andragathius was a Scythian from the most easterly Roman province along the Danubius. He had entered the Roman army of the east and first served with Maximus when the latter was posted as *dux* in Moesia. Scythian officers were uncommon in the army, so Andragathius had few friends and no patrons, something which Maximus swiftly spotted. The Scythian was clearly a highly effective officer, so the duke drew him into his inner circle, treated him with favour and always rewarded him well. As a result, Andragathius was devoted to the duke.

Assembled with him in the greeting party at the porch were Maximus' eldest son, Victor, and his second son, Eugenius. Both were children of Maximus' first marriage to the Princess Ceindrech, the daughter of Rheiden, prince of the northern tribe of the Votadini. They were only fourteen and thirteen years old respectively, still boys. They were in tremendous awe of their father and delighted that they had been allowed this day to be in the reception party greeting him on his return. Maximus was proud of them both and in his mind's eye had fixed both their futures in the army. Habitually, neither boy paid more than perfunctory respect to their stepmother, Elen; at best they were cool to one who was, they felt, an unworthy replacement for their own mother, a southerner who knew nothing of their mother's people. At worst, they could be cuttingly cruel. It caused Elen pain that they rejected the love she tried to offer them. It hurt her that Maximus did not seem to notice their attitudes and did nothing to curb their open contempt.

Today was no different. Victor started to stalk off behind his father with not a word in reply to his stepmother's greeting, a lack of respect noticed by Gerontius. "Be polite and say hello to your mother, Victor," her bodyguard commander prompted.

"Who are you to tell me, the duke's first-born son, what to do?" Victor rudely replied. He turned to walk away again but was brought up short and squealed pitifully when Andragathius boxed his ear.

"Behave like the gentleman your father is trying to bring you up to be, boy," ordered the Scythian. "Give your respects to my lady."

Andragathius had strong arms, so the blow stung. He was an officer who kept himself in good physical shape and there was not an ounce of fat on a muscular body that filled out his dress uniform perfectly. His Asiatic face was blessed with broad, prominent cheekbones beneath dark brown eyes, which to the British looked exotically slanted. He shaved his head to a polish, save for a top knot at its back. He was a formidable man and scared the wits out of Victor, who started to snivel, but did as he was bid.

"Now be off with you," finished Andragathius. "I am sorry, my lady, your son must learn his manners."

"Thank you, Andragathius," Elen said. "I think Victor has learned his lesson."

Victor had indeed learned his lesson, but it was not the one that his stepmother hoped. As he slouched off with Eugenius in his father's wake, he burned with the shame of injured pride at having been not only publicly chastised, but also smacked by the Scythian. He would not forget this; he would find a way to pay him out one day.

Chapter Eight

THE LADY ELEN

As Maximus led his officers into his headquarters to discuss preparations for the campaign, Elen was glad to be able to slip away. Taking only a couple of slave girls to ensure her safety, she evaded the careful watch of Gerontius and his guards, ducked out of the main gate of the fortress and crossed the bridge into the city. Here, too, there was a bustle of noisy activity, but it was of the everyday sort to which she was more accustomed. She could hear many of the languages of the empire in the crush of people on the streets.

The cries of hawkers and shopkeepers advertising their wares and haggling with customers accompanied her as she wound her way through the crowded stalls. She heard the bellowed boasts of slave sellers demonstrating the strength and docility of the Picti and Scoti slaves whom they had manacled and tied to posts on a platform. Crowds had gathered to gawk at these wild and bedraggled captives, who still looked, despite their fetters, so intimidating that only a few citizens were brave enough to offer bids. On another corner she passed people watching a juggler in Moorish costume whose performing monkey collected coppers from the crowd.

Elen hurried on, passing trains of pack animals plodding up through the city from the docks along the river. Through gaps in the tenements that lined the streets, she could see the tall, slender cranes used for unloading the merchant ships that brought wine from Burdigalia in the south of Gallia or cheap household goods from the mouths of the Rhenus and the coasts of the Mare Germanicum. She would not have been aware of the fact, but some of these ships were owned by her recent host, the *consularis* Julian, whose firm employed an agent in the city.

Wherever Elen went, she tried to avert her eyes from the shrines that were everywhere in the city and the temples to an uncountable number of gods, all to her mind houses of unspeakable demons. On every street corner stood idols before which individual devotees left flowers and small offerings of meat and wine to their personal deity. The centre of the city had many large temples, each inside its own sacred enclosure, and in these worshippers bought animals and birds for sacrifice. Some were grand edifices, with flights of steps leading up to porticoed colonnades, from which the scent of eastern incense escaped into the evening air. She heard the chants of priests processing through the streets, bearing the effigies of the gods and goddesses whose festivals were being celebrated that day. As these wound their way through the city streets, cymbals clashing and horns blaring, their devotees danced and writhed in their wake.

Almost every god in the empire, it seemed, was worshipped in Eboracum. The buildings of the state gods dominated the centre of the city. These housed the cults of the emperors and the memorials of past governors. Here were the seats of the Roman pantheon, of Jupiter, Fortuna, Venus, Oceanus and his consort Tethys. A life-sized statue of Mars, the god of war, stood on the corner of the main street. Nearby was the god's temple precinct, which was adorned with tablets erected by generations of soldiers recording their prayers for good fortune in war and commemorating their fallen comrades. Lesser, or less well known, deities had sacred spots further out in the city; as she walked away from the middle of town, Elen passed the temples of local British gods like Toutatis, the god of the Brigantes, and Veteris, a local favourite with the troops; these were gods like the ones she had been brought up to worship in Dumnonia. Other deities were less familiar, having been brought from farther afield, many from the home countries of the soldiers and merchants housed in the city. From Egypt had come the cults of Serapis and the gnostic demon Chnoubis. In the suburbs of the fort, there was a monumental shrine of Mithras, the soldiers' god. A religious mélange of mingled blood and incense hung like a pall over the entire city, and Elen hurried on as quickly as she could to escape all this cacophonous idolatry, her face covered ineffectually by a scarf.

Headed down towards the docks, Elen turned into a small lane where there was a Christian church that was almost hidden by the huge blocks of stone mounting the cranes which unloaded the merchant ships. This was the church of Eboracum's bishop. It was small and poor, much to Elen's dismay, for she had seen the basilicas of churches in other places in the empire, where bishops and the rich among their congregations showed off their ostentatious wealth. There was still little like that in Britannia. She prayed for the day when all the pagan filth in Eboracum would be swept into the river and the church would take its proper place at the centre of its life. Christ the King would rule here and throughout Britannia, she was sure.

Despite the apparent poverty of the little church, she found there a large congregation gathered for a service which was being conducted by the bishop's deacon. Elen stayed at the back of the church and looked around. She could see a very mixed crowd of men and women, facial types that she recognised from all over the empire, black faces from Africa, brown, hawk-nosed Levantine faces from the eastern provinces, tall, Germanic-looking types from the freighters crossing the seas. There were a few whose clothes and jewels, and accompanying slaves, made them identifiably wealthy, for the bishop's flock extended to the owners of villas in the surrounding country. There were few Christians still among their farming people, however. The peasants who formed the mass of the population remained resolutely pagan and had so far violently resisted attempts to destroy their rural shrines and idols. No one yet had shown any interest in converting them.

The bishop had few allies in Eboracum and it was unsurprising that he counted Elen as one of the most important. Spotting her, he came back to meet her, gave her his blessing and led her further into the church to better hear the service. For a while, Elen lost herself in the preaching and the singing of hymns, which were balm to her troubled soul. She was by now in a very highly strung state and desperately needed the assurance of her faith. Maximus had not divulged his plans to her, but, after what had transpired in Segontium, she had great suspicions that her husband was set on a path that was perilous for all of them. She needed to pray to her Lord for protection for her family – she had no illusions about the danger they were all going to be in – but she found it very difficult. To make things worse, she knew that she could tell no one in the church about her fears, as to do so would simply realise them. Neither could she speak to her husband about what he was doing until he deigned to let her know what it was. She had bottled up all her fears inside her, where they ate away at her every waking minute and spoiled her sleep at night. There was nothing she could do to alleviate this other than to pray, so she did so fervently now, raising her hands and opening her palms to her Lord as she beseeched his protection.

*

Elen's marriage to Maximus had been a great shock to her. She was still in her teens when they wed. Until then, still a young, naive girl brought up in a simple way by her father's household in his compound near Isca, she had dreamed of marrying a prince from another British tribe. Then into her life strode this thunderous, physically overpowering Roman, to whom within days she found herself betrothed. Of course, she had played no part in the decision that she should wed; she had not even had any warning of it. After the wedding in the basilica which her father had hastily repaired, Maximus had whisked her away, on her own save for two female slaves, to travel the empire with him and to watch him fight its wars. At the time when she married him, she had no Latin, nor could she read or write any language. She had counted herself lucky that Maximus had a good grasp of the Brythonic tongue; he had long served in Britannia and his first wife had been another British princess. But he had taught her nothing himself, always too busy, wrapped up in his soldier's life, so she had been forced to pick up things as she went along. It had been very hard at first. Her life in Isca had given her no social skills, no knowledge, in fact, of anything that any Roman lady would have recognised as polite or cultivated. Instead, before her marriage, she had lived almost entirely outdoors, riding the hills and hunting game. She could handle spear and bow, but she had no knowledge of a musical instrument or an embroidery frame, had never run a household and was scared into silence by the sophisticated conversation of what she thought were the fine women of the society in which her husband moved.

It had taken Elen many years to feel at all comfortable in her marriage to this strange, selfish and utterly dominating man. She bore him children, sons as well as daughters. This made Maximus happy, as did the fact that she suffered without complaint the trials of perpetually being on the move as he was posted from place to place. He liked what he had. He did not want a wife who gossiped or nagged about household matters. He preferred it that Elen was the demure, shy and unchallenging spouse he thought he had married. When he thought about her feelings, which was infrequently, he believed that she was happy, but that had far less import to him than the fact that his match had achieved its aim.

She had discovered after her wedding that their marriage had been the fruit of an imperial policy developed and implemented by the *comes*, the count, Theodosius, the Roman general whom her husband served. The grand scheme was designed to secure the empire's frontiers by tying to it the tribes who lived on either side of them by marriages of trusted imperial officers to their princesses. These Roman husbands were left in situ to create half-Roman dynasties. Maximus had been married in a similar way five years before, on that occasion to the Princess Ceindrech of the Votadini, the tribe whose lands lay on both sides of the frontier in the north. She had died after giving him four children. A second scheme was then formed to marry Maximus to cement the Dumnonii to the empire. It had not quite worked out that way, as the count had changed his mind and decided to take Maximus with him to Africa, to which Elen had accompanied him. She had been forced to be mother to four stepchildren as well as to the four babies to which she gave birth. She had tried, despite their wandering, to make them all a home in each place they settled.

It was in Africa, where they had been stationed for a couple of years, her husband still working for Count Theodosius as he put down a rebellion in Mauretania, that she had first come across Christianity. She was far from her own gods; they seemed to have lost their power in her life with every league that the ships carried her from her native shores, yet she had found no solace in any of the deities to which her husband paid superstitious and superficial reverence. The local gods had no relevance to her. One day, in the forum, she happened to pass a crowd listening to an oration by a Christian preacher, and she found herself attracted by the deep conviction expressed in the preaching of his faith. The idea that the Christian god was universal, one that might watch over his flock everywhere, was greatly appealing to a woman whose travels had cast her far from any faith. At the time, though, she had not paid very much heed.

Their next move was to lead to a deep change of heart. Maximus had been promoted and posted as the *dux moesiae secundae*, the Duke of Lower Moesia, an area which lay at the far end of the frontier on the River Danubius. He was responsible for keeping the barbarians on the other side of the river. This had gone disastrously wrong during his tenure when the Gothi, fleeing the hordes of Hunni then bearing down on them across the steppes of Scythia, had crossed the river. The Gothi were in a pitiable state. They had lost their lands and most of their possessions and had found little food during their flight. They were imploring the empire for aid and safety and camped in large numbers around the fortress. From the safety of its walls, Elen had watched in horror as her husband's troops despoiled the barbarians of their jewellery and gold, then their property and the wagons that carried it. Finally, the Gothi were reduced to begging for food and became so bereft of the means of life that they began to sell their wives and children into slavery.

To add to this Roman shame, she very soon discovered her husband's part in this looting. In their own house appeared new Gothic slaves, ragged at first and full of hatred. Worse still, she came across the teenage boys her husband kept in the slaves' quarters, whom, when he was in the mood or drunk, he took to his bed. Her anguish at all this seemed to have no end and she could see no way of dealing with it. At that lowest point, she overheard some officer make a sniggering jest about a Christian priest ministering to the starving barbarians. She sought the man out, an act that, in her position, could have been very dangerous. Had she been spotted, it would have been seen as a direct rebuke to her husband's deeds. She watched the priest as he cared for the destitute and she wept. She asked him to clandestinely instruct her in his faith. The more she learned, the more the injustice of her husband's behaviour burned inside her, but she gained hope, for she could now believe that there could be forgiveness and peace if she accepted the risen Christ. After some months, she allowed herself to be secretly baptised and, thereafter, wherever she followed Maximus, she attended whatever church or house meeting that she could find.

Maximus soon knew of this, not from Elen, but from his staff, but he took no steps to forbid practising her new religion. This was neither charity on his part nor a sign of love for his wife. With most of the empire, he had come to see that without professing the religion of Christ it would be very difficult to gain promotion and position. Imperial edicts had begun to make this clear, and whilst the duke was prepared to ally with those of the old beliefs who were bitterly opposed to the Christian takeover, he had insufficient belief in any of those faiths to fight their cause. He could sense which faith would prevail in the long run. His wife's faith, he thought, was something that he might make use of when the time came.

Maximus did not realise, however, how much his wife had come to despair of him for what he had done in Moesia. She feared that he was damned. Yet she kept her silence as a good wife should. She lowered her eyes and looked away, just as she had always done.

*

The sermon in the Eboracum church that day was given by a priest whom Elen had not seen before. The bishop whispered to her that he came from Londinium, where the faith was older and far stronger than in the north. Elen had never heard oratory like his. The man was clearly highly educated, practised in swaying crowds, and he held this congregation in the palms of his upraised hands. He spoke of the freedom of mankind, of each Christian's own responsibility for choosing to accept God and for doing good, and of the fundamental decency that was innate in all mankind. His oration ended:

"God has given man the intellect to choose his own path. What point could there be for God to create a world in which everything his creatures did, or said or thought, had been fixed from the beginning as part of His plan? Is our Father so cruel that he has fixed for eternity that only a tiny few who are his elect should be saved and that the rest, through no fault of their own, should be damned to hellfire? God is the god of love. He gave his only Son that we should all have the chance to be saved. This is the creed that our blessed father Pelagius has taught us. There are many who do not believe this, and, because of what they think is God's omniscience, believe that all has been preordained. Pelagius and his followers, and among them I count myself, do not believe this, cannot believe this. Pelagius has just gone to Roma to persuade our Church fathers of the moral righteousness of his theology. He fights for us all and we shower our blessings upon him. May the holy martyrs Alban, Julius and Aaron be with him in this cause. Pray that he succeeds."

Elen found herself strangely uplifted by these words. She felt great comfort in the idea that she could choose to walk her own path and reach towards the good. She would pray that evening that her husband, too, might at last choose to be brought to the light, and that he might, despite all he had done, find the peace of forgiveness.

After the service, Elen took a few moments to speak to the bishop. "Have you heard, bishop, about the new edicts that his imperial majesty, Gratian, has promulgated banning sacrifices to devils and spirits and taking their money?" Elen asked.

"I have, my lady. The Lord is moving against them, and their last days cannot be long away. God bless and preserve the emperor."

"It will not be long before even the leaders of this godless army in Eboracum must bend, and then our faith will flourish. You know," continued Elen, "that you will always have my support, and I pray that I am here with you to see the day when the temples of the unrighteous are torn down and all their works confounded."

"You will be, my lady, you will be. May almighty God drive your husband's sword in the fight for the truth and the light."

Elen shuddered under her shawl at this, for she could not find it within herself to hold such a hope. She knew full well that her husband's sword would be unsheathed only in his self-interest. She changed the subject to that of the sermon they had heard in the church and asked the bishop who the preacher was.

"He is a follower of the teacher Pelagius," explained the bishop. "His teaching is controversial. Many would deny its validity. I myself am not sure of its orthodoxy, but it is an attractive interpretation of the faith, and it will win many adherents, I think."

Although she could not have known it at the time, the doctrine of love and freewill that she had heard that day would be one that she would keep in her heart and act upon for the rest of her life. The preacher had ignited a small spark of hope in Elen's soul, and she hoped that it would not be extinguished again. She had been a passive spectator in her own life for too long.

It was the first time that Elen conceived the notion that her fate was not written and that she might choose her own path whenever opportunity offered.

She resolved that day that she *was* going to choose.

Chapter Nine

CASTOR AND POLLUX

It did not take the *protector* Gerontius long to discover that his charge had disappeared. He hastily set about a discreet but unsuccessful search of the fortress to locate Elen. After two hours, when she had still not turned up, he was beginning to panic, and it was to his huge relief when she and her maids reappeared in her quarters. Elen tried to pretend that she had been there all along, an excuse that Gerontius gently indicated he knew was untrue. He looked so worried that Elen felt ashamed to have given him the slip. Something she had seen of her favourite young officer now gave her a little confidence to be open with him. During their journey from Deva, she had watched him give alms to a poor man they had come across on the road and had noticed the kindness in his face. She had wondered then whether he was of the true faith. She decided to take a chance. She fell back on the truth and told him where she had been.

"My lady," said Gerontius, "I too am of the faith, so I understand the reason for your caution. Yet it is not safe for you to go abroad like that by yourself. The bishop and his flock will, of course, do you no harm, but there are many in the city who will. What is more, if the duke finds out that I have let you out of my sight for even one instant, he will not be forgiving. For the sake of my position, maybe my life, please do not go off by yourself again."

"I am sorry to have put you at risk by my selfish actions, Gerontius," replied Elen. "No, I shall not do that again."

"If my lady would like to go shopping or to see the sights, however, and would take me with her, I think we still might go anywhere in the city that my lady fancied. My men are very loyal and will not betray your destination."

Elen took the hint, and on her next visit to the church, went with a very unobtrusive escort that hovered at a distance and was accompanied into the church by a single male escort who stuck close by her side, and that was Gerontius.

*

When he got back to his quarters in the fortress that night, having seen Elen safely to bed, Gerontius went straight to the rooms of the commander of Maximus' bodyguard, his friend Claudius Constantine. The two were close friends. They had met while serving the duke in Moesia and had both accompanied the general to Britannia. As Maximus had kept them both close to him, they had been able to continue to serve together for longer than army service usually allowed.

Gerontius was a couple of years younger than Constantine. His sunny, easy-going character complemented Constantine's gravity; he was one of the few men who could make his friend laugh. He had a stunning smile and a charm that melted the hearts of all those upon whom he turned it. People who knew him said that when he laughed it was as if the sun came out. To him, the glass was always half full. Constantine, on the other hand, could not but see that it was half empty. Together, their brother officers said, they would have made a perfect whole.

Gerontius was a Briton, the second son of a decurion from Venta Belgarum, a junior member of the aristocracy of the Belgae. He had decided to join the army after the prospect of inheriting his father's lands had evaporated when his brother, the heir, produced a clutch of children. His family helped him out by buying him the military rank of *protector domesticus*, a rank that took him close to the western emperor. After the Gothic incursion, he had been part of a team sent east by the Emperor Gratian to assess the situation in Moesia. There he met Constantine.

At first, the two had been unsure of each other, their characters being so markedly different. Constantine was conservative in his view of religion, as he was in all things, and cleaved to the old ways. He abominated the lack of toleration spread by the Christian tide that was slowly engulfing the empire. Gerontius, on the other hand, had grown up in a Christian household in Venta and had a simple faith that he followed quietly. He was no extremist, however, and was not an advocate of banning what he viewed as paganism. Had they both had the same faith, they both agreed, they would have gone before a priest and formally sworn brotherhood, but, as it was, they both considered that they were brothers anyway.

Constantine was naturally traditional in his belief in the virtues and civilising mission of Roma. Having been brought up on the Danubius frontier and seen on more than one occasion the chaos that could be unleashed on innocent people when marauding barbarians were not kept under tight control, he held the maintenance of the *pax romana* as the highest good, more important than the protection of any personality or the imposition of any faith. When he fought, he did so for eternal Roma. Gerontius had a more jaundiced view of the empire, and although he was happy to be both a citizen and a soldier, his British roots were dearest to him.

Were he given the opportunity, he always claimed, it would be his tribe and his country that he put first. The pair sparred good-naturedly about these matters, as about much else.

Neither man was married yet, both being still firmly wedded to their careers, so they spent their free time together and were scarcely ever seen apart. Their closeness was a byword in the army; their men called them Castor and Pollux, the heavenly twins, and more crudely would jest about them behind their backs, putting wagers on which of them acted as the man, which the woman, something that would have horrified both of them had they heard it. In any case, Constantine showed little interest in sex. He did not frequent brothels or keep slave women; he seemed cold and aloof to women of his own status, such as the wives of his fellow officers. The army was all to him, and everything else, women included, counted for less.

This was not so with Gerontius. His men had not been wrong when they sensed something different about him, and their ribaldry, had he heard it, would have wounded him deeper, as there was truth within it. The occasional half glance at a handsome young recruit, the choice of the best-looking soldier to be his personal orderly, his total lack of interest in any female company, all of these were clear signs for the percipient. He had found himself falling in love with Constantine back on the Danubius and at times was unable to hide his feelings completely. Constantine did not notice, or affected not to; others did not miss it. Nevertheless, Gerontius was well aware that there could be no sexual relationship between men of their rank, for they were of equivalent status. Any sex act would be a *stuprum*, a crime of shame, and he was fully aware that Constantine would have been repulsed by an advance. So, Gerontius suffered platonically the sharp pleasure of his friend's company and instead would take out his frustrated lust upon the occasional slave boy or willing civilian.

Yet the two were very close. There was little that they would not confide in each other, and due to their different ranks and temperaments it was usually Gerontius who sought the counsel of his more experienced friend. Today, he needed to talk to Constantine about Elen's escape into the city. His friend was alarmed by what he heard, not for Elen, for whom he had respect but no responsibility, but for his friend. He had no doubt that Maximus would react violently if he knew that his wife had sneaked off alone into the city and been away for several hours. His advice to Gerontius was to stay closer and to lean on the slave girls around Elen to give him prior warning should she repeat the escape.

Gerontius had also come to bid a temporary farewell to his friend, who was about to march north on the morrow. Where the duke went, there must go Constantine, but he himself had been ordered to stay behind in Eboracum to protect Elen and the children. He was beginning to think that this was the more dangerous task, for were Elen's excursions to become known, he knew that he would find the duke far more frightening than any number of Picti whom Constantine might come across.

The friends embraced as Gerontius wished his friend a safe return.

"I wish I were coming with you," Gerontius confessed. "It is going to be a lot harder making sure all is well here with the duke's family than your job looking after the duke himself!"

"You are right, Gerontius," replied his friend. "No matter how many political or strategic risks our duke takes, one risk that he doesn't take is with his own body. Our unit will be close around him, all the time. You and I know that this is not because he's a coward, far from it, just that he isn't going to lose it all, to waste all this effort, for the sake of showing off what a hero he is."

"The risks he takes are always calculated, which is why he has always won."

Constantine agreed. "This time will be the same, I think. I don't believe that this Pictish war is anything more than the opening move in a much bigger game. I can't tell you what happened at Segontium, save that it made me realise that something big is afoot. You'll be pleased, Gerontius, too, that what the duke has planned is going to change things here in Britannia. He's going to take your people with him when he goes where he's going. Just wait and see."

"It's not before time that someone did, Constantine. Britannia may have done well out of the empire in many ways. Just look at the riches down south. My hometown, Venta, is doing very nicely out of all the money that selling our grain to the army brings in, not to mention what we earn from the corn and animals we ship across the sea to the troops on the Rhenus. But as for any political or social power, you can forget it. As far as the rest of the empire is concerned, they think we are still living in mud huts at the end of the world."

"Which is just what the duke said the other day," said Constantine, laughing. They parted, as always, off to do their duty in different directions, knowing certainly that this time they'd be back together again soon.

Chapter Ten

THE ROAD TO THE NORTH

Within days, the army's columns marched north out of the city, their long baggage trains at the rear. The duke had assembled a force of nearly 10,000 men, about half of them from his two legions, the Twentieth, which had just marched in from Deva, and the Sixth Victrix, which was based in Eboracum's fort. Pulcher and his Segontienses had joined the main body, along with other cohorts assembled by the duke from the forts of the west and northwest. With them marched troops of *laeti*, mercenaries levied from allied people settled in Britannia, including units of the Alamanni under their aged king, Fraomarius, now an old man, but although frail still eager for war, the plunder it would bring, and the renown it would give him when he divided the spoils between his fighting chiefs. There were Germans of other peoples, too, Saxones, Frisii and Franci from both banks of the Rhenus, all of whom served under their own tribal leaders in return for settlement inside the empire.

Around the duke, to make sure that he came through this expedition unscathed, rode the bodyguard he had personally picked and placed under the command of Constantine. Also close at hand rode his second-in-command, Andragathius, a gaggle of staff officers following him, these led by Promotus, to whom fell the responsibility of planning the detail of the campaign. Also riding with the duke, and this for the first time, was Victor, Maximus' eldest son. It was time, thought the duke, to blood the young man and start to prepare him for his imperial future.

It would take the army more than a week to reach the *vallum aelium*, the Wall, the barrier built across the country on the orders of the Emperor Hadrian so long before. The columns wound their way through the small towns and villages scattered on either side of the great north road, the countryside gradually changing as they marched. They soon left behind them the flat and marshy lands that lay around the River Usa, where flax was grown on large estates for the linen trade. Gradually, the landscape became wilder, wetter and less populated. Vistas of moorland and small, impoverished farm holdings took the place of the rich estates of the south. Only twenty or so years before, these lands, even before that some of the least civilised in the empire, had been devastated by the Picti, who had swept south during what had come to be known as the Great Barbarian Conspiracy. They had burned, looted, raped and enslaved as they came south. Only those inside the walls of Eboracum and some scattered forts outside it had been safe. By the time reinforcements arrived from Gallia, the north had been reduced to a blackened ruin. To this day, while the forts and the Wall itself had been rebuilt, many of the towns, villages and isolated farms still stood empty and crumbling, the fields that surrounded them weed-grown and untilled. As they marched, the men passed the blackened timbers and collapsed walls of small roadside huts and posting stations. The sights of destruction and the plight of the murdered countryfolk angered the troops. The duke was pleased that this put them in good mind to exact revenge.

After some days on the road, the duke and his headquarters staff stopped for the night in Isurium, the tribal capital of the Brigantes. It was a poor enough place, but it was surrounded by a high, very thick wall, studded with bastions, defences strong enough to have prevented it falling to the Picti. There was little, though, to recommend the place to a Roman, for the Brigantes had never recovered from the Romans' slaughter of their tribe when it had revolted against the newly conquering empire over 300 years before. Now, there was still not even a public bathhouse in the town. The duke and Andragathius put up in the scruffy *mansio*.

After their evening meal, Maximus took the opportunity to sound out Andragathius' views of his plans. He trusted his deputy, who had been with him through the troubles in the east. He had already given him the broad outline of what he intended to do. Now, he needed to ensure that Andragathius was clear about how it should be accomplished. The Scythian had often wielded his great common sense and organising ability to put into effect his general's broad-brush ideas. Those ideas were on a bigger scale now, but Maximus was confident that his deputy could handle them.

"I see three phases in the operation you plan after the Pictish expedition, admirable duke," Andragathius responded. "I see little problem in the first two. You hold the strongest military power in Britannia and after this war, north of the Wall, with its rewards of spoil and easy combat, the army will follow you. If we act swiftly, I doubt that there will be any opposition in Britannia. Nor do I see any real opposition in the second phase; the *limitanei*, the frontier forces on the Rhenus, are too weak and are stationed too far apart to offer any resistance. The dangerous part will come in phase three, when we face the *comitatus*, the field army in Gallia. We do not want a fight there, so we shall have to rely upon your ally Julian's money. Are you sure of the man?"

"I am sure," replied the duke. "He is a greedy, frustrated person who sees our success as his route to fame and fortune. He is also extremely rich."

"If we can suborn the field army quickly, before reinforcements can come to its aid, we shall have Gallia. The Emperor Theodosius will not come for you there; he has too much on his hands in the east. There is little risk from the young Emperor Valentinian in Mediolanum. By the time he grows to manhood, your rule will have become rock solid in the west."

"What if we were to ensure that he would never be able to come for us? If we removed one more piece from the board, we would have one less enemy."

"I counsel caution, duke. If you move against Valentinian, you will force Theodosius to take up the cause of his protégé. Better to become yourself the young emperor's patron, to stay in Gallia but exercise influence then power over Mediolanum and so become the real ruler of the west. I think it vital that you do not provoke Theodosius."

"Your counsel, as always, Andragathius, is sound. I thank you for it." Maximus dissembled here. He had no intention of stopping until he had power over all the west, maybe not even then. It would not, though, be a good idea to frighten Andragathius with that prospect. That would be for another day.

The next day, the columns moved on fast. After Isurium, the road went straight as a die, guarded at road junctions and river crossings by a chain of forts. This was a zone in which the military predominated. Each fort was flanked by a small civilian settlement, the populations of which lived off the money the soldiers spent, so the grubby workshops, shops and inns in each were interspersed with alehouses and brothels, which the marching men were not permitted to visit; they hoped for more liberality on their return journey.

The weather was fine and clear, the moorland birds swooped and sang over the marching columns, and there was a spring in all their steps.

*

The days of marching north gave Maximus too much time to think. As he rode, he let his mind sink back into the thoughts that always plagued him when he wasn't occupied. Why was he about to endanger his own life, the lives of his family and doubtless of many others, by embarking on the path of mutiny, rebellion and usurpation? Many had tried it before him, and few, save those born to the purple, had succeeded. Was he insane?

He was enough of a realist to recognise that there was indeed some spur of madness in his motivation, a darkness inside him that had grown unchecked, fed by the grievances he had been nursing for eight years. This fungus had started to fester within him on the day when the new regime of the Emperor Gratian murdered Count Theodosius, his dear patron, the only commander he had ever wanted to serve, the man whom he had followed, honoured, nay loved throughout the first half of his life.

Count Theodosius was the father of the current emperor of the east, who bore his name. Maximus had spent his childhood in the count's household in Hispania and had grown up alongside his son. Although he was the child of a poor and very distant relation, Maximus had been treated as his own by the count. The duke let his memories play back to scenes of his boyhood, when he had grown up on the count's great estate. He and the younger Theodosius were inseparable in those years. They had played together, they had been beaten into literacy by the same tutor and they had sat together in the same classes in the local school. Together they had gone into the army, and, when the old Emperor Valentinian sent the count to Britannia to rid it of the Picti, Scoti and Saxones who had overrun it in the year of the Great Barbarian Conspiracy, both Maximus and Theodosius had gone with him as cadet officers on his staff. It was then, when the count had pushed the invaders back north of the Wall and had re-established Roman control of the tribes to its north, that Maximus had been married to Ceindrech, the first of his two British princesses.

After many years of hard work and some bloodshed, when the count had restored Britannia once more to safety, he had departed. By then, Maximus had married his second British wife, Elen, who went with him to Africa, where the count had been summoned to fight another of the empire's wars. His own son, Theodosius, had been posted to the east, so despite his recent marriage, the count took Maximus with him. In his typically brilliant and very thorough fashion, Count Theodosius had effectively suppressed the rebellion of the Moorish Prince Firmus.

It had been a tragedy that the old Emperor Valentinian, who had always looked upon the count with great favour, had chosen this time to burst a blood vessel and die, leaving the western empire to his son, the fourteen-year-old Gratian. Rather than bring Count Theodosius back in triumph, Gratian's courtiers had seen him, the greatest soldier of the age, as a threat to the throne. They had sent officers to Africa to have the count arraigned on spurious charges and put to death.

Maximus was with him when he was arrested. He had been forced to watch as the man he regarded as his father was publicly beheaded outside the walls of Carthago. It was that deed, rather than any favouritism shown by Gratian to his

Gothi bodyguards, or pretended fears of the young emperor's military incapacity, that was the real cause of Maximus' hatred for Gratian, and why he wanted him, and all those around him who were responsible for the count's betrayal, dead.

The years since the great count died in Africa had only increased the duke's coruscating desire for revenge. As a recognised supporter of a convicted traitor, his career had been stalled. He had risen only gradually, only very slowly taking more senior military posts, and had been appointed not just once but twice to the command of frontier troops, posts reserved for second-raters. Now, he was sure, his career had finally stalled completely. In his own estimation there would be no further posting for him after this command in Britannia's north. His long-cherished hopes of rising to the rank of count, or even to the position of *magister peditum*, commander of an army, had died with his posting to Eboracum. It had not helped, of course, that his first dukedom, on the Danubius, had ended very badly indeed.

When the Gothi across the river implored Gratian's uncle Valens, the emperor of the east, to save them from the ferocity of the Hunni, Maximus had been Duke of Moesia Secunda, stationed in the massive fortress of Durostorum. In what followed, he had let himself down by greed and a lack of humanity, not to mention an absence of any ordinary common sense. Under imperial orders to detail his troops to ferry thousands upon thousands of Gothi into the empire, he had failed to carry out his orders to disarm them. Instead, he had sought to make money from the refugees' desperate plight. He had deliberately made no preparations to feed and house the barbarians and instead had let them starve around the wagons in which they leaguered up in the fields. They had been reduced to such desperation that even their nobles were forced to sell their own children into slavery in exchange for the pieces of dog meat that his men threw at them. Boys had been sold for his own profit and in many cases used for the pleasure of his soldiery. He did not dwell on the fact that he had taken two of the boys for his own pleasure; it meant little to him, and in any case, when he was posted to Britannia he had left them behind in Durostorum. He had not, he congratulated himself, stooped to having their throats slit, but instead handed them over to one of the staff officers who was staying there.

Yet, looking back, he had no illusions about the infamy of his policy and to what it had led directly, which was the death of the Emperor Valens and the evaporation of Roman might in Thracia. For the Gothi, in ever-growing numbers as they fled from the Hunni, brought to the point of destruction by the treatment they had received, had used the weapons they had retained to break out of the reservations in which they had been confined. They had massacred the few troops sent against them and pillaged a whole string of provinces. Maximus had shut himself up in his impregnable fortress and left the civilians to their own devices; a bloody fate for many of them. When the Emperor Valens refused to await reinforcements from the west and impulsively took the field at Hadrianopolis, two thirds of the eastern army perished. The emperor's body was never recovered. It was the worst disaster to Roman arms in hundreds of years. Had so many not died, and the chaos not been so great, his own crimes would, he knew, have cost him at least his post, maybe his life. However, largely due to the fact that no one had been left in charge, he had survived, though tainted, in the general chaos.

To add to the guilt which he felt over his own conduct and its effects, and to the hatred that he felt for Gratian, jealousy had started to gnaw his innards. In the ghastly aftermath of the Gothic victory, the younger Theodosius, once his closest friend, in effect his brother, had been recalled to service by

Gratian's court to rescue the empire in the east. Just as Maximus' career was stalling to a point from which it was not destined to recover, Gratian had made Theodosius an Augustus, Emperor of the East, with his seat in Constantinopolis.

So, to Maximus' contorted mind, rather than avenge his father, as he should have done, Theodosius had accepted elevation to be one of three members of the college of emperors, alongside Gratian, his father's murderer.

Theodosius had let Maximus alone in Moesia and not attempted to bring him to justice for his criminal behaviour. Maybe it was for old times' sake, more likely it was because for many years he had his hands full trying to restore peace. Yet Maximus knew that Theodosius would never trust him again. He also knew that people of rank, those who knew what had happened, especially in the army, whispered about him behind his back and that most who knew of his infamy had as little to do with him as they could get away with. He would never be able to escape the cloud under which he had ruined his life. The love that Maximus had borne his friend had curdled slowly into envy and hatred. The fact that Maximus knew that this was his own fault made it all the harder to bear.

Chapter Eleven

AGAINST THE PICTI

Gnawed by his grievances, although careful to show his thoughts to no man, the duke pushed his army on. At Longovicium, they picked up arms and equipment at the military factory, then marched on to a temporary assembly area at Coria, just south of the Wall. This was the last small town within territory under the direct administration of the empire. Coria was also the Votadini's principal settlement south of the Wall; their lands straddled the frontier. This was the last place where Maximus and his men would see any signs of civilisation before they crossed into the wilder lands of the north. The army pitched camp there to pause and draw breath for a few days.

When Count Theodosius had restored Roman authority in the north, he had vigorously cowed the British tribes who acted as a buffer between the empire and the Picti. To make sure that they kept to their renewed vows of service, he left Roman officers embedded within them. It was in accordance with this policy that he had married Maximus to a princess of the Votadini, which was the eastern frontier region's principal tribe. After she died, and Maximus had been sent off to marry Elen of the Dumnonii, the tribune Catellius had replaced him to reside in the tribe's capital, a hillfort in Manau Goddodin, up on the tribe's Pictish frontier. Catellius and another officer, the tribune Paternus, had been married into the Votadini's ruling house. Among these peoples, inheritance was traced through the female line, so offspring of such marriages were powerful tools for binding the tribes to Roma. Roman officers had also been detached to command the irregular troops raised by the tribe to do Roma's work. Not all of these Romans had survived, but those who did rode down to the Wall to meet the duke. They brought with them Caswallon, the Votadini's ruling prince, the duke's nephew by his first marriage.

More tribal levies soon arrived in the duke's encampment. Led by their Roman officers, men of the two major tribes of the west, the Selgovae and the Novantae, rode in to join his force. Last to arrive, for he had further to come, was the ruler of a fourth tribe, the Damnonii, whose rocky stronghold of Alt Clut dominated the River Clota a long way to the north. This prince had left his troops in his own lands and now clattered into the town with just a small escort, accompanied by Quintilius Clemens, the Roman officer the duke had made resident in his household. The Roman officers with them were naturally glad to be back with the army and, after long absences in the wilds, with men who spoke their own tongue. Though now wielding independent authority and leading often exciting lives, they had volunteered for permanent exile in lands which most would have deemed too barbarous for a Roman.

All these tribes were Roma's allies, tied to her by treaty, bound to provide troops and to act as a buffer between the Wall and the Picti. Twenty years before, their predecessors, in several cases the fathers of those who now rode in to meet Maximus, had betrayed the empire and aided the Picti to attack the south. Their descendants were anxious now to be seen to be enthusiastic supporters. They were, in any case, keen for war, avidly looking forward to the harvest of slaves and plunder it would earn them.

*

When his forces had assembled at Coria, the duke summoned a conference to brief his officers and the princes who had joined him. Before the meeting, Maximus had taken pains to speak to each as they arrived. This had given him the opportunity to give the princes an idea of what was afoot. Over several nights, he had feasted with those who arrived earliest and in the daytimes had carefully inspected their men. Now they all met together for the first time. They made for a crowded and colourful gathering in the marquee that had been erected for the occasion, typical of the great diversity of races that served in the armies of the empire. Both British princes and Fraomarius, the Allamannic king, with their tribal nobles and chiefs behind them and their Roman advisers at their right hands, filled one side of the tent. In the centre, on a low dais, sat the duke with Andragathius by his side and Promotus and the rest of his staff to the rear. Occupying the other side of the tent were the army's principal Roman commanders, Aurelian, prefect of the Twentieth, and Flavius Quietus, commander of the Sixth Victrix, a Gaul who owed his appointment to Maximus, under whom he had served in Africa. Lesser commanders, such as Pulcher of the Segontienses, stood to the rear. Constantine had posted his bodyguards around the edges of the tent to keep a watchful eye on the gathering and had placed more men around its outside to keep unwanted ears from hearing what was to transpire.

Promotus called the conference to order in querulous tones that weren't heard by all, so with a withering look at his chief of staff, the duke rose to speak before the hubbub had subsided. "By now," he boomed, immediately quietening those in the back ranks who hadn't heard Promotus, "you will all know why we are here. It is time to show the Pictish barbarians beyond our borders that the might of Roma is not to be disrespected. For too long, your peoples' lives and livelihoods have suffered from their outrageous attacks. Now I intend that we teach them a lesson they will not forget in this generation and many more."

The duke paused to survey the crowd. "Never since the days of the great Count Theodosius," he went on, "has such a powerful force marched north. I see before me the flower of the empire and her allies. We shall conquer."

There was a rumble of cheering and the thunder of weapons banging the earth. "Our plan is simple," went on the duke, "and you already know it, so I shall only summarise it now. Our main force will march north from the old Wall built by the divine Antoninus Pius. We shall then divide into several columns following the routes our illustrious predecessors have used to harry the north. If circumstances permit, we shall go further than any have been since Agricola's day. On our left will be the men of Alt Clut, on our right the forces of the Votadini, and up the east coast will sail our fleets. We shall destroy everything in our path and kill all the men of the Caledonii and Miathi tribes that we find in our path. The fit women and children we shall bring back as slaves. We shall carry back with us everything of value we find, especially the property these brigands have looted from our lands in the past. You are all going to come home rich!"

Applause broke out again; the idea of plunder gladdened the hearts of everyone there. "As we do this," the duke resumed after the noise had died down, "the ships of the Selgovae will harry Hibernia and those of the Novantae will sail up the west coast, pillaging as they go."

Maximus paused. "You can see in this how important to Roma are you, its allies of the north. It is my intention to ensure that after this campaign is won, this fact is recognised in more substantial and permanent ways. You men of the north already help hold our frontier for us. You have not, however, until now, had any official recognition of your importance in the governance of the diocese. I intend that this changes and I shall give you a place in the sun. I can say no more now of this as my plans have yet to mature. Trust me, however, not to forget this pledge."

This last commitment by the duke was one that had not been anticipated by anyone present and was loudly welcomed. The duke nodded to them all, then stalked out with their acclamations ringing in his ears, leaving Andragathius and Promotus to issue all those present with detailed orders for the campaign.

*

On the morrow, the army resumed its progress north, accompanied now by the British princes of Alt Clut and the Votadini. Within the first day they reached the fort of Hunnum, its massive walls standing atop a hill that guarded the main road north as it crossed the Wall. No matter how many times he saw it, the sight of this ancient defensive frontier, built nearly 300 years before, always took the duke's breath away. He knew it better than most, having traversed its length and inspected its troops many times since he took command. The Wall was massive, with a parapet that stood fifteen feet high, a line of grey stone that wound as far as the eye could see; it stretched, in fact, from coast to coast of the island of Britannia. The Wall's precincts were cut off from all the lands to the south by the *vallum*, a band of land cleared of vegetation along its entire length. All along the centre of this ran a deep ditch and a military road. On the north side of the Wall, facing the barbarians, was another ditch, this one ten feet deep. The forts which lay along its length and those supporting them in the rear housed most of the 13,000 men of the duke's regular command.

Maximus turned to Constantine, who was riding beside him. "I recall what the Wall was like when I first saw it as a young man. Then, the Picti who had overrun it had fled north, leaving fires still burning inside the milecastles they had managed to capture and pillage. The villages that clustered at the gates of all the forts were in ruins and still in some cases ablaze. Many of the troops had abandoned their posts and fled south, leaving the civilian population to the mercy of the raiders. The Picti and their treacherous British accomplices had killed all who were unfit for work and dragged the rest away to slavery. Most of the forts had been able to hold out to wait for relief, for the Picti had no knowledge of siege warfare and were after plunder easily gained. Count Theodosius led our army north until it reached the Wall, sweeping up the deserting soldiery as we came. We found the Wall largely deserted, no longer garrisoned, the gates it guarded to the north stoved in and burned. The men we found trickling out of the surviving posts had held out for months. Gaunt, starving in some cases, they had survived by hoping against hope for a relief that it seemed would never come. It took years to recover and rebuild."

By now, however, Constantine could see no sign on the Wall or its surrounds of any of this destruction. The damage had been restored, the forts regarrisoned and the civilian villages reinhabited. All along its length, the Wall was a bustling hive of the military and the contractors, artisans, small farmers and civilian populations that lived off them. Most of the soldiers of the duke's force had seen it before, and, in good soldierly fashion, were deliberately unimpressed by what they were seeing for the umpteenth time. They marched north through the massive gateway at Hunnum into what all but the British in their number regarded as the wilderness. To many of the accompanying tribesmen, it was, of course, their home.

Two days later, the column passed Bremenium, the last of the Roman outposts north of the Wall, watched as they passed by the troops manning the artillery catapults on its bastions, who saluted and waved. They marched on for another week through the lands of the Votadini, still reckoned friendly territory despite what had happened in the past. Finally, they reached the eastern end of the abandoned wall that had been occupied in the time of the Emperor Antoninus Pius, who had briefly made it Roma's northernmost frontier. There was little left of those fortifications now, though the wall itself and the ruined forts along it still gave the bivouacking troops some protection when they halted for the night. This wall had been abandoned so long before that only the military mapmakers marching with the legions any longer knew the Roman names of its forts. It ran through the land of Manau Gododdin, the northernmost territory of the Votadini. From here on lay only the enemy.

Maximus had a very simple plan, one he wanted to complete quickly, before midsummer if he could. Although he had not indicated this to his men, he intended to lead no army of conquest, more an enormous raiding party with which he intended to destroy as much as he could of the Pictish tribes across the border; enough, in fact, to crush any thought they might have of causing trouble in the north while he took many of his troops across to Gallia. He needed his men for the more dangerous task of confronting the Emperor Gratian, so his plan called for avoiding a major engagement. Along with his British allies, he also had a baser motive, and that was plunder. In the wake of his columns trundled the wagons of slave traders, hard men who would pay for the living bodies of those who fell into Maximus' hands.

*

Aside from Victor, the rest of Maximus' family remained back in Eboracum. The fortress was a good place to bring up her children, thought Elen. There could be nowhere more secure in the western empire, and since her time with Maximus in the east, where she had seen the horrors of the Gothic invasion, the security of her family was one of the principal thoughts in her mind. When she had first come to Eboracum, she had been too frightened to leave the great fortress, and it had taken her months before she would walk outside its walls, even with an escort. Now, she was more at ease, although she feared that her husband's plans would not allow that comforting feeling to last. She tried hard not to show her anxiety to either her husband or her children. Only the bishop of the city recognised her anguish, though none of the reasons why, and was able to offer her only the scant comfort of her religion.

Although four of Maximus' children were by his first wife, Elen had tried to care for all eight of his offspring equally. It wasn't easy. Victor and Eugenius, in particular, were growing into teenagers in their father's image, free-spirited and daring, but selfish and insouciant. Victor, still only fourteen years old, was already copying his father's arrogance and swagger. He ignored Elen and kept as far away from her as he could.

Eugenius, whose name was Owain in the British tongue, was Maximus' second son. He was growing into a tall, strapping youth, who suffered from a condition that caused his lips to darken in colour and led to his British nickname *finddu*, or black lips. He revered his father and on a good day brought himself to tolerate Elen. More often than not following his eldest brother Victor's example, he affected to despise his stepmother. He did not admire her shyness and resented her anxious fussing; he was not inclined to regard her as his mother at all. Antonius, the third stepson, known as Annun by the British, was a year younger again, only twelve at this point. He was a gentler child and happily treated Elen as his mother, as did Magna, the only daughter of the first marriage, who was a sweet and obliging girl. Much to Elen's pain and sadness, all four children were of the old faiths, for Maximus honoured the memory of his dead northern wife by insisting that her children maintain the rites she had observed. All four also spoke Brythonic well, in the northern dialect of the Votadini.

In contrast, Elen had been able to bring up her own children baptised in the faith she followed and, when Maximus allowed a chaplain to be brought into the palace, they attended services, although they did not accompany their mother into the city to the bishop's church. Constantine, the eldest of her children, whom the British called Custennin, was another child who seemed to have been made in Maximus' image. In his earlier years he had been bullied by his older stepbrothers, but he had been hardened by it and by his father's example, so that by now he stood up for himself sufficiently violently that they left him alone. Publicus, her second son, who was called Peblig in the British tongue, was not at all like his father. He had always been a small, weak child, so sickly in his early years that it was doubted he would live long, but Elen had nursed him through every childhood illness, and he'd survived. A dreamy, emotional child, he took much after her and liked nothing better than to sit at her feet and hear stories from the scriptures. His large, dark eyes would light up when she read to him; he looked so very much like her, she knew.

The youngest two daughters, Gratiana and Severa, were still too young to make much of an impression on anyone, being only eight and six. They loved to run through the many corridors and rooms of the fortress and were great favourites of the soldiers. They, like their older siblings, spent their days at lessons with their tutors. Elen intended them all to be literate. The boys were undergoing different stages of the usual course of studies that would fit them into the Roman society that Maximus intended would be their milieu. All but Peblig were also undergoing training in horsemanship and the use of arms, an education that they much preferred to the tedium of the school room. It had been tacitly agreed that Peblig would not have to suffer this. It was clear even then that he would follow other paths.

With Victor having gone north with his father, and in consequence as Owain softened temporarily towards his stepmother, harmony and homeliness prevailed for once in the home. Elen could be glad and drew breath.

*

Maximus' columns carved their way northwards, following in the tracks of all the earlier Roman generals and emperors who had harried the north. Count Theodosius had been the last of these only a few years before and the marks of his pillaging were still evident in the burned-out hovels on either side of their path. As Maximus had intended, the Pictish tribes of the Miathi and Caledonii, having got wind of his expedition weeks before, had fled north with their animals into the highlands. Those men who had not been able to escape, Maximus ordered to be put to the sword and their women and children carted off into slavery. Every village, every isolated farm or fisherman's hut, he ordered burned to the ground. To their east, sailing in parallel to their progress, the Roman fleet that was normally based at Arbeia, at the eastern end of the Wall, sailed along the coast, destroying every craft, burning every timbered hovel and sacking every fishing village they encountered. In front and on the flanks of the army, the troops and ships of the allied British tribes, its eyes and ears, fanned out and looted as far as they felt safe. As they all marched, above them rose the smoke of a hundred burned habitations, and in their wake the crows, wolves and foxes swarmed to feast upon the remains of the dead.

The duke had let his troops be told that they aimed at repeating the feats of the great Agricola and the Emperor Septimius Severus. He gave out that the army's initial objectives were the old Roman campaign fortresses at Horrea Classis and Pinnata Castra, ensuring by doing so that if the Picti decided to stand and fight they would do so further north than he intended to march. In reality, he had no interest in marching even that far.

*

It was towards the end of the campaign, if that is what this extended raid could be called, that occurred the only excitement to trouble Constantine and the men of his bodyguard. The duke had come to watch the Segontienses destroying a Pictish village. It was only a small place, a collection of half a dozen filthy and stinking hovels where the animals ran in and out of the houses as if they were barns. Since the duke had first come across Pulcher's unit in their original post, it had become, for some reason known only to himself, something of a favourite among the units under his command. The duke liked Pulcher, who was a tough, unintelligent officer, a man who was going nowhere but did exactly as he was told, a brutal man with no qualms, a harsh taskmaster after the duke's own heart, although with none of his cunning or intelligence. The duke liked to watch him and his men creating mayhem.

The male villagers had already fled, leaving a few old women and children whose mothers had either also fled or were in hiding. Pulcher was relishing the chance to shed blood and throw his weight around. He had his men torch the thatched roofs of the houses and throw whatever household goods that they'd looted into the flames. In the course of this, Pulcher's soldiers uncovered some grain pits, and in them found two girls hiding inside. They were pulled out screaming and shivering with fright. Cheered on by the duke, the troops dragged the girls into the open, ripped off their clothes and lined up to rape them in the mud in front of their hut, taking them turn by turn.

After each had been raped two or three times, their screaming died away into delirium. It was at that point that an older woman hiding in another pit nearby sprang out of her cover. She was nearly naked, which exposed her skin covered in swirling patterns of blue woad. She was clutching a long, curved knife in her hand. Seeing the duke almost in front of her, she shrieked and leapt at his horse, her arm raised to drive her dagger into his side. In a flash, Constantine was in her way; the thrust of his sword in her rib cage pushed her sideways and her flailing hand managed to sink her weapon only into the horse's flank. She collapsed beneath its belly, writhing in her death throes.

The duke had not flinched and remained seated on his now wounded mount. "I shall not forget that, Constantine," he said. "I thank you."

"Pulcher," he continued, "finish this. I want no one left alive here after your men have all enjoyed themselves."

The duke's instructions were interrupted by the sound of retching that came from just behind him. He turned to see his son Victor vomiting up his breakfast. Victor had seen death, but he had never before been exposed to massacre, torture and rape. His father glared at him. "Get a hold on yourself, boy. This is what I brought you here to see. You'll see a lot worse than this before you're done." He rode off, leaving one of Constantine's men to help Victor wipe the vomit from his uniform and to offer the shame-faced youth a flask of water.

When the raping was over and the girls were dead, everyone left in the village was dragged out and cut to pieces. Their severed limbs, heads and breasts were nailed to trees so that, when they returned, their husbands, fathers and brothers would not have far to look for them.

*

After a month of pillage, the duke's men had their tails up. They and their British allies were well pleased with their spoils. The army was intact and the operation had shaken it down into an efficient military machine. Maximus declared victory and called a halt. Covering his rear with ambushes as he went, and moving so swiftly that pursuit could not catch his army, Maximus marched his men back down to the Wall.

Chapter Twelve

MAXIMUS AUGUSTUS

In his first night back in Eboracum, Maximus lay with Elen. When he was back at base, he still slept most nights with his wife, although by now they had abandoned making love. When he felt the need, he made use of one of their slave girls, or, if he wanted something more exotic, of the African he had made his cupbearer back in Mauretania. Elen had come to accept what he did, although she could never bring herself to be happy about it. Yet she wanted no more children, so it was a compromise that suited her. She believed, hoped, rather, that her husband loved her in his unstated, selfish way and the life they lived together now was much as she expected it to be. Her lot was better than that of most, she thought. It seemed enough.

Maximus had not been easy to sleep with since their journey to Segontium. He seemed plagued by dreams that came to him again and again. One was more of a vision, he had told her, and it had troubled his sleep more and more frequently over the last few months. Was it a dream or was he being told something? He asked himself this question each time but could never get to grips with the idea. He was coming to believe that what he saw, or was being shown, was more than just a dream. He could remember the vision with absolute clarity. When it came, he felt as though he was not just watching but living the vision. He was loath to admit it, but this frightened him. It seemed to him a sign of weakness that he refused to acknowledge. It was other people, weak and foolish people, who had these sorts of experiences. He was too practical, too hard-headed, to suffer that sort of thing. No ghost had ever dared to cross his path. Yet he had a deep superstition and dealt with it by trying to avoid or deflect what he could not understand before having to come face to face with it. He tried this with the dream. Every time it began, he was determined to face down his own fear and avoid being overcome by it. He always failed.

In his vision he was lifted up onto a dais that was so high that from it he could look down on the clouds. He felt as though above the world, mountain peaks spread around his feet. Behind them he saw the blue of an ocean that rippled and sparkled as it reflected the bright sun above. As the vision unfolded, mists would begin to form on all sides and slowly envelop the peaks until they vanished in a roiling, turbulent torrent of white and grey. From these emerged faces like upturned pebbles that stretched all around him to the far reaches of his sight. Somehow, he knew that they all wanted something of him, these faces. He could feel the yearning in their upturned, expectant eyes. When he looked down, he could see faces of all the nations and peoples of the places in which he had served, faces of men and women, faces of the old, the young and of children. He knew none of them. They puzzled him, these people; why were they all looking at him? They seemed to like him, to want him to do something. They began to cry out in ever-increasing noise that became a cacophony as they roared their approval at him.

Then among them he would begin to pick out people he knew, British faces, some who were close to him, members of his families in the Votadini and the Dumnonii. There came Eudaf, Conan and Gadeon. He saw his first wife, Ceindreth, and last of all he would see Elen, just as she had been on the first day he met her: young, fresh, joyful, life itself. He was sure in each of his dreams – and this was for the first time in his life that he had ever had such feelings – that this was Britannia and that he belonged there. Understanding that, his very being became suffused with such a golden feeling of happiness and ease as he had not felt since childhood.

It did not last. Something ominous was gathering behind him. Each time he knew it would come and he dreaded it. There was a looming, dark presence, that he knew he had to turn to see. He forced himself to face the threat, but by now he knew, for he had seen this too many times, that he could not face or defeat whatever it was. Yet he forced himself to look back. Each time he saw, in the distance across waters that were stormy now and rainswept, a heavy, turbulent darkness rising. It swirled towards him. He knew that he must protect his people and his home from this darkness, but he stood before it alone. On it would come, so fast that it enveloped and overwhelmed him. He drew his sword and struck out, but his blade cut through nothing but mist, and he began to suffocate in the blackness that overwhelmed him. It was at that point that he would wake, sweating and wide-eyed.

On this night, as his sword cut through the darkness and he could no longer breathe, he cried out in his sleep and startled Elen awake beside him.

"What is it, Magnus?" she asked. He shuddered, still only half awake, so she took him in her arms and held him close.

"I have had the same vision again, my love," he said. "I do not understand it fully, but I think I have been shown things I did not comprehend before and what my destiny is calling me to do."

"A vision from God, then. He is leading you to His truth." Elen had not yet abandoned the hope in her heart that her husband would at last come to the risen Lord and would be forgiven and saved. Perhaps this vision would lead him at last to Christ.

He dashed her hopes. "There is nothing of any god or religion in this dream, unless the Fates themselves are pulling back the curtain to show me what they plan for me. It is such a pointless vision; I have been shown nothing that might help me in the future. There is nothing in this dream but feelings, at first of such happiness as I have not felt since I was a boy, such a feeling of relief, as if the burden of my life has been lifted. I can see, my love, that the happiness I feel comes from you, Elen, and from your people. I feel for once that I am home."

Elen was taken aback. She had never heard him talk of her people in this way. Never before had he shown any desire to find a home. He had never been a man to say that he loved her or to show often that he did. The centre of his being had always seemed to her to be himself. Maybe this dream meant that he might be changing.

"This is a revelation, Magnus. You have been shown your own feelings. Your feeling of happiness cannot be counterfeit, for whatever power shows you good things is a power for good. Evil spirits do not show you joy and contentment. It is a gift from God, a sign for you to follow him."

Maximus could not shake off the shock of what he had seen in his vision. "Since I left Hispania with the count, I have never felt that I truly belonged in any place where I have been, or that I should cherish anyone other than my family," he said. "Home was where you and I were together. That was all. Why now do I feel that your people are my people and that I should cherish them? How am I to do that? There was nothing in the vision to explain it."

They held each other close until they drifted off to sleep again. Elen had been made very happy by what her husband had told her of his vision. She could not know, however, that he had only told her of the first part of it, and Elen failed to notice that it was something terrifying that had woken Maximus and startled her from sleep.

What was on the mind of her husband was different. He was appalled by the conclusion to what he now firmly believed was a vision he was being shown. He hated the doubt that had been sown in his mind. Would his mighty project lead only to darkness? Was he going to imperil all he now knew and that he held dear by reaching for the purple? And what was this darkness? Was it his ambition and greed? Was it his destiny to fight the barbarian darkness that loomed in the east? Or was something worse going to happen to him?

Although he could not answer these questions, he told himself that he would fight this darkness, whatever it was, and that he would overcome it. He was not the man to give up now and he was going to win.

*

Just after dawn, on a bright mid-summer's morning under a clear blue sky, the northern army was drawn up in review order on the parade ground outside Eboracum's fortress walls. In the sunlight, the gold, silver and brass of the troops' ceremonial equipment glowed and glinted in the sun. The regimental emblems painted on their shields splashed long lines of colour across the front of their ranks. The red cloaks and horsehair plumes on the helmets of the officers and senior ranks of the cavalry moved gently in the slight breeze, the faces of the riders inscrutable behind the gilded masks of their parade helmets. The infantry was drawn up in the centre, only their officers mounted to their front.

Behind the dais, as if for a backdrop to the duke who now stood upon it, were massed the German and British tribesmen who had accompanied his force to the north. Each was parading by tribal unit, dressed in their different furs and leathers and carrying what was, to the Romans, their outlandish weaponry. Close around the dais stood the men of the *bucellarii*, the duke's personal escort troops, commanded by Constantine, standing, as always, close behind his commander. Facing the dais, in the centre of the parade, the standard-bearers held high the eagles and sacred standards of the units on parade.

Just to the rear of the duke and Constantine, standing proudly in miniature military dress with plumed helmet, shining cuirass and a small sword, stood Victor. The boy looked about him haughtily, intent on ensuring that everyone could see him there with his father. His brothers Owain, Annun and Custennin were further back still, all save for Peblig, who sat unhappily with his mother and his three sisters, watched over by Gerontius and his men, whose faces made it plain that they felt there were no honours to be won babysitting and that they would much rather be out there with the rest.

Over the parade ground towered the enormous statue of the Emperor Constantine, who eighty years before had been acclaimed Augustus on this very spot. Even in that day, this had been a place redolent of imperial history, for the emperors Caracalla and Geta had been proclaimed there a hundred years before that. All such acclamations were auguries, it would seem to those who understood these things, for the good fortune of what was about to take place now. From the rear of the parade, the bugles and horns blasted out a salute.

"Soldiers of Roma," the duke began, shouting at full strength to enable his army to hear his words, although in truth many at the rear or on the flanks could not, and had to learn later from their fellows in the front ranks what it was that their commander had said that day. "You return victorious. You have dealt the barbarians beyond our frontiers, those uncivilised murderers who have for long plagued this land, a hammer blow from which they will take generations to recover. Roma thanks you!" The horns blared out again, then the duke continued: "And Roma knows how to thank you. From the wealth which we have recovered from your victory I promise you that each man shall receive his share, a donative that your paymasters shall pay you all after this parade."

There was an enormous roar of approval from the men and a clashing of shields upon the ground. When the thunderous applause had at last subsided, the duke went on: "All of you served with exemplary courage and fortitude in the wet and dismal swamps and barren hills where our enemies lurk, but to those of you whose bravery was greatest, Roma now gives its recognition and reward." On that cue, a file of officers and men marched forward, each to salute the duke and to receive at his hands a golden torc, an armband, a disk for breastplate or a silver spear. The German and British tribesmen were not neglected in this, their best receiving a cup or a set of horse trappings. The bugles and horns called out again, spears clashed on shields and the men roared out their approbation.

The last to be called was Constantine, who had saved his duke's life. He had expected something, an armilla, to wear on his arm, perhaps, or even a golden torc for his neck, but he was completely taken aback to see in the duke's hands a wreath of oak leaves forming the chaplet of a civic crown. This was the second highest award in the empire, given to a man who had saved the life of a citizen, but it was very rarely given outside the imperial family, for it carried with it the extraordinary gift of entry to the senate. Constantine, who had come up the hard way through the ranks and whose forebears were peasants from Moesia, could not believe that this was happening to him. He received the award, saluted and marched back to his place in a daze, roars of approval ringing out across the parade ground. The applause came not least from his friend Gerontius, who, despite a tinge of jealousy at Constantine's good fortune, was nevertheless the most delighted of them all.

Many soldiers on parade that day had seen similar, if smaller, ceremonies, but none could have seen in their lifetime what happened next. From the rear of the saluting platform emerged on horseback a barbaric figure, his shoulders covered with furs, his shield of bronze engraved with the images of his gods, his long sabre hanging from his sword belt. Trotting forward came Fraomarius, King of the Alamanni. He halted his mount in front of the duke, saluted him with his sword, then bellowed in his very basic Latin: "Our duke is great; he is a great warrior and our leader. He is a god to my people and fit to be our true emperor!"

At this signal, Andragathius, the duke's second-in-command, stepped forward. "All hail to our duke," he shouted. "All hail to our invincible leader, the husband and father of Britons, an unbeaten soldier of Roma, defender of her frontiers, the terror of our foes, fitter than any other to rule. All hail, all hail to our imperator, to our Augustus."

There was a vast swelling of noise as the massed ranks of soldiers bellowed their approval. Nothing more could be heard in the din for several minutes, during which the duke was seen to be gesticulating with his hands, making great show of pushing Andragathius away, refusing to acknowledge what he had said. Andragathius, though, would not be pushed away. Instead, he knelt before the duke and offered him a grass crown, the army's highest award. Fraomarius, too, dismounted and began to kneel, at which sign the staff officers and household troops around the dais dropped to their knees, and, in a series of waves, the men of all the units on parade and the tribesmen knelt. The duke looked down now, below him the upturned faces of many thousands of men acclaiming him and demanding that he take the grass crown. He raised his hands to quieten them, then spoke the words that settled his and their fates, the fates of Britannia and of the empire.

"You are my trusted, my faithful soldiers. You are my life and my duty," the duke cried. "I am not worthy to rule, nor fit to be your Augustus. Yet I cannot deny you. You have placed your lives in my hands. You have revealed my destiny. In memory of your victory, I shall forever bear the title Britannicus Maximus after my name." Now his turn came to kneel, and he did so before Andragathius, who placed the grass crown on his head, then turned and raised his arms.

"Behold our Augustus of the new age," cried Andragathius, "he who will keep Roma's eternal light burning, who will defend our hearths and our families, who will destroy our enemies and keep us safe! Behold, our imperator!"

"Imperator! Imperator! Imperator!" thundered all sides.

*

The die was cast; for Maximus, for all of them, there was no going back now.

Chapter Thirteen

THE TRUE FAITH

There was, of course, nothing spontaneous in the acclamation at Eboracum of Maximus as emperor. The affair had been most carefully planned and the parade served only to set his carefully considered plans in motion. Cavalry *turmae* under the command of junior officers, specially selected for their loyalty, had already fanned out across the diocese and at the exact hour at which the duke stood forth to address his troops, they entered the offices of a series of commanders and officials across the land.

In Londinium, a detachment invaded the praetorium of Desiderius, the Vicar of Britannia. He had only a few troops of his escort at his disposal and was not about to argue with the hard-looking tribune who marched briskly into his office, treated him politely and with the respect due to his position, but who had half a cohort to back up what he said. The vicar meekly allowed himself to be taken to his villa outside the city walls, where he was held under house arrest. Also in Londinium was Leucadius, the *praeses* of the province of Maxima Caesariensis, the south-eastern British province administered from the city. Leucadius was a man of an old equestrian family, a Christian and a supporter of Gratian, and he was made of sterner stuff than his superior. He and his household staff made a short attempt to resist, and Maximus' troops had to cut down several of his German bodyguards and slaves before the governor surrendered. He was thrown into jail in the city fort, where the city's German auxiliary guards were also disarmed and confined. He was joined there by the imperial financial officials who were appointed from Gallia and whose loyalty was definitely not going to lie with Maximus.

Further to the south, in a villa near the port of Dubris, the Count Narses was taken in his bed. He was the *Comes Litoris Saxonici per Britannias*, the Count of the Saxon Shore in Britannia. His troops and ships were scattered from the far north-east coast round to the island of Vectis, and the closest of these in Dubris had already been bribed with Julian's money to stay where they were. As the only major danger to the duke's seizure of power, that left the *praefectus* commanding the count's only legion, the Second Augusta, which was based a very long way away in Isca Silurum, but this officer, too, had been bribed to sit tight. Count Narses was an easterner, an officer who knew the sordid history that had brought Maximus to his northern command, and he despised his powerful colleague intensely. Nonetheless, he had no roots in Britannia, no links with any who were influential there and he had no troops close to hand; he was powerless to resist and was taken into custody.

Cavalry troops had also fanned out across eastern and southern Britannia carrying the duke's orders to prevent all ships leaving port. The commanders of the locally based naval detachments of the *classis britannica*, the British fleet, were bribed to conform and they cut communications with their commander, who was based across the sea in Bononia. No news of the coup was to reach Gallia yet.

The cavalcade of Julian, the ex-governor of Valentia, the axles of its wagons heavily laden down with the vast baggage of his household effects, had already departed British shores and was even then winding its way back to his villa in Gallia. All he had left behind was a considerable treasury of gold that he had deposited in Londinium and which he had made available for Maximus to use. He was now setting about amassing a larger pot of treasure to be used when Maximus moved across the sea. Julian's successor had yet to arrive in post in Valentia. That left two governors to account for, the *praeses* of the province of Flavia Caesariensis in Lindum Colonia and the *praeses* of Britannia Prima in Corinium. Neither of these had command of any troops and neither was inclined to resist or flee. They were allowed to remain where they were, now thoughtfully provided with a small military guard by the duke.

The coup had been swiftly and easily accomplished.

*

Maximus moved south swiftly now, pressing his mounted units on before him, while Andragathius followed him with the troops on foot. Leaving the children, Elen came south in a carriage, part of the transport following the main body of the army. Although he had relieved him of his legion to take it with him as he marched south, the duke had left Quietus, the prefect in command of the Sixth Legion, in place in Eboracum with orders to command the north and the Wall in his absence.

Along with the troops who had been sent out to establish control across the diocese had gone messages to members of the diocesan council to convene in Londinium in two weeks' time. This small and select body, containing representatives of Britannia's major cities, had, until now, been pretty much an ornamental body; now Maximus had bigger plans for it.

It was, he had decided, to be an instrument for ensuring the loyalty of the island as well as for protecting it in his absence. To the list of its usual members, he added for the first time invitations to the princes of the major tribes of the periphery, key figures who would owe loyalty to him alone.

Although the closure of the southern ports would, for the time being, prevent news of the coup reaching Gallia, there was no way that every small trading or fishing vessel could be prevented from carrying news of the coup. The closure of traffic would of itself send a warning signal across the water. There was therefore not much time to act, so he ordered his troops to march straight to Rutupiae and Dubris, where ships of the *classis britannica*, supplemented by a fleet of Julian's cargo vessels, were assembling to transport his army to the continent.

*

Maximus' next task in Londinium was to complete his plans for the governance of the island. By now, Eudaf Hen, at last feeling his years, had returned home from Segontium. Conan was already at sea, sailing south, his ships laden with the loot and slaves he had taken in Hibernia, which he would offload to his, and the duke's, profit in Gallia. After that, he would sail with his fleet to Armorica, from which, once established there, he would control the western seaboard and hold the western flank of the duke's enterprise. That left it to Gadeon to ride into the capital to represent his tribe on the council. He came early, as the duke wished to make arrangements with him for the future. They met briefly in the duke's private quarters in the residence of the vicar. After the usual few perfunctory greetings, for, although each respected and now needed the other, they were still very wary, the duke pressed on straight to business.

"So how are your people getting on in the west, Prince Gadeon?" the duke enquired.

"All goes to plan, *dominus*. Conan has made sure that we shall not be raided by the Scoti for many years to come. There is scarcely a boat left afloat on the coast of Hibernia and we have almost all of those who survived our raids shackled in our ships to be sold in the slave markets. He has also filled our coffers with plenty of gold to pay for what he needs to do in Gallia and Armorica. He and our fleet are on the high seas now and he will land in Armorica by the date you have fixed. Segontium is secure and the Scoti inside our lands have had such a drubbing that they will not dare show their heads while you are away."

The duke was very pleased with Gadeon's report. "That is excellent news, Gadeon. We are almost ready to cross the ocean ourselves. When we depart from here, we shall take over communications with Conan's force. You have other tasks, and we need you here. How is our father-in-law?"

"Ailing, I am sorry to say, my lord. He has had to take to his bed back in our own country, and I fear that you may not be able to return in time to see him and bid farewell."

"We are sorry indeed to hear that," said the duke. "Prince Eudaf has been a true friend of ours, and of Roma. Elen will be distraught to lose him. He has, alas, never seen his grandchildren."

The duke had wine poured. "So, let us turn to business. I am leaving Desiderius here in his post of vicar to run the administration of the diocese, though I am also leaving a detachment in the city that will answer directly to me just in case anyone tries to use our absence to cause trouble. Desiderius will continue to head the Council of Britannia, but he will not be the most influential voice upon it. That will be yours."

Gadeon was taken aback by this. Tribal princes had not sat on the council before. It had been stuffed with central government servants and rich representatives of the landowners who comprised the aristocracy of the major towns. Until now, the council had been accustomed to meet once a year in the temple by the river that had been especially built for the purpose, a building opposite the government offices. It housed the altar dedicated to the spirits of the emperors and of Roma. Until recently, it had been served by the chief priest of the diocese, but his post had fallen vacant after the imperial edicts banning pagan practices, and there was now some doubt about what to do with the altar.

Gadeon managed to retain his composure. He knew that the council had never exercised much power, rather was a forum for giving the administration a feel for the opinions of its chief subjects. It would debate and make decisions on domestic matters, and it exercised some legislative authority, but only with the nod of the vicar. It had once been a prestigious body, but the expense of attending its formal meetings had come to be avoided where possible by those eligible to sit on it. As they did in their own cities, the rich resented the waste of unpaid time involved in administration and avoided office where they could. Most preferred to retire to their country estates and evade the cost of elections with their donatives and celebratory games. They were also very successful at avoiding taxation. This un-civic approach to urban life had worsened over many years as towns had been forced to pay not only for the fortifications made obligatory by law, but also for the mostly German guards who had to be hired to man them. Instead of building forum, basilica and bathhouse, the principal citizens of towns now had to finance walls, bastions, artillery and soldiers. None of this was paid for, of course, by the foreign magnates who, increasingly, had been buying up estates in the lowlands from which to profit by selling corn to the government and the army. The diocesan council was not something that anyone of influence had recently shown signs of wanting to sit upon.

"The core of the council is going to sit permanently while I am away, to be my eyes and ears. I am going to appoint you to this body, of course, but I shall also appoint the princes of the chief tribes. Vitalinus of the Cornovii and Dobunni will be a member, and I am asking the nobles of the Atrebates, the Belgae and the Cantii to join as full members. The princes of the north and west will be asked to send representatives. You can see, I think, that this is the beginning of something completely new. As I have enlisted the aid of the peoples of the border to defend the diocese, I am now enlisting the aid of Britons to rule their own island. It is my intention that in future the government of this land should include its princes, men upon whom I can rely and who have no imperial bureaucratic career to feed their ambitions or lead them elsewhere."

This concept was to Gadeon so radical that he for once could find no easy response. He was amazed. There had never been a permanently sitting council before, and no tribal prince from the periphery had ever been invited to attend. He could immediately foresee that this might cause trouble with the imperial administrators and the lowland aristocracy, most of whom regarded those who lived on the frontiers as almost as barbarous as those who attacked it. But he could also see that this plan would give Maximus both huge support in Britannia and a reliable way of controlling events while he was overseas. He could also see opportunities of profit and power lurking tantalisingly in the future that Maximus had conjured. The levers of power could always be pulled for a profit. Eventually, he found the right words: "My lord, you are proposing something enormously propitious, an advantage that we of this island have never before been offered."

"In giving you and your fellow princes this gift, Gadeon," continued Maximus, "we are also ensuring the safety of our rule here. You have a unique role to perform for us. You will make sure that no one arises here to stab us in the back or betray our enterprise. You will be our eyes and ears, here, prince. Use them well and write to us as often as you can."

"I thank you, lord, and vow that I shall work to make your grace and this land secure."

Both men rose, well satisfied with the course that events were taking.

*

In the council chamber in the temple, over a hundred members waited for the newly proclaimed Augustus to take his presiding seat. Desiderius, now Maximus' reappointed vicar, and the three surviving provincial governors sat to his right and left. There were enough military officers present in the chamber, the alarming-looking Andragathius, Aurelian and Promotus among them, to make it clear where power lay, so none there, of course, was prepared to step out of line and the flattering panegyric read before Maximus by the best of the orators available in the capital was loudly applauded. The council members acclaimed Maximus as "imperator" and "Augustus" many times in pre-scripted shouts.

Proceedings went as smoothly as Maximus required. The previous council members affected to show no surprise, rather to demonstrate a very happy agreement, when confronted with the fact of the inclusion of Gadeon and the other princes as full members. Representatives of the northern frontier tribes – the Votadini, the Novantae and the Selgovae – and of the Silures from the west were, at least on the surface, made welcome. Business now had to be translated from its Latin, for some of the tribal members spoke only their own tongue. The new arrangement of a permanently sitting council, cast in the form of a standing committee, was announced by the vicar and received unanimous approval. On this were to sit Gadeon, Vitalinus and other princes alongside him. Desiderius, who was perfectly aware that he was being sidelined and supervised, managed to look as though this was the sort of thing that happened all the time.

"Our intention," announced Maximus, "is that Britannia be more closely tied to the empire by its leading families, who will now be given roles in its administration through this council. It is high time to recognise the service they have given in building and defending the diocese. We shall expect more local officers to hold post here in the imperial administration, and fewer will be posted in from abroad. We are delegating to you, the principal citizens of Britannia, a share in the governance of this island, just as we have now delegated to the peoples of the periphery the defence of all of us."

This statement was met with renewed acclamation, only in part officially scripted, for these plans were highly attractive to the native leaders present that day.

The newly acclaimed emperor took some time to expound his reasons for seizing supreme power. The empire was in peril, he told them. In the west, it was not in safe hands; the Emperor Gratian was too young and incompetent to deal with the issues that faced them all. In replacing him, Maximus claimed the support of the Emperor Theodosius. To prove this, he waved a roll of parchment at the council, affixed with the imperial seal. There was a gasp of surprise at this. If the eastern emperor was in favour of a change of regime, then almost all danger of subsequent retribution would evaporate, and they could voice their wholehearted support. Which is what they did, unanimously and in once again pre-scripted chants.

There was, of course, no such letter and no approval from the east. It was a lie that would one day come back to bite the person who uttered it.

It was during the second day of the council that an issue arose which would have unexpected effects. The session took a petition from the Christian bishop of Londinium that the temple they were sitting in be turned into a church and that the altar to the emperors be rededicated to the Christian god. Had the newly acclaimed emperor not been there, the argument would no doubt have been fierce and even, perhaps, the occasion for subsequent violence and the trashing of the building, but there was an awkward reticence in the air that day due to the fact that one of the emperors to whom both temple and altar were dedicated was sitting before them. Council members were not to know that Maximus had little interest in the religious issues under debate, nor in the future of what he regarded as merely a lump of carved stone, but he himself very rapidly realised that they needed him to declare his view. Most of the council members from the cities were loud in their demands to follow imperial edicts banning sacrifice to the old gods. Maximus could also see that many of the military members and almost all the British tribal aristocracy were against such radical change. He curtailed the debate by deferring a decision until his new regime had clarified its stance, but the tumult in the hall opened his eyes to the power of this issue to mould men's loyalties. It also made him uneasy; he was beginning to realise what he was about to face across the seas, where he knew these struggles were even more fractious than those in Britannia.

*

Maximus retired to the nearby palace only to find the debate he thought he had stifled in the council rear up and bite him in the person of his wife. The bishop had hastened to brief Elen while the council was in session. His colleague in Eboracum had sent him word that in the new empress he would find a supporter, so, whilst the debate raged in the council, he had called upon Elen. The bishop was a clever, even a cunning, man, who had not been long in his post, a Gaul who had trained under the acclaimed Bishop Iustus of Lugdunum, so one who knew enough of imperial politics to choose his words carefully. He planted the idea in Elen's mind that she should take actions that she would otherwise never have contemplated.

"With your influence and with God's grace," suggested the bishop, "the altar in the temple can be made a thing of the past. There is more, too," he claimed. "Were he to seek the help of almighty God, the new emperor's cause would triumph. Intervene now, my lady, I beseech you, the time is ripe!"

Elen had never sought a voice in any of her husband's policies and quailed before the thought of doing so now. This was, however, a matter of the saving of the emperor's soul and thus of great import to the whole empire. With more than a little trepidation, she awaited her husband's return.

By the time Maximus joined her on what was to be his last night before marching to war, she resolved that she must take what might be the last opportunity to convert her husband. Ever since the sermon she had heard in Eboracum, she had been watching for a chance to choose the path which her life would follow. She saw such a chance now. She prayed to her Christ for strength and the ability to find the right words.

"My lord, how was the council today?" she asked innocently. "Did you achieve what you wanted?"

"We did, my love, it was all a great success. We can leave in the morning with everything here secure."

"I am glad to hear that. I know that Gadeon will be too. I've also heard, my lord, that the stone in the temple is going to cause us trouble while you are away," she went on. "I can see the people here are very hot to pull it down or turn it into an altar of the Lord Jesus."

"We can see that, too, Elen. We must not be long in making up our mind, but we think that we do not need to do so before we leave."

"Perhaps not, my husband, but if I may say so, there is more to this issue than one piece of stone. Your decision here will show the world what you believe and what they can expect from you when you sit on the imperial throne. It seems to me that the tide of the true faith is too strong now in the empire to reverse it. The Emperor Julian tried, years back, and he failed and perished. Even Gratian's attempt at toleration proved too much for people to stomach. You have a great fight on your hands now in Gallia. Do you really want to count all the Christians of the west among your enemies? Would you not rather be seen as their God-given saviour and supporter?"

Maximus paused. He had not expected such political sophistication from his wife. She had never uttered such a long speech before. He found that she had given voice to the possibilities that had run through his mind during the debate in the council.

"Remember," she went on, to her husband's even greater amazement, "what happened when the great Constantine saw the words 'in this sign conquer' in the heavens. When he had the Chi Ro symbol of our Lord Jesus Christ painted on his men's shields, he won a great victory."

"He did indeed, my love, at the Milvian Bridge, and so won the whole empire."

Elen grasped Maximus' arm and looked him full in the face. "Do the same, then, my husband. Christ will protect you and give you victory. He will protect all of us."

Maximus reflected that no religion had played any part in his vision. There had been no sign in his dream of any Christ or Christian god. Nor was there any faith inside him driving him on. What other people believed had always been a matter of indifference to him. Yet he could see now the cold, hard fact that his lack of any real faith might very well be a disadvantage in this world of troubled belief. In his lifetime, he had watched the growing strength of the Christian party as it spread its influence across the empire. He found most of its faith's adherents desperately unattractive, weak moaners who in their foolishness believed that their god alone could save them. He wasn't at all attracted by their religion. He temporised still. "We leave tomorrow, my love, it is too late to act now."

"Not so, my lord," his wife responded. "Londinium is full of priests. We can bring the bishop here and baptise you tonight. Announce your conversion before you sail. Tell the world that God has called you and that you fight in his name."

To his own amazement, Maximus found that he was persuaded by his wife's argument. For the first time in their marriage, he decided to act as his wife advised. "You speak true, my love. It is indeed time."

*

The baptism was done that night by Londinium's bishop in the flickering light of the torches around the palace bath in which Maximus was immersed. That night, the imperial temple was stripped of anything that Christians regarded as idolatrous; the imperial altar now had a cross on it, and the imposing building found itself reborn as the new church of the Apostle Paul. The bishop put the word around the city, so that on the next morning, when Maximus rode through the south gate to cross the river, he rode through a cheering crowd saluting him and blessing him on his way.

When he reached camp at Rutupiae, before the whole assembled army, Maximus had a wooden cross raised. Although there was no time to have new symbols painted on the shields of his soldiers, as the fleet was to set sail on the next tide, when they did sail, the cross went before them in the bows of his ship.

Chapter Fourteen

USURPATION

Just off the south coast of Armorica, two sleek patrol galleys sliced through the choppy waters of the *mare gallaecum* and came alongside both port and starboard of Conan's ship. He was out ahead of his small fleet of twelve vessels, some of them lumbering freighters that were rolling in the swell, and the galleys had no trouble catching up with them.

"What ships are you, where are you from and where are you bound?" demanded the Roman officer in the starboard galley, shouting loudly to be heard against the blustering breeze.

"We are Dumnonian, with a cargo of slaves from Hibernia bound for the markets of Burdigalia," Conan bellowed back.

The galley on the port side dropped a cutter which swiftly carried a landing party across the gap between the vessels; an officer and half a dozen armed sailors clambered over the side.

"Feel free to look around," Conan invited them. "We have slaves on board, as does each of the vessels of my prince's fleet."

The Roman sailors were used to meeting Dumnonian vessels and accustomed to seeing slaves in them. There was nothing new to see here, so after a cursory inspection and the pocketing of a small amount of silver coin, the boarding party rowed back over to their ship. The gallies pulled away and headed northwest.

Conan, too, was very used to this procedure and was not in the slightest worried by the encounter. He chuckled at the fact that he would soon have the crews of those galleys working for him. *Time to get back some of that silver with which I've greased so many of their palms*, he thought, and laughed at the vision he had of the utter surprise he'd see on their faces when he let it be known that he was the new western emperor's *mare dux*, the ruler of the western seaboard. He couldn't do that quite yet; first, Maximus had to land in Gallia, but Conan allowed himself to savour the prospect of the title, the wealth and even the opportunity for a little revenge that the position was going to bring him. More than all that, he looked forward to the fun he was going to have destroying anyone who got in his way.

He could not recall when he had been blessed by the gods with so many good months of pure pleasure. He was operating entirely on his own, in command of everything he was doing. Now down south on the open sea, the weather was unusually fair and the sea had claimed none of his ships or men. He, and they, had been having fun with the most beautiful of the Scoti women every night since their capture. They were fierce, wild creatures, but a sea journey tied to wooden beams had tamed them somewhat and after Conan had thrown overboard one who had thought to fend him off with her teeth and nails, there had been no more trouble from that quarter.

As the Roman vessels disappeared into the distance, Conan's half-brother Erbin joined him by the tiller. Conan had taken him with him to act as his second-in-command on their expedition to Hibernia. Erbin was a warrior much after his own heart. Physically strong, a man who liked his mead and was often noisy in his cups, Erbin was, like himself, a victor of many sea fights with Scoti raiders, whom he loathed with a similar passion to Conan's, and whom he enjoyed killing. Together on this voyage, they had plundered the coasts of Hibernia, killed a creditable number of its inhabitants and captured more, whom they had crammed into the navels of their ships, ready for the slave markets of southern Gallia.

Some days later, the fleet steered up the sluggish estuary of the Garunna towards Burdigalia, where Conan intended to offload his slaves. They would make him a profit easily sufficient to cover whatever expenses he would face over the next few months. Burdigalia was a western terminus of the slave trade, well connected by road to the south of Gallia and to Massilia, which was linked by sea to Italia and the east. Slaving had given his fleet a perfect excuse for cruising down the western coast. With his slaves offloaded, with gold and silver in his ships' coffers, all he had to do was to await the date that Maximus had fixed to cross the ocean, and then he would land in Armorica.

*

Events in Britannia had caught the imperial administration off guard. It had been an opportune moment for Maximus to make his move to take the purple; he was either very lucky or a very good judge of events, perhaps both. The Emperor Gratian was in Italia, with most of his *palatini*, the units of the army that operated close around him. These were moving to join his younger brother's *magister militum*, the commander-in-chief Arbogastes, who was assembling troops at Verona to march north to block an expected invasion of Pannonia by the Alamanni. Gratian had unfinished business with that German tribe. Four years before, when he was just twenty, his army had defeated one section of them at Argentovaria, on the Roman side of the Rhenus, wiping them out and killing their king. The Alamanni had many sections, however, and they had continued to raid over the frontier, as they were trying to do again. Gratian wanted to finish them for good, this time.

The emperor had left one of the chief supports of his reign, the *magister militum* Merobaudes, in charge of the Gallic *comitatus*, the field army. This was based around Lutetia, a long way from the emperor, so neither Gratian nor Merobaudes could come to each other's aid quickly. This was because, two years before this, Gratian had moved his imperial capital from Augusta Treverorum on the Mosella to Mediolanum in Italia, placing his court far from events in the north. He had left in Augusta the praetorian prefect of all his domains, Decimius Magnus Ausonius, the head of his civilian administration.

It was Ausonius' responsibility to watch the west, but it took him a few weeks to understand and react to the alarm bells that were beginning to ring in Britannia. Imperial couriers and their ships had continued to depart for ports on the island, but so far none had returned. The regular roulement of officials posted into Britannia had continued, but after the ex-governor Julian had returned to Gallia from Valentia, no one else had followed him back.

Ausonius was a rich landowner from Aquitania in the southwest and a much-published writer, a poet and focus of literate culture in the west. This had caused the late Emperor Valentinian to make him tutor to his son, Gratian. The young man and his mentor had become very close, so close that, when Gratian became emperor, he appointed Ausonius to head, first the administration of Gallia, then that of the entire western empire. Ausonius, however, knew little of the military. In all of his pampered life, he had not been schooled to deal with a crisis. He had spent his four years in office growing rich by stuffing the administration of the entire western empire with his friends, relations and clients, contacts from Aquitania and cultured men of similar minds to himself. None of these were suited by experience, temperament or ability to react decisively against a military threat from a ruthless opponent like Maximus. Ausonius was also well past the age when he could have acted with the vigour of middle age, let alone youth, for he was now sixty-three years old. Crucially, he dithered now.

From the senior civil officer in Gallia, the praetorian prefect Proculus Gregorius, who was the British Vicar Desiderius' superior, Ausonius received rumours that had been picked up along the coast, vague news that the British ports had been locked down and that no ships had been allowed to sail. Nothing, neither message nor routine correspondence, had been received from the Vicar Desiderius for weeks. After some days of indecision, Gregorius warned Ausonius that he suspected a security threat. Now at last Ausonius sent out messengers warning the emperor, the *magister militum* Merobaudes and the civilian authorities that something might be afoot and that they should watch and report. He had left it fatally late.

The general Merobaudes, then in command in the west, was an old soldier and a man made of much more decisive stuff than Ausonius. He did not need telling that something was definitely not right in Britannia. Though now in his fifties, he was an experienced and tough operator. He had been fighting the empire's wars for over three decades, having first risen to favour in the army under the Emperor Julian, whose corpse he had escorted back from Persia. The Emperor Valentinian had raised him further to command the army of Illyricum, and later Gratian had advanced him again by giving him the command of the armies of Gallia. He was a proud man, of royal Frankish blood; his brother, Priaros, ruled the Franci settled inside the empire in Toxiandria, south of the mouth of the Rhenus. He was greatly in the young emperor's favour, and, despite his barbarian origins, he had just been made consul for a second time.

Merobaudes was a man against whom Maximus had a grudge, for he had been involved in the show trial and execution of Count Theodosius in Africa. When Maximus was created Duke of the Britannias and given the north to rule, he had not been pleased to find that this had made Merobaudes his direct superior.

From the fleets that he controlled off the coast of Gallia, the Frankish general heard talk of British ports being closed and messengers not returning. He sent couriers now to Maximus and to the Count of the Saxon Shore to find out exactly what was happening. He was not really surprised when no answers to his messages returned, and he was now grimly aware that he was facing a threat from across the water. He warned the border forces under his command to be on the alert.

*

The warnings from all sides indeed proved too late and insufficient. When Maximus' fleet was spotted about to enter the harbour at Lugdunum Batavorum, the base at the mouth of the Rhenus that supplied the German frontier for hundreds of miles up the river, the troops in the fort assumed that it was the regular British flotilla bringing grain, horses and equipment. They were only disabused of their misapprehension when troops landed along with the supplies and swiftly took over the fort and the harbour below it. The border troops were relieved to find that they were left unharmed to carry on with their duties.

Maximus treated the *praefectus* who was their commander with respect. He summoned the officer and politely asked him to send a message down the *limes*, the line of the frontier, that the Augustus Magnus Maximus had arrived from Britannia at the invitation of Emperor Theodosius to take over from the incompetent boy Gratian and to prevent the Gothi spreading across the west. With this message went personal ones to the commanders of the two legions based up the river, the Thirtieth at Vetera and the First further south at Bonna. These he assured of his favour, asking them to remain in their posts and to carry on guarding the frontier as before. Maximus knew that neither commander had sufficient troops to oppose his invading army, and in the event his confidence was well founded, for both proved very happy to accept the very large bribes that accompanied the couriers.

With the frontier secured, Maximus headed south across the low countries. His cavalry, commanded by Andragathius, swept in an arc before him. They marched through country that was now settled largely by the Franci, who had been moving there from across the border for over a century by now. His troops faced no opposition, despite the number of small forts and watch towers spaced out along the roads. Only four small and understrength units were stationed in his path, and none were prepared to resist him. Entering the provincial capital at Forum Hadriani, Maximus received a polite and correct, if chilly, reception from its civilian authorities.

*

As Maximus reached Forum Hadriani, Conan landed his troops in Darioritum, the best harbour on the coast of Armorica. This was a place very well known to the crews of his ships and, as it was the location of one of Julian's family agencies, they were expected there. To cover all eventualities and, as it were, to give an official stamp to proceedings, with him by now was a tribune from Maximus' force who had brought a detachment of men with a herald.

The port was the provincial capital of the Venetii, a tribe that Julius Caesar had almost destroyed centuries before during his Gallic wars. The town had recovered since then and was renowned for its maritime academy, an institute that instructed sailors and navigators using the western seaboard. The capital and its surrounding lands were, however, now in grave decline. This was the case for pretty much the whole of Armorica, which had suffered hugely from Saxon raids over the previous few decades, so much so that the bulk of the population had been evacuated further into Gallia. Some cities in the peninsula had been abandoned completely and their streets were now eerily empty, overgrown and haunted by wild beasts of the forest. Great swathes of farmland had returned to wilderness, untilled since their workforces fled.

There was a fort in Darioritum and some small outposts and signal stations along the nearby headlands, but it was very lightly defended against sea attack. The troops stationed there were in the command of the *dux tractus armoricanus et nervicani*, the Duke of the Armorican and Nervican Region, whose headquarters was a long way off at Grannona, north of the peninsula. Only two small units of barbarian troops manned the dozen or so forts all the way around Armorica's coast and there was nothing to oppose Conan when he presented the prefect in the fort with the credentials of *mare dux* given him by Maximus. In this capacity, he had been made the superior of the Armorican duke, and the prefect of the troops in Darioritum decided, wisely, that he was not going to do anything to risk his neck by opposing him, particularly as his acquiescence was sweetened by the jingle of gold coin. He did, though, surreptitiously get messages off to both Grannona and Lutetia.

*

By now, Merobaudes was well aware of the peril he was in, but he was not a man to panic. On the face of it, he held the upper hand. The troops of his field army outnumbered those of Maximus by at least two to one. Were they reliable, though? They were a very mixed bag, miscellaneous small units of many nationalities, of whom about forty per cent were of barbarian origin. Had the emperor, to whom they were probably personally loyal, been present, they would have had a figurehead whose standard they would have followed. Gratian, alas, was far away. It would be weeks before he and his troops could arrive.

Merobaudes knew that he was not much loved by his men, rather, he had always been a figure to inspire their fear. A strict, even brutal commander, a non-Roman at that, he had accumulated a lot of enemies in his slow rise to power. He was also short of cash, for Gratian had taken the treasury with him to Italia, so he had insufficient funds to be generous with men he needed to ask to put their lives on the line to fight for him.

It did not look good. He was now faced with two forces invading from opposite directions. The most serious threat was clearly from the north, with Maximus bearing down on him along the well-maintained network of roads that led to Lutetia. Rather than try to strike at this force or to attempt to mop up the incursion in Armorica, it seemed that the best approach was to stay where he was and await reinforcement by his emperor.

Merobaudes was a good soldier but did not have much flair as a commander. He ordered his troops to take up defensive positions around Lutetia then sat there, inactive inside his defences, waiting for Maximus to arrive.

*

Way to the south in Italia, the Emperor Gratian found that he had little immediately to hand with which to come to Merobaudes' aid, save his own person. He was a brave, impulsive young man and had no second thoughts in deciding to ride north to reinforce his general. With only an escort of 300 Gothic cavalrymen, he took the road, leaving his palatine troops to follow as fast as they could. He took this risk believing that Merobaudes was strong enough to hold Maximus off until he reached him and that, with his presence and the size of the field army in Gallia, they could jointly see off Maximus' threat. He was to find that he had been sadly mistaken.

*

Maximus reached Lutetia to find Merobaudes' force entrenched, but he did not attack and merely allowed his skirmishers to range around the imperial forces to keep them inactive and alert. Under cover of that and the next four nights, he had special couriers sent to the commanders of the opposing field army, messengers who were armed with promises of future imperial favour, of promotions and appointments, and, which was more to the point, with bags of gold coin worth amounts that he promised to double. The first unit to agree to defect was from the imperial cavalry, a unit of Moors, some of whose officers had served with Maximus in Africa. More units followed, and on the fifth day, led by the cavalry, these began to cross the no man's land between the opposing forces to join Maximus' army. Seeing their comrades deserting, the remainder laid down their arms.

Merobaudes now found himself helpless. When he saw that the game was up, he attempted to flee, but he made it no further than the line of Maximus' skirmishers, who killed his small Frankish escort and placed him in fetters. He was thrown into the wooden hut which he had been using for his headquarters. Maximus ordered him to be held there until he had seen the Frank himself. When he reached the hut, he had Merobaudes dragged outside. He wanted to humiliate the man before he had him killed.

"I had expected a better fight from you," he jeered. "Your failure is abject and it has doomed your emperor to the fate that now befalls you. It is a fate that you inflicted on the best and most loyal general in the empire, the Count Theodosius. Your officers in Africa made me watch while he was paraded and butchered. Now, I shall watch your death and the count will be avenged."

Merobaudes did not attempt to argue. He spat on the ground. "Your turn will come, usurper," he growled. "You will not last long on the throne of the west. The might of the empire will hunt you down. Your great count's son will come for you, his father's son or no."

"Perhaps," retorted Maximus, "but I shall have more than enough time to enjoy your agony." Turning to his troops, Maximus ordered: "Throw him back into the hut so that I can listen to his screams." The Frank was dragged back inside, the door barred, and the hut set on fire. It took only a few minutes before the thatched roof and wattle walls collapsed. Merobaudes, however, uttered not a single sound.

As the charred remains of the Frankish general were dragged out of the smoking ruin, Maximus ordered: "Throw what's left of him into that ditch for the dogs and birds. There is to be no word given out about the Frank's death. The consul," he sneered, "has merely ceased to exist."

*

Reaching Lugdunum in the centre of Gallia, Gratian heard the news put about by Maximus that his troops had defected and that Merobaudes had fled. The emperor could not believe that his Frankish *magister militum* had betrayed him. He would go to his death without being disabused of the idea that it was Merobaudes who had deserted him. With dismay, Gratian saw that he had no choice but to try to reach his palatine troops, which were now marching back from Verona and had yet to enter Gallia. There was nothing for it but to flee. He sought the advice from Lugdunum's governor, who suggested that Gratian make for Gratianopolis, a city only recently renamed in his honour, which was at the foot of the mountains. There, suggested the governor, he would find supporters who would assist him to cross back into Italia. If he took this route, the governor advised, he would shortly catch up with the party escorting his young wife, Lacta, who was on the road fleeing from Augusta. Her litter, he added, was travelling on the same road. This news was false, but fatal.

Gratian had no way of knowing that the governor had been suborned by Maximus' gold coin. When his party came across a small escort with a litter carried by mules, Gratian took it for his wife's party and stopped to rescue her. He dismounted and pulled back the litter's curtains. To his horror, inside the litter was not his wife but Maximus' general, Andragathius, who took advantage of Gratian's amazement to leap forth and disarm him. At that signal, the troops placed in ambush fell upon Gratian's Gothic escort and cut them down.

Andragathius had orders that Gratian was to be killed, orders that he could not fail to carry out. He was not a cruel man, nor one who had any grudge against the young emperor. He was an officer who had been brought up in the service of Gratian's father, Valentinian, and he pitied the late emperor's young son. He could not bring himself to slay him out of hand, so he had him taken back to Lugdunum. Yet he knew that Maximus had a burning hatred of Gratian, and that, if he could, he would inflict a horrible death upon him. So, he caused the governor to invite Gratian to dinner, and at its end, he left with moist eyes as the governor's men smothered the young man to death. He had Gratian's body embalmed, then rode back north to join Maximus, escorting the corpse, sorrowing at the world and what the Fates led a soldier to do.

Andragathius could not shake off the premonition that this deed would bring nothing but ill fortune. He had seen enough of imperial politics to know that Gratian would be avenged. He prayed to Pharnucus, the mounted god of his own people, that he would not be called to account for this crime.

Chapter Fifteen

AUGUSTA TREVERORUM

The suborning of the field army and the death of Gratian stilled any further opposition in Gallia and Maximus was left to enjoy entering Augusta Treverorum peacefully. The garrison of the city turned out to line the route into the city and its officers made haste to register their recognition of their new master. Just to make sure that no one was tempted to hold out for the old regime, Maximus had the *comes* Vallio, the commander who had been left in charge there by Gratian, tracked down and killed. He was one of those officers around Gratian whom Maximus blamed for the death of Count Theodosius. He was traced to his residence, where he had withdrawn to await events. Pulcher and his Segontienses surrounded the house. They broke down the door and dragged the count out into its courtyard, then hanged him from the rafters of his outhouse. It was the sort of task that Pulcher relished, as Maximus had long before appreciated. Pulcher made Vallio's death as painful as he could, making sure that the twisted cord cut into his victim's neck. The emperor had it made public that Vallio had hung himself, too weak and cowardly, it was added, to use his own sword.

The old regime's praetorian prefect, Ausonius, had managed to flee back to his estate near Burdigalia and was not pursued. Julian, who had pretensions to being his literary friend, had asked Maximus for his life. There was, in any case, no further need for bloodshed. It was time instead for a display of pomp to announce the arrival of the new regime. Maximus entered the city riding at the head of his army to a cacophony of horns and trumpets, his officials showering small coins on the people of the city, who welcomed the new emperor with roars of approval. At the gates of the imperial palace, Maximus dismounted to allow himself to be taken into the great basilica on a chair carried at shoulder height by eight of his tallest soldiers. Before him marched his standard-bearers, trumpeters and Constantine's bodyguards, who were now dressed in the traditional dazzling white uniforms that designated the imperial presence. Two slaves carrying ostrich-feathered fans on high poles came before the throne, two more followed behind, then in a long procession came the chief officers of the army and the state. Guards threw open the vast gilded, wooden doors to the basilica, the *aula palatina*, to let the procession march up its great length. Inside, against each of the great walls, stood officials and servants of the court. Reaching the apse at the far end, the chair was set down to allow Maximus to mount the steps to the throne, where he sat to listen to the proclamation of his assumption of imperial power. From high against the wall of the apse, he looked down, as if divine, upon the sea of faces who were massed on both sides of the hall. Once again, his vision flashed back in his mind.

"Flavius Magnus Maximus Augustus, Britannicus Maximus, imperator," chanted the herald, "by conquest and with the approval of the Augustus Theodosius, rightful ruler of Gallia, Britannia and Hispania, restorer of the eternal light. Acclaim your sovereign lord!"

Over and over again, the throng shouted their acclamation. "Maximus Augustus! Imperator!"

The empire was truly at Maximus' feet.

*

News of the successful end to the campaign in Gallia was quickly received by the council in Londinium. The vicar convened a special meeting to agree a despatch congratulating Maximus, who was now, for the time at least, undisputed emperor of the west. Desiderius could afford to feel a little more secure in his seat now. Were Maximus to fail, he would be, in all probability, held accountable for his acquiescence in the usurpation. Were Maximus to succeed, on the other hand, the emperor's gratitude for his passivity would be guaranteed. It seemed that he had bet on the right horse.

The lack of actual fighting in Gallia was something that council members could feel happy about, for none wished to see Roman blood spilled by Romans, and they could now look forward to the return of most of the troops that Maximus had taken across the sea. Their return would ensure the resumption of payments to landowners and tradesmen for the produce and goods that supported them. The renewed minting of coin in Londinium, which Maximus had just ordered, was also regarded as a very good sign. The British princes were by now becoming used to participating in the political events of the diocese and so were also pleased, as the news cemented their newfound status.

Chief among these was Gadeon, who had a greater grasp of the overall picture than any of his fellow princes, and who was in regular contact by messenger with Maximus in Gallia. After the council meeting called to congratulate the new emperor, Gadeon waylaid the Prince Vitalinus outside the council chamber. Vitalinus, whose British name was Guidolin, was an important tribal chief. His main seat was the thriving and very Romanised city of Viroconium, the tribal capital of the Cornovii, situated beside the River Sabrina in the most western lowlands of the island. He controlled a great swathe of territory in the west. His family had, several generations back, married into the tribe of the Dobunni, the lands of which included the colony of Glevum, the hot waters at Aquae Sulis and the provincial capital of Corinium. He was thus the richest and most influential British prince of the day. Gadeon and he were, as were most British princely families, distantly related by marriage. It was Vitalinus' men whom Maximus had called upon to reinforce the garrison of Deva when he took away most of the Twentieth Legion. Vitalinus held important patronages and Gadeon wanted to bring him a little further now into the web which Maximus was spinning.

When they were in a quiet room away from the chamber, Gadeon began the conversation: "Are you happy, cousin, with the turn of events in Gallia?"

"I think so," replied Vitalinus. He was a sensible man of notable gravity, who took his responsibilities to his people very seriously. "We can only hope that Maximus' luck holds. Without his presence, at the best things here will certainly revert to the old normal, at the worst they might endanger our lives."

"His luck seems to be holding so far."

"Yes, it does, and that is pleasing my people. The presence of the princes on the diocesan council has gone down very well. Maximus is becoming a popular ruler because he has delegated so much to us, not to mention the helpful fact that he has a British wife and a brood of half-British children."

Vitalinus had not, Gadeon knew, a grasp of the bigger picture and had clearly not thought through the deeper purposes behind Maximus' British policies. "The new emperor is relying on us to prevent any loss of these islands while he is away in Gallia. It seems a sensible policy to me, for one can never rely totally on imperial army officers to stay loyal to any absent emperor. Maximus knows his history; usurpation can breed usurpers. With us not only involved centrally, but now also militarily on the western seaboard, he is stronger than before."

Gadeon wanted to go further now, to make an ally of this important prince. "I see many opportunities for us here, cousin. Our island has, for centuries, been a home for a tenth of the imperial army. It has produced emperors and would-be emperors. As in Gallia, our landowning families have made huge profits from the empire. But unlike in Gallia, no British family has ever wielded influence at the centre, or even been elevated legally to the purple. There have been Spaniards, Moors, even Syrians on the imperial throne, who with them brought wealth and influence to families from their homelands. Under the old Emperor Valentinian, the court was full of Pannonians. Gratian's accession swamped the state with the offspring of many Gallic families. Yet here, even the families who own the vast agricultural estates of the east of our island have never wielded any influence in the empire. Now, I think, under this emperor, our time may have come."

"I had not thought of that," confessed Vitalinus. "It would indeed be a happy prospect were it to come to pass."

"I mean to do what I can in this council to make it possible," said Gadeon. "I wanted you to know that I am keeping in close touch with the emperor, and would wish, cousin, if you are happy for me to do so, to recommend you to him. You no doubt have suitable candidates for imperial favour, as do we in Dumnonia, and I intend to seek that favour for them."

"I would of course be willing, and I shall let you know the names of those you might recommend. Give me a few days to think of this."

"There is one other issue I would like to broach with you," went on Gadeon. "The emperor's children are still young, the oldest still only in their teens, but it seems to me that there would be great advantage were they to be married into some of the chief families of our country. The Romans have done this before; the emperor's two wives are recent examples. Extending that policy further to include his children would benefit all parties. I have yet to raise this issue with my cousin, Elen, but now, I think, is the time to do so. If we do not move swiftly to get Maximus' children betrothed, they will be married off somewhere else and we shall lose the chance to tie ourselves to what we hope will be a new imperial line."

"You are now several steps ahead of me, Gadeon," the prince replied. Gadeon was rapidly earning his respect. "You are right, though. I can see that clearly. Let me give this matter some thought. I shall get back to you within days so that you may set these things in motion. My only unhappiness," added Vitalinus, "in all this is the fact that Maximus has espoused the Christian faith. I had nursed hopes that he might restore tolerance."

"Those were my hopes, too," responded Gadeon. "I believe that my cousin, Elen, may have had a hand in this. She has become cloyingly devout. We are, alas, stuck with this now. All we shall be able to do is to maintain our observance of our own gods in our own lands. I do not think that anyone in authority here in Britannia has yet the power to challenge us on that."

"We are becoming too useful for anyone to poke our wasps' nest with that stick," agreed Vitalinus. "Let us work to maintain that state of affairs." He chuckled. "We need them to fear us, just a little!"

They parted, Vitalinus with the dawning idea that changes bigger than he had imagined were now afoot, Gadeon with quiet confidence that he had both made an ally and furthered his own plans.

*

In Gallia, Maximus was rapidly transforming himself from the bluff, rugged army commander that he had seemed hitherto into an emperor whose every attribute carried an aura of the divine. He was now God's elected representative here on earth. His person, next to God or the gods in the empire, was deemed, at least officially, sacred. Every aspect of his administration, even his bedchamber and his privy purse, were held sacred. As emperor, he was surrounded by men who bowed, scraped and flattered. Not only his slaves but even the senior officials of his consistory were not permitted to look him in the eye. His new staff, many adopted from the old regime, fawned upon him and lauded every small decision that he made. He had come to Augusta intending to sweep away the effete and the idle, to simplify and strengthen, but he soon succumbed to the expectations that an emperor must behave and be treated in a truly imperial fashion. A sign of this, one that was noted throughout the court, was his attitude to eunuchs. When he mounted the throne, he had given vent to his soldierly contempt for those who performed many of the duties at court, whom he had hitherto characterised as whining half-men, by exiling all eunuchs from the precincts. Within months, they had insinuated their way back, seemingly without any further distaste on the part of their emperor. There they were now, fawning about him.

The maintenance of imperial prestige by ceremony and show made incumbency of the imperial throne immensely gratifying to anyone who achieved it, but the hubris and detachment from reality that came with it were dangerous.

Unfortunately for Maximus, he failed to remember that it was not those who always agreed with him who were the best counsellors, or that those who attempted to point out the flaws in his policies might just be more loyal than the flatterers.

Imperial power also brought with it a host of minor irritations, the need for perpetual formality, the necessity of deciding minor and tedious issues, the difficulties of taking any initiative. Religion made things far, far worse. Maximus had been on the throne for only a matter of weeks when he was to discover some of the difficulties that being a Christian emperor could entail.

*

Elen lived her days now in a state of perpetual anxiety. She had little belief that what her husband was doing would lead to anything other than the destruction of them all. Maximus had called for her once he had reached the imperial capital, telling her to bring all their children, but she had for once disobeyed him. Victor had crossed to Gallia with her husband and was now ensconced in the palace. Elen left the other children back in Eboracum. All the brothers, even tiny Peblig, had clamoured to be allowed to travel with her, but Elen was firm and, leaving orders for their continued instruction, bade them farewell at the palace gates. The boys fumed and the girls wept.

Elen travelled uncomfortably by ship then carriage across the north of Gallia, surrounded at each stage by Gerontius' cavalry escort. As they travelled, she was left alone with her fears. Gallia was peaceful now, but there was a cold reserve about the welcome she received at each major town on their route. She could see that few people of any note turned out to see her. The rich and important of Gallia were still holding their breath about her husband's usurpation. Few, too, had any respect for this semi-barbarous British princess from a remote tribe.

Nonetheless, the great imperial city of Augusta Treverorum gave her the official welcome now due to Elen as consort of the emperor. The city was full of her husband's people, so that it at least felt safe, but it was too grand a place to feel much comfort. Now that she was an empress, Elen found that she was unable ever to be fully alone. Surrounded by ladies in waiting and maidservants, she was sure that there were spies in her household, so she was now always careful of what she said. Her days were plotted out for her relentlessly by the secretary and aides appointed to her chamber. There was no one she knew in Augusta that she could trust.

The palace was full of civil servants and soldiers and hummed with business. To Elen, the whole place seemed foreign, eastern; the court reeked of the perfumes and customs of Constantinopolis. No one came near her without rendering deep but cold obeisance. Supplicants would drop before her, full face on the floor. The huge, magnificent throne room, its dais staggeringly high and richly decorated, dwarfed any human crossing its floor. The imperial throne in the apse at its end was so high off the ground that when Maximus climbed it, rather than a Christian emperor, he seemed, to those placed far below him, an Olympian deity. She shivered every time she was called upon to enter the place.

Elen tried to tell herself that her husband's plans were actually working out, just as Maximus bragged to her in their private chambers at night. The administrations of Gallia and Hispania had indeed swiftly acknowledged him as emperor; Julian's gold had gone a long way. So peaceful had the transition been that there had been no need for any purge of opponents; the officials who had held office as friends and clients of Ausonius bent like willows in the wind, and none of them gave any indication of disloyalty to the new regime. In any case, the principal officials among them were being rapidly replaced; they were allowed to return home to their estates. Maximus decreed some shuffling of provincial boundaries, but ventured nothing more serious in the way of reform. Britannia was quiet and under the control of the diocesan council that Maximus had appointed; Gadeon kept Elen well informed of all that happened there. Elen could see no sign of any revolution in government or of any opposition to her husband. Yet still she felt unsafe. She found herself shivering uncontrollably at times and could not shake off the feeling of dread that overshadowed her days. At night, she slept fitfully and clung to her husband when he came to share her bed.

Just after Elen arrived in Augusta, her eldest stepson, Victor, was proclaimed the Augustus Flavius Victor. The acclamation took place in a lavish ceremony in the basilica attended by the whole consistory. Despite his being aged only fourteen, in one leap Victor had been elevated past the rank of Caesar to be co-emperor with his father. From now on, he would be attributed semi-divine status, only slightly lower than that of his father. Maximus issued an edict ordering that Victor's portrait appear on the gold *solidi* and silver coins that he was having minted to mark his accession. This all went swiftly to Victor's head, and the cruel streak, which those close to him had always known him to possess, began to break out more noticeably. The boy began to take a perverse pleasure in hurting those attached to his household. Humiliating and flogging his slaves seemed to give him a sadistic thrill. He never saw his stepmother now, save on official occasions, when he never looked at her.

Maximus noticed none of this. His usual self-confidence had been enhanced considerably by the ease of his success.

It seemed to him that none now stood against him and that he truly possessed divine favour. He sent back to Britannia most of the troops which had accompanied his expedition, for both the Gallic field army and the imperial palatine troops of Gratian had come through the usurpation unscathed and they were now back in station in Gallia. Taking no chances, however, Maximus had placed some of the troops he returned to Britannia under the control of a senior officer appointed by him to a new post. This officer was to be styled the *comes britanniarum*, the Count of the British Provinces, and he promoted to it Aurelian, the prefect of the Second Legion, whose troops had accompanied him to Gallia. The mobile force allocated to the new count included six cavalry and three infantry units, some of them transferred from the Army of Gallia. For the first time, there was now a count commanding a field army in Britannia, just as there had long been in Gallia, Italia and in the east. In doing this, Maximus sought to strengthen his British base whilst ensuring that in future no single senior officer would be able to wield the full strength of the forces in the British diocese as he had done himself.

Sufficiently confident was Maximus of the solidity of his position that he sent his *praepositus sacri cubiculi*, the chamberlain of his bedchamber, on an embassy to Theodosius in Constantinopolis. He bore the eastern emperor an arrogant missive dictated by Maximus himself, taunting him either to accept the situation or to make trial of it in war. Maximus rightly calculated that Theodosius was so troubled by the threats surrounding him that he would be unable to intervene. Only in the previous year had the huge disruption caused by the ingress of the Gothic tribes into Thracia been settled by treaty. Further east, war always threatened from the Sassanids in Persia.

Maximus was right in this, but it was a short-term gamble that he was taking. Theodosius was indeed unable to do more than ask for guarantees of the security of the imperial family in Mediolanum. Having achieved this, or so he was led to believe, both he and the administration of the twelve-year-old Valentinian II issued official recognition of Maximus as Augustus in the west, and they had this recognition recorded by the erection of statues to him across the empire as far afield as Alexandria. This, Maximus fooled himself, showed that Theodosius had not forgotten their lifelong personal relationship and Maximus' love for his father, whom he had avenged. He made the unwarranted assumption that he had made Theodosius accept him as his equal.

Andragathius made the mistake of pointing out in council that it was merely the pressure of circumstances, and certainly no affection for Maximus, that was preventing Theodosius from marching west.

The emperor was displeased and showed it. "Come, Andragathius, my statues are now being installed in all the major cities of the east, inscribed with my status as co-emperor. Would Theodosius have ordered this if he intended to oppose my elevation to the purple?"

"My lord, Theodosius and his advisers may indeed be seeking to allay your suspicions. They may very well be playing a long game. Statues are more easily pulled down than they are erected."

The Augustus Victor saw the look of anger on his father's face and took his chance to pay back the barbarian who had so humiliated him in Eboracum. "Father, Andragathius knows nothing of the friendship you enjoy with the emperor of the east. How could he? He is but a barbarian soldier of no political experience. None here can make this assessment other than you."

"Theodosius is my friend. You are right, Victor. I am the only man here who can make this judgment."

The issue was passed over, but seeds had been sown in that council that were to sprout later to ill effect. Elen watched her husband growing more confident and authoritarian as the days went by. She could not reciprocate his blind belief that all was going his way. She tried hard not to believe that out of the east would come retribution for the murder of Gratian, but deep inside herself she knew that killing a lawful emperor had been a grievous sin. Alone together in their bedroom, Elen couldn't hide her fears. "Are we safe now?" she asked her husband.

"We are safer now than since my master, the great Count Theodosius, was murdered," he replied. "We were never really safe from Gratian and those around him. They had not forgotten where my loyalties lay."

"But in the future?" she pressed him. "They will not forgive Gratian's death. They will come for us and our son."

"Theodosius knows me. We grew up together and we were together for half our lives. I killed the men who had his father slaughtered. He will not come for me." Maximus laughed. "Besides, he has so many worries in his lap that he will not have the strength to move against us. We shall grow safer as time passes. Do not fret, my love, you and Victor will be safe and our family shall prosper. Our house has a glorious future."

Elen could not find it in herself to say more. Maybe it was the Dumnonii blood in her veins, something her new faith made her loath to recognise. Whatever it was, she felt a heaviness that she could not shake off. She prayed that night and every night afterwards for her children and her husband. Try as she might, her Christ gave her no answer or sign. That was about to change.

Chapter Sixteen

TWO CHRISTIANS

At the time of Maximus' accession, but almost certainly unknown to him then, there were two very famous Christians who personified the dichotomy in the orthodox Christianity of the west. In the city of Mediolanum, the boy Valentinian II's imperial capital, its fiery bishop, Aurelius Ambrosius, was the first of these, a cleric who was a ruthless politician, the apostle of a deity who was uncompromisingly the god of wrath and power. Ambrose was a scourge of those he called devil worshippers and pagans. He had instigated the almost total destruction of their temples and shrines all over his diocese and egged on the harassment of their priests, who were beaten up by his followers, prevented from sacrifice and worship, and driven out of the city. Ambrose visited his wrath equally upon those he regarded as heretics, especially upon the Arians.

Argument about the nature of Christ was widespread among Christians across the empire. Those who held to Ambrose's beliefs accepted the creed that had been made orthodox at the Council of Nicaea sixty years before. Now in the majority, the adherents of this creed characterised as a heretic anyone who denied that Christ was co-eternal with the father. Those who believed otherwise, who were derided as "Arians" by the orthodox, believed that Christ had been created by God and so was subordinate to him. Arians had been prevalent in Mediolanum for many years before Ambrose's consecration as its bishop. His predecessor in the see, Auxentius, had been a prominent Arian theologian who had been declared a heretic by the bishop of Roma. Friends in high places, however, had protected Auxentius, who had been left to die unscathed and in post, so when Ambrose took over, he viewed it as his task to clean the Arian stables he found polluting the city. He instigated a struggle that was reflected across the empire, for members of the imperial dynasty, including the late eastern Emperor Valens and the young western Emperor Valentinian II, were Arians. There were many Arians inside the army, including Gothi who had been recruited in increasing numbers after Theodosius' wars against them. The struggle between orthodoxy and Arianism was bitter.

Ambrose had the skin of a rhinoceros and seemed unaffected by the enemies that he made in his fight for what he believed was holy truth. By nature arrogant, stubborn and argumentative, he was nonetheless a very brave man and a marvellous orator who made open use of his popularity in his city to resist the imperial authorities when they tried to impose their will upon him. In this, he was perhaps the first cleric ever to publicly defy his emperor and live to tell the tale. This had earned him an iconic status unmatched by that of any other cleric in the western empire, even that of the bishop of Roma, who, although the patriarch of the west, its most senior bishop, found himself relatively eclipsed.

Ambrose lived in a grand style in cathedral, palace and city. He dressed in splendid robes. When he went out, it was always in procession, surrounded by acolytes and followed by crowds of the devout. He was a hugely persuasive speaker, an orator who could sway crowds from his pulpit. Absolutely sure of the power that he believed God had placed in his hands, he was utterly confident in exercising it. He had held great power over the Emperor Gratian. For Maximus, still in the uncertain glory of his imperial status, it was lucky that Ambrose was a long way away from his court and any possible offence he might cause the priest.

Much closer to Augusta resided the other major Christian of the age, the holy Martin, bishop of Civitas Turonum. Martin was Ambrose's opposite in almost everything, save for the orthodox Christianity he followed. He was regarded with awe and affection by western Christians, who acknowledged him as the holiest man in the western empire. Martin saw his saviour Christ as a benevolent, forgiving deity of love. He regarded it as his duty to live in poverty and to fight for anyone in need whom God put in his way. Not for him was the enforcement of obedience using the weapon of excommunication or physical threat. Although he, like Ambrose, was unafraid of any authority other than God, his tools were meek persuasion and love for all. His only sanction against the wicked was to refuse to break bread with them.

Martin had been a soldier under the emperors Constantine and Julian, a cavalryman who had famously divided his cloak to give half of it to a beggar. He had taken his discharge from his unit on the German frontier to travel into Gallia to sit at the feet of the holy Hilary of Pictavium, the most eminent western Christian of the years of Martin's youth. When Hilary so upset the imperial authorities that he was exiled, Martin began a long series of wanderings, preaching the faith as far afield as Pannonia and Illyricum, and he returned to Gallia only when Hilary was reinstated. At Hilary's death, Martin was so bereft that he allowed himself to be elected bishop, a dignity he did not seek and did not want, preferring to live in poverty. His preference for the simple life of a hermit eventually led him to resign his see and cross the river from his city to an isolated rural spot where he could live alone. Here, however, he was unable to fend off the world, for, as his fame spread, he gradually accumulated so many disciples that he was forced to make order out of the growing chaos by establishing rules for their joint lives. So was born Majus Monasterium, the first Christian monastery in the west. The numbers of monks still increasing, Martin founded a second monastery near the city. These were historic foundations, the first monasteries in the western empire.

Martin was older now, but still active. He carried on travelling widely in Gallia, converting pagans, helping the destitute and speaking truth to power. That power was now the new Emperor Maximus, so Martin travelled by cart for over a week to meet him. He had another reason for his journey, a mission of charity. He had been fed information by the Gallic circle of Ausonius that in the imperial dungeons in Augusta Treverorum were two imprisoned Christians who were in need of his help. He set out to free them.

*

As empress, Elen, to her dismay, was forced to endure attendance at audiences and to be present on the frequent ceremonial occasions held at court. In the apse of the basilica, her throne was set lower than her husband's and Victor's, but it was still high enough to make her isolation complete. What went on before her eyes involved men she did not know and issues of which she had no comprehension. Much of the oratory spoken before the throne was in a language more complicated than she could understand. She frequently relapsed into troubled daydreams. It was at the end of one of these well-choreographed occasions that she heard the new chamberlain announce that the holy Martin was in the ante chamber and was requesting audience. Elen sat bolt upright. Martin was a man of whom she had heard much and who, for once, was a figure she really did want to see.

She watched, fascinated, as into the vast throne room of the *aula palatina* walked a man of late middle age, bearded, slightly stooping and leaning on his staff. He was accompanied by only one young man, his presbyter, who walked several paces behind him. Martin's robes were made of dun-coloured, home-spun cloth; his sandals were scuffed and worn. Poverty cried out from his every inch, but he was by no means abashed to stand before the court. He knew the forms and saluted the emperor with confidence. He did not prostrate himself on the floor. As Martin stood humbly, way below the thrones, seemingly lost in the vast expanse of the black and white marble floor, Elen felt a grace and light emanating from his calm, gentle face. Her breath caught in her throat.

Maximus felt none of that, but he did recognise with pleasure the bearing of an old soldier, and with more than his usual kindness, beckoned his visitor to approach.

"Lord, I come to you in the name of the risen Christ to seek your mercy on his servants," began the holy man, his clear, unwavering voice echoing up into the void of the basilica over a hundred feet above them.

"Holy Martin, your fame precedes you," replied the emperor. "We are glad to meet you and we are honoured to welcome you to our court. Since I was baptised before coming to Gallia, I have heard much of you, especially from my wife," and he turned to introduce Elen with a gesture of his hand.

"My good lady." Martin bowed his head. "You will know, then, lord, that our Lord Jesus enjoins us always to turn the other cheek, and that after his passing he has broken the chains of many of his captive followers, including those of the apostles Peter and Paul. He has taught us that it is the nature of the almighty God always to have mercy. You, the ruler of our empire, are appointed to rule for and through Him, to act justly, righteously and with mercy."

Maximus nodded solemn ascent to Martin's words, which had touched a nerve even under his thick skin. When he thought of such things, Maximus had indeed begun to accept the idea, repeated to him endlessly by the officials of his consistory, that he was the agent of the Almighty here on earth. It was a flattering idea. Also, he was wise enough to know that, in these increasingly Christian times, the occasional exercise of mercy could bring with it an element of popularity.

"Lord," went on the holy Martin, "when you came to Gallia from across the seas you brought with you two men of the faith, men whose solemn oath to serve the last emperor they could not in their consciences break, two men who were prepared to suffer whatever penalty you, my lord, might impose upon them rather than break their word, men who would not dishonour themselves by betraying their oaths of office. I speak, you will understand, I am sure, of the *comes* Narses and the *praeses* Leucadius, who are held, lord, at your pleasure in your prison. I have come before you to pray that you may release them to return unharmed to the bosom of their families, for in truth you would, my lord, expect all of us to serve you as honourably as they have served your predecessor."

It had dawned upon Maximus, before the completion of Martin's short oration, that this man of God was offering him a way out of a predicament in which he had found himself since his seizure of power. He had, in truth, not known what to do with the two officers whose release Martin was seeking. He had not been able to leave them behind to cause dissension in Britannia, but he had not wished to have them killed; neither was his enemy. Therefore, he had ordered them brought, caged in a cart, all the way to Augusta, and they had been in the fortress dungeon ever since.

"Indeed, God has sent you to us today, Holy Martin," he now responded, "to deflect our sword with his mercy. It is in our mind to release these men into your charge so that they may be sent home to their families, without mischief to ourself or to the state. If they swear to do us no evil, will you take them?"

Martin was slightly taken aback by the ease of his small victory, but he took up the challenge immediately. "I shall, lord, and I shall make sure that they reach home as you direct."

"So let it be done," Maximus ordered, and members of the imperial staff scurried away to do his bidding. "Holy Martin, it would please me and my wife greatly were you to stay and dine with us before you depart."

Martin was unafraid to look the emperor in the eye. "I cannot, lord, eat with a man who has killed his emperor." Unabashed, he watched as Maximus started back in surprise and anger. Elen urgently placed her hand on the emperor's arm.

Maximus glanced at his wife and paused, then drew breath and replied: "We ascended to the purple straight from the font of salvation by our baptism. My acclamation as emperor was by divine will and the successful outcome of our mission has been proof that we have acted according to God's will. As God has so favoured us, I pray that now you, his most holy priest, will favour us also, and break bread with us."

Martin had not been unaware of the reverence with which Elen had been regarding him throughout this exchange. There was a purpose at work in her, it seemed to him, that had to be divine. So, against his better will, he bowed his head in acceptance of the invitation and stayed for supper. When the emperor paid Martin the high compliment of seating him at his right hand, then passed Martin his own cup, Martin passed it to his presbyter to drink first. Maximus surprised himself by being impressed.

After they had dined together on this first occasion, Martin left the capital in his ancient cart, taking with him the two freed captives travelling unmolested to their freedom.

*

It was only a few days later that a very different sort of visitor arrived at the palace. Maximus was conferring with his senior officers about the growing problem of insecurity along the German frontier, where the tribes, sensing some instability, had started to attack river traffic and raid across the river into lightly held areas on the Roman bank. Andragathius was advocating swift reprisals to stamp Maximus' imperial authority across the border early in his reign. The conference was just arriving at the consensus that something would soon need to be done were the situation not to get out of hand, when there was a raucous blast of trumpets from the courtyard below.

Word of an embassy from the imperial administration in Italia had reached the capital some weeks before, and this news was swiftly followed by requests for safe conduct for its leader, Bishop Ambrose of Mediolanum, and his retinue. These had clattered into Augusta the day before, but had sent to the court neither notification of their arrival nor accreditation of their mission, instead had moved into the city where Ambrose, who had been born there, still kept his father's house. There the imperial delegation had established itself. Now, it was clear, it had decided to arrive at court, though without any prearranged schedule for an audience.

Stung by this disrespect, Maximus mounted the throne, while his officers and high officials assembled around the dais, principal among them Evodius, the new praetorian prefect of Gallia, and the *magister militum* Andragathius. Members of the imperial household scurried to get into place, led by the acting *praepositus*, the eunuch Gallicanus, who had been appointed in place of the old man sent on embassy to the east. At hand were several notaries ready to take minutes and draft edicts. Around the dais, as well as at the edges of the basilica, the bodyguards mounted sharp watch, their arms displayed. Ambrose might be a priest, but he was an emissary from Mediolanum, and no one here trusted anyone from that city. Maximus gave instruction that no favour be shown the delegation and he had the enormous veil that could be hung to separate his presence from the court pulled across in front of his throne.

The vast doors swung open to reveal not just an ambassador but a procession. At its head stalked a priest bearing a huge golden cross. Behind him came two acolytes swinging censors, spewing incense that spread a sweet-smelling fog across the already scented room. Behind them walked two parallel rows of deacons singing hymns, then bearers of the imperial insignia and the imperial trumpeters whose instruments had blared out a fanfare in the courtyard. They repeated this now in the echoing hall. Finally, after all these had spilled into the basilica, Bishop Ambrose entered, carried aloft on a chair by six tall attendants. He was gorgeously enrobed in scarlet and green, rings of bright gold and rubies on his fingers, a tall mitre on his head. His chair was set down before the throne. He did not kneel but gave the merest inclination of his head to the emperor seated way above him.

"Ambassador, you are most welcome to our court," opened Maximus after a pause felt by all present. "We had word of your coming and had prepared quarters for you in the palace, but we are told that you are accommodated elsewhere."

"We are, lord," replied the bishop. "I have a house nearby in the city, and it seemed best not to impose upon your hospitality." In truth, the bishop had thought it less awkward not to have to break bread with a man whom he regarded as a usurper and the murderer of the rightful emperor. Maximus was, of course, not unaware of that fact.

"We trust, then, ambassador, that you are well provided for there. We hope that your return to the place of your birth is a happy one."

"Were you to grant the request that is the object of my visit, it will be," replied Ambrose, getting straight to the point. He had become used to dealing with figures wearing the purple and by now had such confidence in the protection of his God and in his own ability to carry all before him that he had dispensed with what he regarded as elaborate and pointlessly indirect diplomatic discourse, let alone any form of politeness. He was also becoming angry and frustrated at having to address the emperor through the veil that obscured all but his outline.

"And what would that request be, ambassador?" asked Maximus, continuing to refuse to acknowledge this emissary as a bishop and so denying him any moral edge arising from his cloth.

"My imperial master, the Emperor Valentinian II, asks you, as a true Christian, to surrender to him the body of his brother, the late and much-lamented Emperor Gratian. His mother, the Dowager Empress Justina, is in mourning for her stepson and wishes to be able to bury his body alongside that of his first wife, the Lady Constantia, who has most recently been laid to rest in Constantinopolis."

"Ambassador, we had not learned of the burial of the Lady Constantia. We are, however, unable to accede to this imperial request," replied Maximus, "though it gives us no pleasure to be unable to do so. On the death of Gratian, his body was embalmed and brought to this city, where it now lies at rest and where it will remain. When you return to Italia, you will inform my imperial colleague that the body is no longer in a state fit for such a journey. But you will, I trust, give the emperor my fraternal greetings. Now, we shall ensure that you are escorted back with honour to your father's house."

Maximus rose, and before Ambrose was able to attempt any further argument, indicated by a wave of his hand that the audience was at an end. The bodyguard fell in at the front and rear of the bishop's procession and marched the by now infuriated and exasperated bishop and his men out of the hall. Ambrose was not accustomed to being so slightingly dealt with and resolved that this afront would not go unanswered were he one day to find an opportunity.

On his return to Mediolanum, the failure of his mission would bring grief to the Dowager Empress Justina and her son Valentinian. Ambrose's failure would also worsen the relations between the Italian imperial court and himself, relations that had already reached breaking point. In his death, Gratian's body was already beginning to make flesh the fears that his murder had inflicted upon Andragathius and the Empress Elen.

*

Had Elen been able to overhear a conversation happening over 1,500 miles to the east, her worst fears would have been confirmed. In Constantinopolis, the Emperor Theodosius had convened a council of his closest advisers to discuss what to do about Maximus' usurpation. They met in the splendour of the imperial palace, its wide windows overlooking the sharp blue of the Bosporus. The unanimous advice was that what had happened could not be tolerated, on the grounds that the usurpation had overturned the divinely appointed governance of the state. Not to intervene, all were convinced, would bring eventual destruction down upon themselves. No one present believed that Maximus would be content to rule only what he had already attained. All were agreed, however, that now was not the time to act. The east was still too unsettled to withdraw sufficient troops to overcome the armies of the west. The problems of the Gothi infesting the empire and the Persian threat to its east were still too pressing.

Theodosius dismissed his councillors and left the chamber to sit under the shade of trees lining the terrace overlooking the water. He was sure that they had reached the right decision, but he was still unhappy about it. He was a man of firm principle who cleaved to doing things correctly. His whole life had been one of adherence to duty. He lived by his personal code of honour and in all things he rigidly attempted to fulfil the dictates of his Christian religion. Maximus' usurpation offended every one of his dearly held principles. He could not let it pass. It was not so much that he needed to avenge the death of his co-emperor, Gratian. The young man's death was a loss; he had shown distinct signs of promise, but it was the overthrow of an emperor appointed by all the proper forms that Theodosius found unacceptable. The usurpation had rocked the foundations of his world.

What of Maximus, his boyhood friend and colleague in Britannia? Theodosius found that he had no sympathy left for this man. What Maximus had done five years before on the Danubius had been a betrayal of his duty to the empire. It had led to the death of the Emperor Valens and thousands of his soldiers. It had opened the door to the Gothi, who had burned and looted everything in their path in Thracia;

countless citizens had lost their lives or had been forced to flee. Theodosius had spent the last five years trying to restore some order to the region, and he had not yet fully succeeded. He had been forced to accept a treaty allowing the Gothi to settle under their own rulers and laws, and to bear arms. No barbarian had been so leniently treated before.

Maximus had yet to pay for any of this. To grind salt into his wounds, Theodosius had just been told that Maximus was claiming to have his support for the murder of Gratian and his usurpation of power. He found this direct lie unbearable. He would make Maximus retract that before the end. Had he been able to act now, he would have done so. Because he could not, he must dissemble, something he hated. The opportunity would come, he knew, but he would need to wait.

Chapter Seventeen

THE ALTAR OF VICTORY

No pompous, self-important cleric troubled Conan in his fortress in Darioritum. There was, he was surprised to discover, very little to trouble him at all. The imperial military and naval forces in Gallia had now sworn allegiance to the new emperor of the west, so armed with Maximus' decree appointing him *mare dux*, Conan had taken command of all the vessels and military installations of the *dux armorica* as far south as Burdigalia. He had extended his reach even further south, into the diocese of Hispania, establishing a naval station in the estuary of the River Masma in the province of Gallaecia, a patrol base from which his fleet was able to control the southern approach to the western seaboard. He christened this small settlement Bretona.

The decree from Maximus had also given into Conan's charge the naval vessels and establishments of the *classis britannica* that were based on the Gallic side of the sea, along with coastal units of the *dux belgicae secundae*, the Duke of Lower Belgica, the officer who commanded the coast from Granonna as far as the mouth of the Rhenus. Both of the two dukes in place on Conan's assumption of power had swiftly been replaced by men loyal to Maximus, but even before that their subordinates had shown no indication of doing anything other than acquiesce in the usurpation of power. In any case, none had sufficient means at his disposal to oppose the change.

The British troops and sailors in Conan's fleet had been taken aback by what they found in Darioritum. A good deal of the city was empty and, in places, falling into decay. Many of the landowners of the big estates around the city had moved further into Gallia to escape the destructive raids of the last forty years. Those who had made a living in their employ, or in the commerce and industry of the city, had followed them into more strongly fortified cities in the interior, such as Condate and Rotomagus. Many of the streets of Darioritum were eerily empty of people, and a lot of the fields in its hinterland were untilled. Wild animals from the forests in the spine of the peninsula were encroaching now into what had been zones of human habitation. There was land here for the taking.

At sea for most of the first months of his appointment, Conan had plenty of time to ponder the several messages he received from his brother Gadeon, who, as always, was thinking well ahead of the game. Gadeon was currently with their uncle in Isca, having travelled there to discuss with the old man the opportunities for their people that were opening up across the water. He was ambivalent about Maximus' long-term prospects, but he had begun to see that not only had Maximus given temporary military power to the Dumnonii, but that he had also given the tribe the chance to double the size of their territory. If Armorica was as open to settlement as Conan had reported, then it seemed sensible to reinforce him in Darioritum with families sufficient to hold the land, whether Maximus survived or no. The time to move was now, while they had imperial support. With his father's blessing, Gadeon began to gather shiploads of families from across Britannia, people who were willing to make the crossing and create a new life in Letavia, which was what the British had traditionally called Armorica.

Some settlers had arrived even before Conan got back to Darioritum after establishing his control up and down the coast. Erbin had managed their arrival, and he was egging Conan on to expand the influx. Erbin was a prince who chafed under any man's direct control and he nagged at his cousin to give him his head to take ships of the fleet to set up another colony on the peninsula's north coast. On their voyages around Armorica, they had noticed that the more remote parts were far more desolate than the area of its capital. Some quite large towns had been completely abandoned and their remaining people gathered in smaller, more easily defensible outposts, usually near the sea. Even these were largely cut off from the aid of the nearest military support.

Erbin had his eye on an almost deserted tract of what had once been the tribal lands of the Coriosolites. That tribe existed pretty much only in name by now, and their capital, once at Fanum Martis, had been moved to Aleto on the coast. "We could recreate our homeland here, a second Dumnonia," Erbin prompted his half-brother. "The place dominates the north coast, and it sits right opposite our own home ports," he added.

"I have more than enough to keep me busy here at Darioritum," responded Conan.

"I know, brother," Erbin replied, "but our numbers are growing and I have now less to do to help you here. Let me go and work for you in the north. If you give me the same sort of letter that Maximus gave you, I can set up our rule there and secure the line of passage to our homeland."

Fortunately for him, Erbin made his plea not long after Conan had received a letter from Gadeon saying pretty much the same thing. Gadeon had suggested a "new Dumnonia" and had recommended new settlements around the northern Armorican coasts. Conan was persuaded, although he was not absolutely sure that allowing Erbin to build a separate mini state, so far out of his control, might not be asking for trouble. On the other hand, it would get Erbin out of his hair.

"Fine, Erbin," he responded, "go north and build a new Dumnonia, but remember your new homeland is part of a bigger new Britannia here in Letavia, not some independent part. If you are properly appointed, I can delegate you control of Aleto and the north coast as far as Grannona. The emperor must be informed, of course, but I do not think he will object. This fits well with his original plan."

Which was true, except that Maximus had not envisaged the emigration of British families in the wake of the military control he had given Conan on the coast.

*

Well satisfied with the results of his financial investment in Maximus' expedition, Sextus Rusticius Julianus sent his co-conspirator word that he was now launching the next phase of their joint enterprise. For him, this meant ascending the ladder of imperial appointments, which would lead, he intended, to the recoupment of the outlays of gold he had made so far. Not that supporting Maximus had to any degree bankrupted him; his family's business was making more money than ever before up the western seaboard, as his ships carried Maximus' troops and supplies and sailed on the errands of his officers, all paid for by the state at more than the going rates. Julian's agents in Britannia had pre-empted the coup by buying up surplus corn and animals, which he had sold to the state to supply the army on the move, again at a good mark-up. So, despite his large outlays, he had not been forced to sell even a single estate or to liquidate any asset. Julian set out from his estate in Gallia with a light heart and much jingling in his money chests. Even were things to go badly wrong for Maximus now, he had personally not shown his hand, nor committed any traceable treason.

Julian had not told Maximus of his other intention, and that was much on his mind now. For generations, his family had grown rich through the protection of the goddess Artahe. Their ships still carried on their sails the goddess' emblem of the bear. Their agency offices all housed small shrines to her. In Aquitania, where the family originated, Julian was one of the main sources of support for the goddess' chief shrine, which he had repaired, then rebuilt after two attempts by local Christians to destroy it. Before setting out on any journey, including this one to Roma, he and members of his family habitually made prayers and offerings at the shrine. A small element of the profit from any journey they made always went to the goddess in some way. Julian and his family had no doubt that their good fortune had stemmed from her favour. Coincidentally, the bear was the emblem of the royal line of Dumnonia, and it now fluttered on Conan's standards over Armorica.

When word had reached Julian that Maximus had been baptised a Christian before setting out on his expedition, it had been a shock. Religion had not figured in any of their earlier negotiations and discussions. Julian had believed that Maximus was of the old religions; he had never appeared the sort of man to be swayed by a faith of meekness, poverty and charity. Julian hoped that this baptism was merely a tactical move of the moment. Whether that was so or no, the baptism put in danger his secondary aim, which was the rescue of the practice of the old religions by the reinstitution of tolerance. It had been the Emperor Gratian's abandonment of toleration that had finally turned Julian against him.

Arriving in Roma, Julian established his base at the villa he kept in the hills outside the capital. When he had recovered from the dust and fatigue of the journey, he straightaway wrote to the offices of Quintus Aurelius Symmachus, the urban prefect, seeking an appointment with the great man. Symmachus was the most powerful figure in Roma, appointed through the patronage of his old friend Ausonius. Now that Ausonius had been displaced, he was perhaps now the most important civilian in the west. He was immensely wealthy and, due to the perquisites of his office, was growing steadily wealthier. It was his post that Julian coveted. Part of his arrangement with Maximus had been his replacement of Symmachus, but the time had not come for that yet and for now Julian was content to make use of the man.

Symmachus was no Christian, rather a follower of the old religion of the state, and he had stuck his neck out two years before by penning an elaborate despatch to the Emperor Gratian, petitioning on behalf of the senate for the restoration of the Altar of the Goddess of Victory. Gratian had ordered the altar's removal from its traditional place in the senate chamber. The majority of the senate feared that its removal would lead to the loss of the goddess' protection and so to disaster for the state. In his epistle to Gratian, Symmachus blamed the removal of the altar for a famine that had arisen and argued that the peace of the empire was best served by tolerance for traditional religious practices. Unfortunately for the senate, Gratian was also in receipt of a letter from Bishop Ambrose, whom he regarded as his father in Christ. Ambrose strongly opposed the restoration of the altar, so Gratian dismissed Symmachus' petition out of hand, humiliating him and causing consternation in Roma.

The removal of Gratian had left the youth Valentinian II nominally ruling Italia from Mediolanum, although power was actually exercised by his mother, the Dowager Empress Justina, and the generals surrounding her. Unlike the orthodox Gratian, Justina, her son and most of their court were Arian Christians, and so were at odds with the founts of Christian orthodoxy whose principal voices were the bishops of Roma and Mediolanum. Justina had taken steps in the provinces under her son's control to prevent any further despoliation of pagan temples or theft of their funds. Now, with Gratian dead, it seemed to Symmachus that there was an opportunity to restore the Altar of Victory and maybe even build on that to reimpose toleration.

The despatch of the letter from Julian announcing his arrival was reciprocated by an invitation to visit Symmachus' offices, the *secretarium tellurense*, on the Oppian Hill. These were a sprawling set of buildings housing the civil service administering not only the city, but also a large area around the city, including the ports that supplied it. Politically, the urban prefect's most sensitive responsibility was the organisation and distribution of the grain supply for the city's inhabitants, who numbered over a million. Symmachus' personal suite was in a vast building that looked out over the city through a colonnaded portico. The mosaics on the floor, the wall paintings and the statuary were all still resolutely of the old faiths. Despite his own wealth and magnificence, Julian could not help but be impressed by the opulence. He encouraged Symmachus to take up the fight for toleration once more and offered his financial support.

Julian reported the subsequent events to Maximus in a letter he despatched after his return from the north, in it embroidering his own part in the affair to increase Maximus' view of his importance in them.

"Symmachus was sufficiently encouraged by our meeting," wrote Julian, "and by the swell of support he got in the senate, where the majority of the senators are not Christian, to have a motion passed appointing him to lead a delegation to petition the Emperor Valentinian for the restoration of the Altar of Victory. I went north in his party, travelling to Mediolanum to be given an audience by the court. Unfortunately for Symmachus, also at court that day was Bishop Ambrose, intent on ensuring that the current imperial authorities' religious inclinations would lead to no backsliding into the old religion. It seems that he had been warned of the senate delegation by its Christian members and by Damasus, who is currently what they call the patriarch Bishop of Roma."

The imperial court in Mediolanum was housed in a fortress enclosing a vast area of palaces, baths, offices and barracks that were separated by walls from the city that surrounded it. All here was on a more magnificent scale than the comparatively spartan Augusta Treverorum.

Julian's letter continued: "The delegation was given audience in its basilica before the young emperor and his mother. When we were given entry to the presence, we found that Ambrose was already before the throne, and he had evidently got at the dowager empress before the audience. He stood next to the throne, a stately, lowering presence."

Julian had watched in silence, standing to the rear of the delegation, unrecognised by anyone at the court. Even though he was a believer in the old gods, ever the realist, he could perceive that what he was looking at was the conflict between the old Roma and the new. Julian continued:

"The thirteen-year-old Emperor Valentinian II," he wrote, "sat high in his appointed place; the fact that no veil had been drawn before him revealed his lack of interest in the proceedings. He fidgeted throughout, playing with the accoutrements he wore, his military dress seeming sadly inappropriate and ill-fitting. His face bore an arrogant yet unintelligent expression that does not bode well for the future of his empire. By his side, but her chair just below the throne, sat his mother, the dowager empress, warily keeping a close eye on the debate."

Justina was even now a very beautiful woman, despite being in her late forties. Her hair was piled high in the latest fashion and her body sparkled with jewels adorning the silks of her gown. She was every bit the dowager empress and looked exactly what she was, the power behind the throne of her son. She had love for neither party before her. This was a conflict she would much rather have avoided. As a Christian, she believed that the Altar of Victory in the senate House was simply a pagan artefact that should be destroyed. Her late husband, the Emperor Valentinian I, had despised the effete and self-serving aristocracy in the senate and had exposed their corruption in order to pull a good few of them down. In their turn, they had hated him, and that antagonism still echoed in her mind. To her, the senate was an irrelevance in the governance of the empire, its members interested only in the accumulation of honours and wealth. On the other hand, Bishop Ambrose was a Nicene Christian who believed that, as Arian Christians, she, her son and many of their household were heretics, to be denied mass and entry to orthodox churches. She bitterly regretted the fact that she needed to keep the bishop on side, as he had tremendous power over the population of the city in which they had their imperial seat. More than that, she wanted him to go back to Maximus a second time to plead for her stepson's body. To her, the outcome of this debate was already a forgone conclusion.

Julian's letter went on: "Standing one step down from her throne, the *magister militum* Arbogast watched the proceedings, and all taking part in them, with visible distaste. The Frank is a dominating figure, a man seemingly built for the armour that he wears, whose scarred face attests to the battles he has fought for the house of Valentinian. He scowled at both senators and Christians alike."

Arbogast had no belief in any Christian god. His god was Roma itself, its power and military might, and, if he held any belief at all rather than just fearing inchoate superstitions, it was that anything that guaranteed Roma's continued victories should remain as it always had been. Although he did not yet have sufficient power to show it, he despised both the indolent youth who sat on the throne and his wily mother. He longed for the days of her late husband, whose rages and steely determination were characteristics he admired. The old emperor had been a man whom he would have followed into hades. He had no truck with this overblown windbag of a bishop who thought he could tell his emperor what to do and he itched to be able to take the man's head.

When Gratian had proposed the removal of the Altar of Victory four years before, Arbogast had supported his superior, another Frankish general, Flavius Bauto, in opposing the move, but both had been overruled. The Emperor Gratian, he thought with distaste, had been in Ambrose's pocket. He had not forgiven that. He also knew that Bauto, the most powerful general of his day in the empire and a man whom he venerated, had just written to the dowager empress to lend support for the restoration of the altar, and this had strengthened his own resolve to intervene.

"Stretching back from the base of the thrones along both sides of the basilica stood the officials of the consistory." Julian's letter described the scene. "The floor between them had been kept clear for our party, and we lined one side of the space reserved for petitioners."

The senators were alone in wearing togas, which, coupled with the ages of the members of the delegation, gave them an out-of-date air that did not fit well in such a militarised assembly. On the other side of the open space, facing them, stood Bishop Ambrose, alone, armed with a heavy gilt and bejewelled crozier. The court chamberlain indicated to Symmachus that he should begin.

"The urban prefect," Julian's letter went on, "had spent days honing a speech that fulfilled all the tenets of classical oratory. He spoke sweetly and persuasively, ranging back over Roma's history and the defeat of all her enemies granted to the city by the Goddess of Victory. Symmachus had judged every cadence, sifted every subtlety in his prose, selected every quotation, but he spoiled it all by going on far too long. I watched appalled as I realised that Symmachus had totally misjudged his audience. He was treating a teenager and an empress as if they were a public crowd or a group of senate literati. As Symmachus droned on, I could see Valentinian fidgeting increasingly and looking distractedly about him. The boy was clearly not comprehending any of the references that Symmachus had so carefully chosen. He kept whispering to his mother. Finally, he nodded off to sleep. Symmachus at last noticed the effect his words were having and wound up his argument, visibly dismayed."

Ambrose had seen this, too. When invited by the chamberlain, he moved to the centre of the room then hit the floor so hard with the tip of his crozier that he chipped the marble. The emperor woke up with a start. The bishop thundered, "What is proposed is a sin for which we and the empire will pay." Cleverly, he abandoned his customary long-winded sermonising and went straight to the point; he knew his audience. "The so-called Goddess of Victory does not exist, and if I am wrong and she does, then she is a demon, and all demons are evil. Roma owes nothing to demons, it rose by the will of God, who gave it strength. Roma needed, and needs, no idol or fictitious deity. Roma rules the world through the Almighty God, his son Jesus Christ and the Holy Spirit. The great Constantine knew this, and in the sign of the Son of God conquered at the Milvian Bridge. The late Emperor Gratian of blessed memory saw this when he ordered the removal of this stone from the senate. If we permit his just act to be reversed, we shall sin. You, emperor, and you, Lady Justina, will sin, and fostering this idolatory will take you and all of us to hell." He inclined his head to the throne, then stood back.

Julian's letter continued: "Arbogast moved to speak, but Justina waved him away and whispered in her son's ear. 'The stone will not be restored,' was all the boy said before he rose and flounced out of the hall, followed by the empress and the household. Symmachus and we were left forlornly watching them depart. Ambrose smirked in our faces, gave a perfunctory bow to Symmachus, then turned his back on us and stalked out of the basilica. Arbogast, clearly smarting with humiliation, lingered to talk to his officers.

"For a second time, Symmachus has found himself worsted by Bishop Ambrose. Bitter, with our tail between our legs, we returned empty-handed to Roma."

The court had lost important allies that day, but it would be some time before the empress and her Arian household would realise that by yielding to him over the Altar of Victory, they had by no means earned the support of the Bishop of Mediolanum.

Concluding his account, Julian summarised events and their import. The outcome had not surprised him. His religious beliefs had certainly been cavalierly set aside, but in another way he was not disappointed. "I can see things turning to your advantage in what happened in Mediolanum. The senate has been badly offended by the court and the stock of the Emperor Valentinian and his mother, Justina, is now very low in Roma. Symmachus, on the other hand, has yet again been shown to be lacking in influence and to have been outmanoeuvred by a Christian bishop. With the loss of his patron and ally Ausonius, and with no other support, he is now very vulnerable. It will not be long before the opportunity will arise to replace him as Prefect of Roma and for you to make the next move."

This was a letter that made Maximus very happy indeed. Events in Mediolanum were playing into his hand.

Chapter Eighteen

PRISCILLIAN

"Welcome, come ashore," cried Erbin from the breakwater that sheltered the harbour of what was now his city of Aleto. "Welcome to the new Dumnonia!"

Entering the harbour mouth was a small flotilla of half a dozen sailing vessels that had just made the crossing from the old country, each packed with people, animals and supplies. Erbin and his escort greeted them as they disembarked onto the quayside. From the ships emerged whole families, some of whom he knew personally. By the tools and implements they carried with their bundles, he could see that the men were tradesmen whose many different crafts would be useful to the new colony. In some ships were farming people, who had brought with them sheep, cattle, chickens and bags of seed. In others were smiths, carpenters and labourers. Many of the women had brought with them the items they needed to crush corn, to spin and to weave. There was even a doctor and his family on one of the ships, his children clutching their father's rolls of surgical implements and bags of potions. Erbin's men took the newcomers into the town to be temporarily housed until they could be allocated more permanent living spaces, or, in the cases of the farmers, land.

"Prince Gadeon continues to do us well," Erbin remarked to one of the ship's captains.

"Aye, my lord, his words have gone out throughout our land and there are many now seeking to cross the ocean to make better lives for themselves. His instructions have been followed very strictly; only those who can support themselves and their families are being given passage."

"All these people whom you have brought look very useful to us," added Erbin. "There is so much to do here."

"You will have little difficulty filling up this land, lord," replied the captain. "Prince Gadeon's words have gone out up the western seaboard, and we are finding that people from the Silures, the Dobunni, the Durotriges and the Cornovii are coming south to join us. Anyone who has no land, or has lost it to the great landowners, thinks that Letavia will offer them a new life."

His words were true enough. The centuries of Roma's rule in Britannia had imposed peace on what had been a warlike group of tribes, and populations had risen with the growing prosperity. Yet as the great estates with their luxurious villas spread across the best agricultural land, many small landowners had sold up their holdings or had lost them due to indebtedness. The tribal areas had accumulated many people who had been forced to move west. The influx to Armorica included many good people of this sort.

Aleto was beginning to recover the look of a functioning town. Houses were being patched up and the streets and public utilities repaired. Farming had resumed in some of the areas around it. There was little local opposition to this colonisation. Although the newcomers and the locals did not speak a language that was mutually intelligible, with the use of pidgin tongues they had enough in common to be able to communicate with each other. Erbin had given firm instructions against theft or the appropriation of property. There was room for all, both old and new. He had also taken pains to ensure that the small Roman unit in Aleto's fort, the *militum martensium*, was made to feel that the colonists posed no threat. The improvement of the city and the increase in the produce which the colonists had at first brought with them, and were now busy creating, promised to make the soldiers' lives a little more comfortable in what had been, until the Britons started to arrive, a rather forlorn outpost.

Things were not, Erbin knew, quite so easy on the other side of Letavia, and he thought himself lucky to have been allowed to establish a new life where he was. In Darioritum, Conan was living in Armorica's capital, where there was still a Roman administration operating, one which, whatever the provisions in the edict from Maximus, reported back to the civil authorities in Gallia Lugdenensis. The army unit in the city, an African unit, the *militum maurorum benetorum*, was one of the most effective in the province and its prefect resented the British intrusion. Conan therefore tended to send new colonists to more remote parts of the southern coast of the peninsula, where people were scarce and further away from Roman interference. Only a few had been settled so far in or around the town of Darioritum itself.

Rather than deal with the local officials, who habitually attempted to place countless bureaucratic hurdles in his way, Conan preferred to take to the sea. His special project in Bretona gave him the opportunity to sail further away still. There, his colony had been founded around the agency that Julian's family had established long ago. This, too, was almost an empty land.

*

Elen was beginning to find her feet at last in Augusta Treverorum, helped by the fact that her husband and Victor had gone on campaign on the Rhenus, where the Alamanni had resumed raiding into the territory of the empire. She was encouraged by the realisation that Maximus was quite happy, rather keen in fact, that she should become a patroness of the holy Martin. This had given her a way of expressing her deeply felt religious faith. Being empress allowed her to use many of the facilities of the state to help Martin and further his work. She was, at last, beginning to feel more secure, even, when she didn't catch herself feeling so, happy.

According to his last despatch to the court, Maximus was now at Moguntiacum, intending to move south to Nemetes from where he was going to cross the Rhenus. Aside from chastising the Alamanni, there was another reason for the direction of his line of march, which was to block any moves from the imperial armies of Italia and the east. Emperor Theodosius' *magister militum*, the Frankish general Flavius Bauto, had moved up to the Danubius to conduct a campaign against the German tribe of the Juthungi, who, at the same time as the Alamanni were raiding across the Rhenus, had invaded the province of Raetia. This abutted the provinces controlled by Maximus, and from it Bauto's troops and their Hun and Alan mercenaries could threaten him from the south.

Left alone in the palace, Elen invited Martin to stay for as long as he could to preach in her chapel and in the main Christian basilica of the city. He accepted the invitation and while in Augusta undertook to instruct her in the faith. This took the court by surprise. Not only had imperial ladies not been in the habit of inviting destitute clerics to teach them, but this empress in particular had, to their knowledge, never made any request or invitation without the prompting of her husband. Gentle dissuasion by officials failed to change her mind and the invitation had gone out by imperial courier. Martin's monasteries near Civita Turonum were over 400 miles away, a journey that would take Martin over a week. To help him on his way, Elen ordered a carriage and escort to collect him.

Elen was there at the gate to the palace to welcome the holy Martin when he arrived. At the first opportunity she heard him preach the gospels to her, her household and the court. Martin also preached all over the city, something not much to the taste of the local bishop, who resented the intrusion of someone who was evidently much more renowned, and probably a good deal holier, than he. Everywhere Martin went, crowds gathered to hear and see him. He touched many who were ill or disabled and the people claimed many miraculous cures. The empress hung upon his every word. When Martin permitted himself to be taken to dine with her, she outraged the court by serving him herself, even going to the kitchen beforehand to cook his dishes.

On the last day of his visit, when Martin had been invited to dine alone with the empress, Elen astonished the court by calling for a basin and water. When these were brought, she knelt to wash the holy man's feet and unwound her long tresses to dry them. She then stretched face down upon the ground in front of him, grasping his ankles. Her servants, at Martin's gentle insistence, were eventually forced to pull her away. The next morning, she went down into the palace courtyard to bid the holy man farewell, then walked with him to the city gate to watch him being carried back to his hermitage in the carriage in which he'd come. The fame of Elen's devotion to Martin and her humble piety quickly spread throughout Maximus' dominions. Her husband heard all this when he returned from the frontier and was astonished. Whilst he was none too pleased that his wife had abased herself before the holy man, and told her so, he was secretly pleased that the bright light of her newly won reputation was shining to the benefit of them both.

*

The short campaign against the Alamanni had been a success, so much so that the retribution Maximus exacted from the tribe gave him a fearsome fame that spread north and south along the river. He had cleverly brought with him to Gallia the unit of Alamanni that Fraomarius had led with him north of the Wall. Fraomarius was too old by now to have made the journey, so his men were led by his son, Chrocus, who proved adept at persuading many of Maximus' adversaries to volunteer for his service. On the emperor's triumphal return, these marched in his wake into camp outside Augusta. The emperor returned to the city in high fettle, feeling very pleased with himself and his settlement of the Rhenus frontier. The imperial threat from Raetia had also evaporated, as Bauto and his army had returned eastwards. Maximus was beginning to feel safe and to behave as if he were invincible.

*

The emperor's return coincided with the eruption, or rather the re-emergence, of one of the Christian disputes that festered in the empire of the day. At the time, cults of various offshoots of Christian beliefs continued to emerge across the empire, despite the efforts of councils of the church to give explicit direction as to what was orthodox and what heretical. This case was about what the Gallic clerics claimed was a dire heresy which had emerged in Hispania. It had been brought before Maximus for judgment before he had marched to the frontier.

At that point, he had no interest in the case and attempted to dispose of the matter by referring it to a synod of bishops in Burdigalia. This had not put a stop to the controversy and on his return, he found the Gallic bishops still clamouring for him to resolve it. With Elen's rapidly growing reputation for sanctity casting his own religion in a deceptively warm light, Maximus now felt the confidence to deal with the case. It struck him that here was an easy way to gain credit with the church, something he very much wanted for the next phase of his plans. Things did not, however, turn out quite as he had hoped.

Priscillian, the leader of the heretical sect, and his chief followers were in imperial custody. This man was the bishop of Avila in the province of Lusitania in Hispania, whose radical reinterpretation of Christianity had spawned a sect that appalled the orthodox. He preached a doctrine based on gnostic ideas that had originated in Aegyptus, ideas postulating the existence of two kingdoms, one of light and one of darkness, both of which, he claimed, were manifest in man. To this, Priscillian had added other beliefs strange to orthodox Christianity, one of which was that Christ had come to earth in a heavenly body that only had the appearance of mortality. Orthodox Hispanic bishops led by Ithacius, the primate of Lusitania, and Hydatius, Bishop of Merida, had excommunicated Priscillian and had attempted to drive him and his episcopal supporters, Instantius and Salvianus, from their sees. In this they had been unsuccessful, as influential figures at the imperial court had protected them.

The synod called by Maximus to meet at Burdigalia had duly condemned the heretics. Now, and this was a novelty in the empire, they had brought the accused before the praetorian prefect Evodius in his court at Augusta Treverorum, charging the accused not with heresy, but with the crime of using magic.

Under torture, Priscillian confessed that he had held nocturnal meetings with shameful women and had prayed while naked. Egged on by Felix, the bishop of Augusta, Evodius sentenced Priscillian and the other two bishops to death.

The sentence caused immediate outcry across the western Christian church. Never before had any cleric accused of heresy been executed by the state. Siricius, the new Bishop of Roma, and Bishop Ambrose both condemned the interference of the civil authorities in a theological case and bitterly attacked the bishops who had brought Priscillian to criminal trial. Martin, too, became involved. He came to Augusta, and when finally granted an audience with the emperor, who was very reluctant on this occasion to see him, begged that he exercise his mercy. His plea seemed to have been successful, for Maximus gave a verbal promise to rescind the order for execution and asked Martin to supper. The emperor, however, was being cowardly and he did not sign an order cancelling the executions, which duly went ahead for five of the accused, then later for another two more. In addition, two of the convicted clerics, including Bishop Instantius, were exiled to the Insulae Sillinae off the coast of Dumnonia, and others of their adherents were exiled internally in Gallia.

Martin was taken aback by this imperial duplicity. He could forgive neither the way he had been deceived nor the executions themselves. Maximus tried to explain himself by saying that he had been legally unable to alter the verdict and sentence of a criminal court; to him, he claimed, the issue was one of maintaining the law, not one of theology. This did not wash with the holy Martin, who was never to forgive what he saw as the emperor's betrayal of the direct promise made to him. He never came to court again.

In the upshot, bishops Syricius and Ambrose publicly condemned Maximus and ensured that the bishops who had brought the case before the prefect lost their sees. The emperor's involvement in punishing heresy did him little good. He wrote to the Bishop of Roma stressing his own orthodoxy and his reasons for allowing the criminal case to continue, but what came to appear as his overzealous repression of heresy lost him the confidence of the key orthodox clergy of the west. It also set a horrible precedent for the future.

The executions also proved counterproductive in Hispania. Rather than proving the religious credentials of the new regime, the executions were highly unpopular. When the bodies of the executed clerics were returned home, they were treated as martyrs and the number of adherents to their sect increased. Particularly resented was the seizure by the state of all their properties. Maximus was accused, with some justice, of coveting the wealth and estates of Priscillian, who had been a very rich man before he became a bishop. The case left a very nasty taste throughout the western empire. For Maximus, it had exactly the opposite effect to the one he had intended.

*

As the bodies of the five slaughtered Priscillians trundled in a cart out of the gate of Augusta and headed south to Hispania, Maximus reviewed his position. He had been badly stung by Christian reaction to his execution of Priscillian and his followers and felt insulted by the holy Martin's castigation of his failure to keep his word. That had not gone at all well. It was a real lesson in how dangerous it was to dabble in religious controversy; he would need to be more careful in future. However, aside from Priscillian's case, things had gone very well so far, and he felt justified in being very pleased with himself. He now ruled most of the western empire and had been recognised as its rightful Augustus by Theodosius, the only man who could oppose him. His empire was at peace; in Britannia and on the western seaboard, things were working out exactly as he had intended. As he had with the Picti and Scoti, he had put the fear of the empire into the hearts of the German tribes across the border. He was recouping the financial outlays he had made during his ascent to power and in any case had no intention of paying back the gold that Julian, his major creditor, had given him; grant of office would suffice there. He could also feel rather pleased with his wife. Elen had always been an asset in Britannia. Now she was a celebrity in her own right in Gallia and beyond, and her famous piety, he hoped, would make up for his own religious blunders. The stage was set for the next phase of his plan, and he was almost ready now to implement it.

*

The nature of that plan was known only to a very few, and knowledge of it had not filtered down to anywhere near the level of officers like Constantine and Gerontius. Had they been aware of what was in the emperor's mind, they might not have been feeling quite so carefree on the spring morning when they rode out together on the hills above Augusta. It was a glorious day, fresh and sunny. The scenery was breathtaking. From the bridle path through the hills, they looked down over woods and vineyards to the city below and to the River Mosella, which twisted its way through the landscape. Nestled in one of the river's bends, the imperial palace shone clear in the morning air above the smoke from a thousand breakfast fires that rose slowly upwards into the clear blue sky. It was a place to make one rejoice to be alive.

The pair had more reason for elation than the weather and the scenery. Since the award of his civic crown, which he was now obliged to wear in his uniform and on all public occasions, Constantine had been promoted to command one of the five regiments of the elite *scholae*, units that accompanied the emperor everywhere in his palatine forces. He was now a tribune commanding the *senior armaturae*, the fifth regiment of the corps, a post carrying with it the prestigious rank of *comes primi ordinis*, count of the first rank, one which would honour him for the remainder of his life.

Gerontius, too, had found imperial favour. As soon as the empress had reached Augusta, he had been relieved of the burden of guarding her and her children. Elen was not at all happy to lose his smiling, handsome face, his occasional practical jokes and the games he had played with her children back in Eboracum. Most of all, she missed his evident care for all of them. Gerontius, however, could scarcely contain his pride and pleasure in being promoted to Constantine's old post, or rather to one that was even better than his friend's had been, for he now commanded the *candidati*, the emperor's personal bodyguard. These were forty of the most carefully chosen soldiers in the army, the elite even of the elitist *scholae*. They wore dazzling white to distinguish them and make them stand out around the throne. There was one fly in this new ointment, which was that all but two of his men were barbarians, Franci or Alamanni, and the other two were Romans from the provinces. He would have preferred a better balance and in particular the inclusion of one or two Britons; that was something he had promised himself to rectify.

The two friends dismounted to look at the view while their horses grazed apart. Since they had got back from the short campaign on the border, this was the first time that they had been able to have a private talk. Constantine started the conversation. "My brother, is it not amazing how our fortunes have changed. Only a few months ago we were living a very simple life in Eboracum. Now, look at where the Fates have brought us."

"How complicated things are now, though," responded Gerontius. "I am unsettled in this place. The politics is poisonous, not only between our emperor's court and Italia, but inside the court, too. One can never know who is trustworthy. I can never understand the real motivation behind what people say. I shudder every time I cross paths with one of the flock of sycophantic eunuchs who are now waddling in and out of the imperial apartments."

"The thing I dislike most," said Constantine, "is all this religious controversy. The only likeable cleric I have seen so far here is the holy Martin. The empress is right to revere him. He is a thoroughly good man. You can tell he was a good soldier in his day. What a great pity that the emperor did not keep his word over Priscillian; we shall not see Martin at court again, I fear. The rest of them are place servers and hypocrites, very ugly men who seek their own power. The worst of all is that Ambrose from Mediolanum. The emperor has at least got that right; I am glad that he treats him with such open disdain."

"All in all, brother," replied Gerontius, "this place is a snake pit. We must watch each other's backs if we are to do our duty and keep safe. I intend, if you are happy with this, to keep you informed of things that I see and that disturb me." What concerned Gerontius now was doing all he could to protect his sworn brother.

Constantine was very glad of this suggestion. He would not have imposed upon his friend by asking for this boon, but Gerontius had offered it, and he was grateful to accept. His promotion had taken him away from the centre of the court and he was feeling exposed, vulnerable even. He could feel there were new winds blowing and he did not know where they were heading. When he saw the emperor nowadays, which was infrequently, he detected a change in him. Maximus had always been an imperviously self-assured man, but he had always taken note of his subordinates and listened to what they said. Now, Constantine had detected a tendency to grandiloquence and a greater condescension to those around him. He had abandoned his old habit of talking with his soldiery and no longer visited his troops informally. The men were kept always at a great distance from his presence, just like all the rest. Perhaps there was no other way to be an emperor, but it worried Constantine, nevertheless. Their future, and that of all they held dear, was now dependent on the judgement of this one man. They had to hope that his judgment would stay as sound as it had proved to be so far.

Chapter Nineteen

BLOODLINES

It had been two years since Maximus set in train his usurpation of power, and he was confident now that his success was based on firm foundations. He could safely leave affairs in Gallia and on the German frontier in the hands of the officers he had appointed and turn to his plans for the governance of Britannia, as well as for the future of his family. Maximus told Elen that they were going back home.

Gadeon had just written to his cousin to follow up the conversation he had initiated with Prince Vitalinus at their meeting after the British Council. The success of that discussion had led Gadeon to meet or contact the other princes of the island, with all of whom he made similar points and to which he had received mostly encouraging replies. He had forwarded the results of all this to Elen, putting to her the advantage of tying Maximus' dynasty by marriage to the principal British houses. Elen did not need much persuading of the sense of this. She had long been anxiously considering how to secure the future safety of her family and she was very clear that the snake pit of imperial politics was a danger to them all. She was realistic enough to understand that now they were committed to Maximus' imperial project, there could be no avoiding the fact that at least some of their children would need to marry into families of power, but she still hoped that she could control the marriages of the others to keep them from harm. Marriages of as many of them as possible into the royal houses of Britannia seemed the safest course.

Victor, however, who had just reached sixteen, was already condemned to his future. Having been acclaimed Augustus, it was now inevitable that he would marry a highborn bride from another imperial family or the Roman aristocracy, so there was no possibility that he could be made safe other than by the victory of their cause. On the other hand, if Magna, their eldest daughter, now thirteen, married similarly highly, it was likely that she would survive any collapse in the fortunes of their house. That would not be the case even for the younger boys, for if Maximus were to fall before establishing supreme power, any male child of his would likely suffer his father's fate. For these reasons, she hoped to persuade her husband that the other boys should marry in Britannia, where they could vanish, if need be, into the western mists.

There was a difficulty here, for their children were not yet of marriageable age. Maximus' second son, Owain, had reached the age of fifteen; Annun was fourteen, Custennin twelve and Peblig was still only eleven. Of their younger daughters, Gratiana was now ten and Severa eight. All of them were still at Eboracum, ministered to by governors, tutors and slaves. Elen nevertheless believed that their family's circumstances demanded that steps be taken to have betrothals arranged now for all of them.

Maximus' plans for his family happily coincided with those of his wife. His intention was to found an imperial dynasty with a British base, much as his predecessors had founded Spanish, African or Pannonian imperial houses. He had begun to take advice from his consistory about eligible

Roman spouses for Victor and Magna. Sending word to Julian, who had remained at Roma, he asked him to forward proposals for marriageable suitors. Julian was well placed to manage this but did not find it easy. Until Maximus' long-term future was clear, marrying a daughter to the son of a usurping Augustus would bring with it possible imputations of treason from which respectable families would shy away; for the moment, Julian could make no headway on behalf of Victor. For Magna, he was more successful. Now that her father was so wealthy, and given the added amount that could be asked to hedge the danger of marrying the daughter of a usurper, she would bring a large dowry, and that was attractive to many.

Before crossing the ocean back to Britannia, Maximus issued an edict establishing the Dumnonian settlements in Armorica as *terrae laetiae*, lands of allies, which meant that the settlers were now officially recognised and permitted their own separate identities alongside those of the indigenous inhabitants. As was the custom, the emperor appointed a *praefectus laetorum* to administer the *laeti*, as such tribal groups were designated. Unusually, in this case, Maximus appointed not a Roman official but Conan to the post, which gratifyingly made him the governor of an almost independent people, one left to its own devices save for its obligation to provide military service to the state. The administration of the west could justify this by pointing to the recent precedent created in the east, where the empire had found for the first time that it needed to incorporate and settle the Gothi as a self-ruling people. Conan now had the legal authority to act independently of the imperial administration in Armorica, and he immediately began to settle immigrants around Darioritum in greater numbers than before.

When the imperial couple departed, Victor was left behind in Augusta in nominal charge. Despite his elevated status, Maximus had not permitted Victor any real authority. His father had refused to let him relinquish either his military training or his schoolwork. Maximus intended that his firstborn son be better educated than he had ever been. In reality, business was in the safe hands of the praetorian prefect Evodius and of Andragathius, the *magister militum*. This, of course, added to Victor's resentment against Andragathius, who did not, as did Evodius, seek to win the mind of the young man by flattery and unctuous deference.

*

The enthusiastic, almost joyful reception that Maximus and Elen met when they disembarked at Rutupiae was very different from the grim efficiency with which the expedition had set out from there over a year before. The local elements of the *classis britannica* escorted their ships into harbour. Horns and bugles blared, soldiers of the Second Augusta clashed their arms on their shields and crowds shouted cries of "Maximus", "imperator" and "Augustus". On the quayside, a welcoming party awaited them, the new Governor of Maxima Caesariensis leading the province's dignitaries, among them the princes and principal men of the Cantiaci, the area's tribe. Elen was delighted to see a Christian element in a party that was led by the bishop of the tribe's capital, Durovernum Cantiacorum, and included a choir of boys singing hymns and carrying banners embroidered with the Christian emblems of the fish and the Chi-Rho. There was no pagan priest in sight. Things here had changed, and Elen could feel pride that her small part in persuading her husband to be baptised had helped spread the faith.

All along the road up to Londinium, they were met by crowds jostling to get a view of the emperor and his British empress. Maximus rode very splendidly on horseback, making himself visible to the people, waving and saluting as he passed. Gerontius was with him, keeping a wary eye open for any troublemakers in the crowds; he was very happy to find none. Soldiers of the Second Augusta provided cohorts to escort the cavalcade. The emperor seemed genuinely popular. Elen followed in a closed carriage, mostly invisible to the multitudes strewing flowers in front of the procession. At the outskirts of the capital, however, she pulled back the curtains so that all could see her waving shyly to acknowledge the roars of acclaim. Desiderius and the chief officers of the diocese were waiting for them on the steps of the vicar's palace, where a guard of honour was drawn up in salute. There, too, were the members of the council, Gadeon leading the British princes in welcoming back their lord. Thousands of the city's inhabitants flocked to the square to see the imperial couple, held back, in some cases roughly, by the city's Saxon security guards.

The council met that day in the redesignated Basilica of the Apostle Paul. On behalf of the diocese, Desiderius presented the emperor with a speech of welcome and led the assembly to acclaim their sovereign. All swore their oath of loyalty. In response, Maximus gave his thanks to the people of Britannia, who, he declared, had supported his ascension to the imperial throne. "Britannia is our real home," he told them, "even though we must reside away from it. Our wife and children are British and we are happiest here." The applause he received was loud, and Maximus was gratified, even touched, by the genuine warmth of their reception. He had not experienced anything like this in Augusta Treverorum or in his marches through Gallia.

After the council's formal meeting, the emperor held a private session with Desiderius and his key officials, then a separate one with the British princes. "We are greatly impressed," he told the latter, "with the way you have shouldered responsibilities in the administration, as well as," and here he gave a direct nod to Gadeon, "with the way you have responded to our call to send settlers to Armorica and Hispania." Gadeon managed not to show any reaction to the emperor's recognition of his role in the settling of Letavia, although he was secretly pleased.

"The ships of Dumnonia," the emperor continued, "have secured the western seas for the empire, and now settlers from many of your peoples are repopulating the empty lands of Armorica, a place nearly ruined by the Saxon raiders. You will be glad, I know, to hear that we have just officially recognised your settlers as *laeti* and have made them responsible for their own affairs by appointing Prince Conan as their prefect. We encourage you to select more of your surplus but useful families to follow those who have gone before. They will make new lives for themselves."

After the meeting, Maximus invited Gadeon to visit him and his wife in his private quarters. He wanted to take the prince's advice about the marriage of his children. When Gadeon was announced, Elen rushed forward to greet her cousin with a warm embrace. "How is my father?" she asked him. "Does he do well?"

"He is ailing gradually, but he is still strong enough to rule our people, although he no longer goes out and about. Everything now has to come to him. His joint pains make him grouchy, but then he was always so, was he not?" Elen smiled and acknowledged the truth of Gadeon's remark.

The prince was prepared for what he knew they would ask him. He had taken the advice of his fellows and had a course to propose that he knew would not offend the most powerful of them, which would gratify most of them and which would be of advantage both to the new imperial house and to his own.

"In your gracious correspondence with me, lord, you have indicated that your eldest son and daughter should both marry into Roman families. That, of course, is as expected. The Augustus Victor is your heir. That leaves sufficient children to marry into the families of our British princes."

"You are aware, prince," replied the emperor, "that in these engagements we shall seek the security of our own family as well as of the island of Britannia. It is important to place our children where their descendants will help hold this diocese to the empire for generations to come."

"I am, my lord," replied Gadeon. "That is why I recommend alliances with the chief princely houses of the west and the north. Those who have offspring of the right age, I would suggest, are the Cornovii, the Silures, the Novantae and the Selgovae, as well, of course, as the empress' own Dumnonii."

Elen had already talked these suggestions through with her husband and had gained his approval of them. Maximus knew all these tribes and was confident that Gadeon had chosen well.

The prince went on: "To be more specific, the princess of the Silures, currently living with her father in his capital of Venta Silurum, is the heir to his principality, which is a rich one and controls the southern coasts of the west of our island. The prince has no sons. His daughter is the right age to make a good match for your divine majesty's second son, Eugenius."

Maximus nodded. Gadeon went on: "Vital for control of the north-western seas are the lands of the Novantae, which is, as you know, secure land north and west of the Wall. They also hold the strategically placed island of Maenavia, which is vital for control of the Scoti raiders coming out of Hibernia. Their prince also has no sons, but has several daughters of an age to marry your son Antonius. He, too, would stand to inherit there.

"We Dumnonii are more fortunate in having a prince to inherit our line. Tudwal, my very young grandson, is really too young to be betrothed, but he would nevertheless make a suitable match for your daughter, Gratiana, and could be pledged to the match. Your other daughter, Severa, is of an age to betroth to Vortigern, the Prince of the Cornovii, grandson of the current prince, Vitalinus, who is one of your greatest supporters in the council and," he went on self-effacingly, "the greatest British prince in the land."

"These marriages and betrothals," Gadeon continued, "would tie your line firmly to every tribe that matters in the west. In the north, we have found a bride for your son Constantine in a princess of the Selgovae. She is not going to inherit her father's place, though it seems that her brother, who will, is sickly and unlikely to produce an heir. Constantine's children are likely to inherit there."

Again, Maximus nodded his agreement. "And what about Publicus?" he asked. "Where shall we find a bride for him?"

"I do not think that we should make plans for Peblig," Elen interjected. "I have heard from his guardians over the last few months that he has become more and more devoted to the Christian religion. He is often found deep in prayer or talking of the faith with his chaplains. His tutors tell me that he is a rapid learner and has excellent Latin. Peblig has told them that he wants to follow the calling of the holy Martin and to sit at Martin's feet in his monastery. I think we may have our first bishop in the family. I do not think we shall see Peblig married in the conventional way."

Maximus had already seen how his youngest son was inclined towards the spiritual. Publicus had always been a frail boy who did not excel at anything physical; no warrior would he be. Yet having a Christian priest in the family might give greater advantages than producing yet another soldier. He had seen enough of imperial politics now to understand that religious controversy was going to disrupt the empire and dog its emperors for a long time to come. An ally inside the church would come in useful. Maybe one day, thought Maximus, he might replace the Bishop of Mediolanum.

The important business of the day resolved, they retired to supper, to less serious talk and, for once, to relax in familiar company. Gadeon had brought his son and heir, Guoremor, Tudwal's father, to meet the imperial couple, and conversation flowed about their homeland and about Guoremor's exploits in the garrison of Segontium and in his harrowing of the Scoti across the western sea. The conversation was polite, rather than warm. Neither the emperor nor Gadeon much liked the other. For Maximus, Gadeon was just a little too clever to be totally trusted; for Gadeon, the emperor was a man concerned only with himself and his reputation, and a greedy one at that. Nevertheless, they needed each other, and as both Elen and Guoremor had enough genuine warmth and humour to cover any gaps, the conversation was kept flowing until all parted content with what had been said and agreed.

*

Over the next two months, Maximus and Elen went on a grand tour of the island, something no emperor had done in this generation. They travelled rapidly around Britannia, both for the emperor to inspect the island's defences and also to formally fulfil the marriage plans that had been made with Gadeon. Maximus was accompanied on the journey by Gerontius and his bodyguard escort. Few Britons had seen an emperor in the flesh and this one, who had a British wife and spoke their tongue, was different from any they had ever heard of, so everywhere Maximus went, he and Elen received the acclaim of city authorities and the adulation of large crowds. Gerontius was glad to see his emperor relax and even soften a little now that he was back in Britannia. He treated the officials he met with courtesy and listened with interest to their reports. He praised those who deserved it and only gently chastised those who he felt had failed in some way. The emperor smiled at the crowds who lined his route and made generous speeches in the cities he visited. Elen, by his side throughout, had never had such a delightful time. She was gracious and warm with all she met and was loved for it in return. Her fame spread.

The couple first went north to Eboracum to be reunited with their children, who were delighted to see their parents after more than a year apart. It was Maximus, of course, whom the three older boys could not wait to see. He arrived now in the splendour of his imperial rank and the entourage that followed in his wake treated them as princes of the imperial house, which was something that their tutors and the palace household had not done, and which would have gone to their heads had not Elen immediately taken steps to prevent it.

Back in her old home, she found time to talk with Gerontius, free for once of the supervision of the court. "Are you glad to be back in Britannia?" she asked him.

"Of course, my lady, although it looks from the plans I have seen of the emperor's itinerary that I shan't be able to see my family in Venta. I have, though, received a letter from my father, who says all is well in the city. He, and from what he wrote many of those he knows, are enthusiastic about the emperor's new policies of delegating authority to the people here and of giving us greater opportunities for advancement. They are praying for his success."

"That is good to hear, Gerontius. I hope one day that I might meet your father. I would like to tell him what a fine son he has."

"Thank you, my lady. He would not agree with you if he were to hear I had lost you in the city!"

Elen laughed. "With all this talk of marriage in the air, Gerontius, are you not tempted yet to marry yourself?"

"Not yet, my lady. Guarding your husband takes more time than any marriage. If I may, though, please keep an eye open for me for some unattached princess as you travel the country."

"I shall indeed, Gerontius, nothing would give me greater pleasure."

*

Leaving Elen in the fortress, Maximus set out after a few days on the next stage of his journey, with him his second son Eugenius so that he could be married at Venta Silurum. The princesses who were to be married to the emperor's sons should by normal custom have been taken into their husband's households, but of course none of the emperor's sons were yet old enough to be able to provide a permanent family home. Gadeon had thought of this, and, with Maximus' approval, had purchased land near Venta where Eugenius could be left after his wedding to establish his own household, guarded until his coming of age by detachments from the Second Augusta and by levies of the tribe.

With Eugenius' future secured, Maximus travelled to Viroconium to rendezvous with Elen and their daughters, who had been escorted down from Eboracum. They stayed in the city for two days for the performance of Severa's official betrothal ceremony. She would, until she was twelve, wear the engagement ring that the tiny prince Vortigern had to be persuaded to put on the third finger of her left hand. Vitalinus' lands and great wealth meant that the ceremony was a lavish one, attended by all the chief men of the Cornovii and the Dobunni. For the first time, Elen met Vitalinus' son and heir, Vitalis. She took to him immediately. He was a confident, powerful man who was clearly swift to grasp the import of the circles into which his son, Vortigern, was to marry. Vitalis made sure he sat next to the empress at the betrothal feast and turned his ample charm upon her.

"My lady, the betrothal of your daughter to our house does us great honour. My son has more good fortune than he is capable of realising today, but when he grows older, he will understand the historic nature of this alliance."

"I am very glad to meet you, prince," Elen responded. "From the magnificence of the feast your father has given us all, and all the arrangements you have made to make us so comfortable here, I know we have made the right choice for Severa. She will be very happy with your son, I am sure."

"I have a feeling, my lady, that we shall be seeing a good deal more of each other in future. The fortunes of our houses are now linked. We shall all be wishing the emperor continued good fortune in whatever he sets out to accomplish. We shall," and here Vitalis laughed, "be travelling ever upwards with him."

"Indeed, our children shall have a good future, prince," Elen replied, and smiled in acknowledgement of what Vitalis had said.

His son Vortigern was too small to really understand what was happening, but Severa bravely carried out her part in the ceremony and behaved as she considered a proper princess should amongst these strange and maybe barbarous people. She showed neither fear nor bashfulness, which went down very well with the assembled chiefs and warriors of the two tribes. After the ceremony, Severa was to return to the protection of Eboracum to stay there until coming of marriageable age, so was sent back there with an escort. Maximus then departed on his journey to the north, while Elen's party took Gratiana south to Isca Dumnoniorum, where she would manage the betrothal by herself.

At Deva, Maximus was joined by his sons Antonius and Constantine, who travelled with him to the Wall. In Luguvallium, at the Wall's western end, they found the princes of the Novantae and Selgovae waiting to give away their daughters. As his brother Eugenius had been at Venta, after his marriage, Antonius was left to set up with his new bride in a villa that was more of a farmhouse than a grand estate, just south of the Wall. Constantine was still two years from marriageable age, so after his betrothal ceremony, Maximus left him to be escorted back to Eboracum, where he was to rejoin Severa and remain under the care of their tutors. The emperor's children had always been close; they had always lived together. Now they were splitting up for the first time.

Duties of state then took priority. The emperor rode east to the port of Arbeia at the far end of the Wall, where he saw a small fleet of ships assembled to conduct a punitive raid on the Picti of the eastern coastlands. The Picti close to the Wall had been sufficiently overawed by the viciousness of his earlier campaign to have caused no trouble since. Those who lived further away had yet to feel Roma's might, and the emperor watched the fleet sail north to obey his direction to sink every Pictish craft, burn every Pictish village and kill or enslave every Pict they came across, all the way up the eastern coast.

Chapter Twenty

TWO BETROTHALS

As her husband journeyed north, Elen travelled south to Isca to meet her father for what she was sure would be the last time. It was clear that he had little time left now to live and she was sure that her own future over the next few years would certainly be in Gallia. Eudaf was, however, still able to hobble about, and he came to watch Gratiana's betrothal to the very young Prince Tudwal in a civil ceremony in the basilica in which his daughter had married. Like her sister Severa, Gratiana now wore her engagement ring on the small middle finger of her left hand.

The ceremony was conducted in Roman fashion, as Maximus had directed, but as the emperor was not present Eudaf insisted that his nephew also be betrothed by the old rites. Tudwal was of the princely house and on current reckoning would be its head one day, so his marriage was of great import and needed to be done properly. Before the betrothal ceremony made the deed irrevocable, Eudaf insisted that they follow tradition, which, according to Diviacus, who was by now very aged but still Eudaf's druid, was absolutely necessary to protect the marriage and the tribe from evil. In the druid's mind, nothing that was to come was firmly fixed, rather the future had the fluidity of water and thus could be deflected into different channels if the right methods were adopted. For this, it was necessary to seek the guidance of the gods before the ancient betrothal ceremony. He and Eudaf knew that Elen would not approve of this, so they didn't tell her of their intention to divine the future; in any case, neither she nor Gratiana needed to be involved until the ceremony of betrothal itself. Diviacus had secreted in his pouch a lock of the girl's hair that had fallen as it was trimmed for the Roman ceremony, and that was all he needed.

Eudaf's wooden hall was built inside a fort which sat astride a low hill that looked out over the river several miles north of Isca. This had been one of the tribe's major settlements before the Romans came. Eudaf liked to live here away from the bustle and stench of the city, which he could see down below his fort. It was in his own hall that he intended to see Tudwal properly betrothed. Just outside the low earthen rampart of the fort was a grove of oak, in the centre of which was a massive tree, venerably old, its spreading branches dotted with the mistletoe which Diviacus and his acolytes ensured continued to thrive there. It was here that the druid, alone, would consult their gods.

The druid had his people collect the items he needed: a few living creatures including a squirrel, a frog, a cockerel and some twigs of mistletoe. To these he would add two vials of evil-smelling liquid, concoctions he himself had prepared. These were for a sacrifice to encourage the gods to tear a rent in the fabric of this world and show what might or might not befall. Before they left the druid alone in the grove, his assistants built a fire under the central tree. His people retreated back to the hillfort as he suspended a bronze cauldron on a tripod over the fire. Slowly, he mixed the contents of the charm, allowing the vapour to rise into the branches above him. He slit the throats of the squirrel and the frog and dripped their blood into the mix, darkening the potion and making the smoke pungent. Seizing the cockerel, he held it aloft to the tree, and with one swift slice of his knife cut off its head, then threw its body upwards. The death throes of the bird kept its wings flapping and carried it into the boughs closest to the ground, where it became entangled in a bunch of mistletoe and hung there, its motions becoming feebler as its blood drained onto the tree. The bird had had a good death, thought the druid, the omen he had hoped for. He let the bird's blood drip into the cauldron, turning the mixture darker still. Squatting on a tree root under the canopy, he waited.

Imperceptibly, as the fumes from the cauldron sifted slowly upwards through the tree, a mist gathered in the upper branches. Its thin, translucent tendrils descended slowly, silently until they absorbed the sacrificial fumes, the lower boughs, the cauldron and at last the druid himself. His eyes closed, and he rocked back and forth on his heels. "Dumnonos," he muttered, "you showed me before the blood and death that follow in the wake of this Roman girl's father. You showed me the struggles and success of our line of princes. Show me now what this girl means to our people."

Diviacus opened his eyes to peer into the mist that enveloped him. A face, Prince Gadeon's face, gradually coalesced, the princely circlet of the tribe upon his head. The vision dissolved to be replaced by the face of Guoremor, whose head also wore the circlet. He, too, slipped away, to be replaced by a couple that were recognisably Tudwal and Gratiana, then more and more faces came, each in turn wearing the gold circlet until they, too, receded into the mist. As face succeeded face, the mist became red as if with swirls of blood, but the line of faces did not break and ran continuous until Diviacus lost count of their number. The scene blew away. In its place he saw Gratiana giving birth to a strong, healthy boy, who wailed lustily. This, too, dissipated and vanished, then the figure of a warrior appeared, one who wore no circlet but who instead wore a wreath of victory. He seemed mightier than all the others Diviacus had seen, although his visage was old and sad. This was the last vision. The mist lifted, leaving the druid cold and drained. His joints chilled and stiff, he rose and walked back to the enclosure.

"Is all well, Diviacus?" asked Eudaf, who was waiting outside the hall.

"My prince, it is well. I was shown that this marriage will carry on your line over generations too many for me to count. I saw their healthy child, a new prince of your people. From your line, carried through Gadeon and Guoremor, then through Tudwal and this half-Roman girl, there will emerge a mighty warrior who will triumph in his day and live to grow old. Dumnonos also showed me once more what he revealed the last time, the blood and struggle that will befall many of those who succeed you. Yet he showed me that this marriage will be a good one for your people and for Prince Tudwal. I believe it is well."

"Good. So be it. I thank you, Diviacus."

The prince entered the hall where Gadeon, Guoremor and Elen had been waiting. There Tudwal and Gratiana joined hands in the ceremony of betrothal that had been practised since time immemorial by the tribe of the Dumnonii.

*

Now that she was home, Elen had one plan of her own to put into effect, one of which she had not informed her husband. It concerned a girl being brought up in Eudaf's hall, the daughter of Donaut, the Prince of Cornubia, whose death a few years before had given Conan his small sub-principality. Donaut's only offspring was still only a very young teenager, who went by the name of Ursula, a nickname rather than her proper name, but the only one that anyone remembered as it was so appropriate. Its meaning was "little she bear", for she was a wild youth, who had so far spent her childhood riding free through the woods and on the moors, hunting deer and flying hawks to catch geese. It was in Elen's mind that she would make a fit consort for her cousin Conan, who was currently without a wife and had never produced an heir. Elen found little difficulty in persuading her father to let her take the girl with her back to Gallia. Eudaf was glad that he might see the back of her, for, having lost both her parents at a very young age, she had long been ungovernable, way beyond even his control.

Eudaf had her brought in to meet Elen. When she finally appeared in front of them both in his hall, she was still covered with mud and tares from the hunting expedition from which she had been recalled. Ursula, of course, had no say in the matter of whether she accompanied Elen or more importantly of her marriage. She was by no means frightened of Conan, her firebrand of a relative, or of any man for that matter. She had no desire to marry and was quite prepared to say so.

"Uncle, I do not wish to marry cousin Conan or any man." She spat on the hall floor. "My life is here in Dumnonia. I have no wish to see foreign lands. Please ask cousin Elen to change her mind."

Eudaf scowled. He was about to issue a curt rejoinder when Elen cut in. "Ursula, you cannot stay here forever growing into an old maid. You have to find a man who is your match. There are few worthy of you, but your cousin is one. Your match will bring back Cornubia to your family and you will have hunting a-plenty there and in Letavia."

"So where is my suitor, cousin?" Ursula replied. "Why is he not here seeking my hand himself? Does he think so little of my fitness to marry him that he proposes by proxy?"

Sometime before, Conan had reluctantly sent Elen word that he accepted this match and would await Ursula's arrival in Letavia, but he was clearly lacking in enthusiasm for it, knowing all too well Ursula's fiery reputation. He had sent no gift or word to his intended bride. The girl had divined this straight away and was doubly offended at being exiled to a place where she wasn't going to be welcome.

"If you come with me now, you will be the companion of the empress and wife of a ruling prince. God will show you your destiny and I shall have with me someone I can trust, in whom I can confide, who will support me, and who I can come to love. Will you not join me?"

Ursula did not know her aunt at all but found herself attracted to her sweetness and touched by her appeal.

"Besides," went on Elen, "you will not have to wed your cousin yet. He is off conquering the world for my husband and has no thought of marriage now. You can live with me at court. There's good hunting in the hills around Augusta."

Ursula looked at her uncle, who was, she could see, ailing fast. If he died soon, she would be left to the devices of his successor. She knew this would be Prince Gadeon, whom she knew well enough to know that it would not be long before he made use of her by marrying her off to a prince she might not like at all. Conan might be a brute, but he was a fine warrior, nonetheless. She made one last plea. "Uncle, I wish to stay with you and take care of you in your last years. You have been good to me. I owe this to you."

"And I owe you your freedom, Ursula, and you will find it across the sea. Do not worry about me. I am well taken care of by my whole people. Go with your cousin."

Ursula could think of no more to say. Yet when she set forth on the road with Elen, she was resolved in her own mind that this marriage, nay any marriage, would never happen. She would, however, trust her cousin for her fate.

Eudaf was at the gate of his compound to bid them farewell. It was a tender goodbye for both women, for they knew that it was unlikely that they would ever see the old man again.

*

Just as their caravan was taking to the road, despatches from both Julian in Roma and from the court in Augusta reached Maximus at the Wall. They gave news from Italia, where there had been a mighty falling out between Valentinian's court and Bishop Ambrose. It was time, Julian counselled, to set in train the next phase of their plan.

Maximus had been waiting for this and he reacted immediately. Fast to horse, he rode south to Eboracum to collect Magna and Publicus, then spurred on to Rutupiae, sending an order to intercept Elen and telling her to bring Gratiana to meet him to make the crossing.

When all the members of the family had gathered in the fort at Rutupiae, including Ursula, whom the emperor scarcely noticed, Maximus gave the order to cross immediately. At high tide, they sailed past Dubris, the chalk cliffs white in the bright morning sunshine. Whether any of them would ever return there was, Maximus knew, now in the hands of the Fates, or maybe of his new Christian God.

He muttered prayers beneath his breath to both, just in case.

Chapter Twenty-one

THE FIRST MONASTERY IN THE WEST

The news from Italia concerned events in the imperial capital at Mediolanum. After the return of the failed senate delegation, Julian had stayed in Roma, using his money to make contacts and gain influence by throwing fabulous parties in his magnificent villa, as well as by sponsoring both a chariot team in the circus games and gladiatorial contests in the arena. Gradually, subtly, he worked his way up the social scale, taking care still to stay in Symmachus' shadow. All the time, the agents of his firm fed him news of Maximus' progress and of what Conan and Erbin were up to on the western seaboard. In turn, he fed Maximus any gossip that came his way about people and events in Italia, always keeping an eye out for circumstances that would enable them both to move to the next stage of their plan. Since their failed delegation, ill feeling towards the imperial court was growing in the senate, and Julian had picked up information that this was also the case inside the army. His despatch warned Maximus to come back to Gallia to be ready for the right moment to strike.

The Dream of Magnus Maximus

*

By the time Maximus and Elen reached the palace, something of significance had changed in Augusta. Maximus had called his brother, Marcellinus, to join him from Hispania, where he was a relatively insignificant officer serving in an unimportant post. The appearance of Marcellinus at court upset the balance of influence, for although not of any note as a soldier, he was an adept schemer who had a much greater opinion of his own abilities than did most of the world. He arrived determined to take advantage of his brother's eminence. He coveted the rank of *magister militum* and set about making allies to help him achieve it. The first he cultivated was his nephew, Victor, whom Marcellinus affected to treat with the exaggerated respect due to the boy's rank of Augustus. It was an easy task to turn Victor's head and, in the young man's hatred of Andragathius, Marcellinus saw a way to kill two birds with one stone. In any disagreement in the acting council, Marcellinus took Victor's part against the man whom Maximus had left in charge of him. The second potential ally was the praetorian prefect Evodius, who had already been worming his way as far as he could into the emperor's favour and now adopted Marcellinus as an ally to undermine Andragathius to his own benefit.

Yet by the return of the imperial party, Marcellinus had had little opportunity to do direct harm, and at present he was prevented from developing his schemes further due to the appearance once again of Bishop Ambrose, who arrived on a second embassy from Mediolanum. Ambrose's party arrived within days of the emperor's return. His embassy had the same subject as his first, the recovery of the body of the late Emperor Gratian. The court in Mediolanum, appreciating its vulnerability and playing for time, was making efforts to appear conciliatory towards Maximus, to the extent of making

Evodius a consul that year alongside Honorius, Emperor Theodosius' son. The dowager empress' choice of Ambrose as her ambassador, however, was once more an infelicitous one.

On this occasion, Ambrose tried a different, more tactful approach. He gave due notice of his arrival in Augusta and asked for lodgings in imperial quarters. It did him little good, however. The court chamberlain, of course on the emperor's direct instructions, refused him a private audience and insisted that he address the throne in public in the basilica. Ambrose had got into the habit of demanding private audiences with Valentinian II and his mother, the dowager empress, and expected Maximus to grant him the same favour. Maximus had no intention of being browbeaten by this troublesome cleric who had just condemned him over the execution of Priscillian. At the only audience Ambrose was granted, he was told, again from behind a veil drawn across the throne, that Gratian's body could not be sent to his stepmother due to its condition. He was summarily dismissed and once again left in a fury. To drive the message home, and to humiliate the bishop by indicating that he did not believe that he would pass on his exact words to the empress, Maximus sent his brother Marcellinus with him to Mediolanum. For the time being, away from his brother, Marcellinus was unable to drop poison into his brother's ear.

Despite issuing this rebuff to their ambassador, it suited Maximus to continue to portray himself as a colleague of Valentinian and Justina, as well as of Theodosius, and so he covered his real intentions by instructing Marcellinus to behave with courtesy and restraint. He was to offer friendship to the Mediolanum court. Marcellinus was no more a politician than he was a competent soldier, but he was adequate for an embassy which was not meant to do more than keep up appearances, and coming from the emperor's brother his words carried a weight that they did not deserve. He presented his brother's warm, fraternal greetings to the Emperor Valentinian and in return was hospitably received and sent back to Gallia with gifts and a warm message. Unfortunately, the success that Marcellinus achieved in his mission gave him an increased credit with his brother and reinforced his over-high opinion of his own abilities.

*

Now, Julian was sure, the time had come to act. Dissension had broken out in the court at Mediolanum accompanied by disaffection in the army. On a day when Marcellinus was smoothing his way around the imperial court, Julian lay reclining on a couch in the cool of the morning, under the shade of the colonnaded walkway that ran on three sides of the water feature in his garden. As he looked out across the city, spread out in a confusion of noise and smoke below him, he dictated to the Greek slave who was his secretary a despatch to the Emperor Maximus. Julian could read and write in good literary style, but his thoughts flowed better, he believed, when dictating. He was recounting now what he had learned at the dinner party he had given for some prominent senators the night before. These had included Symmachus, who had been very indiscreet.

"According to the urban prefect," dictated Julian, "there is considerable dissension inside the court in Mediolanum. The dowager empress feels great hostility towards Bishop Ambrose, whom she blames for failing to recover the body of her stepson, Gratian. She supported the bishop over the Altar of Victory but has got nothing in return except opposition from the bishop and the contempt of Arbogast and the army.

"The situation is now at breaking point, and, as so often nowadays, the issue is religion. The dowager empress, as you are aware, requested that Ambrose hand over the Portian Basilica and a smaller church in the suburbs for the celebration of Easter by the imperial court. I should explain that the basilica is significant. It is the largest church in Mediolanum and it was built as an Arian church by Bishop Ambrose's predecessor, Auxentius. It can be said, therefore, and it is being said by the Arians, that the orthodox have stolen their basilica. The court sent officers to hang up imperial escutcheons to decorate the church before the arrival of the emperor, but Ambrose barred the door and refused them entry, much to the fury of the Arian elements in the army, especially of the Gothi, who all seem to be Arian. Justina got her son to summon Ambrose before a tribunal in the court. At that, the bishop instigated a riot of his orthodox congregation. The Gothic troops attempted to force their way into the basilica, but Ambrose himself stood in the doorway to prevent them. The Gothi wanted to cut him down, but an order from the court prevented it; it seems that the empress feared an uprising and the outbreak of violence around the imperial palace. According to Symmachus' spies, who, he says, have so far proved totally reliable, the general Arbogast warned her that if she allowed the Gothi to attack orthodox citizens, the Roman elements in the army would attack them.

"That humiliation was about to be repeated. Justina tried to get the law on her side by enacting legislation to rescind the previous laws against heresy and to proclaim universal toleration. Ambrose, of course, would be in contravention of any such law, for he is the last man in the empire to tolerate toleration. He again barricaded himself in the basilica and was shut up there by the army. Ambrose got the better of the court by spending his time inside the basilica digging into its floor and unearthing, or so he claimed, the bodies of two ancient martyrs. This aroused the populace, who rejoiced when it became public that a letter from the eastern emperor Theodosius had arrived suggesting strongly to the dowager empress that she back down. Which she did.

"In this affair, the court has shown itself to be weak. Even an unarmed Christian priest has been able to defy it with impunity. The dowager empress has lost the support of the army. The *magister militum* Arbogast is said to be smarting still at being ignored over the Altar of Victory, and now many of his men have been refused the right to practise their religion. There is growing dissension in the ranks between the Arians and Christians of the Nicene variety, something which is deeply troubling Arbogast.

"On another matter, the impression is growing that Valentinian will never be fit to rule. He is developing into an idle, petulant wastrel who thinks of nothing but gratifying his own pleasure. Even his mother despairs of his rudeness, arrogance and failure to attend to business. As was the case with Gratian, whispers are circulating that the young emperor is far too free with his favours towards members of his Gothic bodyguard, all of whom he has handpicked for their muscular, handsome appearance.

"In sum, were you, my lord, to take the line that orthodoxy was under threat in Italia, and to publicly support the stand of Ambrose against the court, you would be welcomed with showers of flowers by the orthodox Christian people. If you were to move swiftly now, perhaps having put your usual feelers out to the senior officers of the army, you would not, in my estimation, find much opposition to your assumption of power here. I believe that it is time!"

Any doubt that Maximus had that he should move swiftly now to take power in Italia was removed by a subsequent despatch from Julian, who reported that Justina and her son had received the Arian bishop Auxentius the younger at court.

Encouraged thus, they had again ordered Ambrose to hand over a church in Milan for Arian worship. Once more, Ambrose and his congregation barricaded themselves inside the church and the imperial order was humiliatingly rescinded. Few had any faith any longer in the resolve of the imperial regime.

By the time this second missive reached the emperor, Andragathius was already assembling his troops on the other side of the mountains.

*

It had never been Maximus' intent that his seizure of power should end in Augusta. He knew that if he stayed there, he could never be secure from eventual attack. Previous usurpers who had stayed passively in Gallia had all perished ignominiously. Italia was right in the centre of the empire and from it every one of Maximus' dioceses could be threatened. There was more, too, on Maximus' mind. Roma and Italia gave credibility to a western emperor in a way that Augusta and Gallia simply could not. Maximus wanted to be Theodosius' equal and for that he needed Roma to match his old friend's throne in Constantinopolis. He and Julian, who had his own reasons for needing a change of regime in Italia, had therefore always planned on a second phase to their plot. Julian had not risked his money simply to see Maximus rule in Augusta.

After the fall of Gratian, Maximus had two potential enemies, the first and most dangerous of them being Theodosius in Constantinopolis, who, he believed, would eventually come to accept him. The eastern emperor was indeed showing every sign of conciliation and had gone so far as to visit Mediolanum to broker a peace between Maximus and the Italian court. The second enemy was the certain one, the court in Mediolanum, where Valentinian and his mother were close family of Gratian, the emperor he had murdered. He knew that they would always seek his downfall. Added to that, the *magister militum* Arbogast, who held the central imperial armies in his power, was no friend of his. Arbogast had forged his way to high command in the train of his mentor, his fellow Frank Merobaudes, whom Maximus had killed. He, too, would not be forgiving. Maximus concluded that it was the regime in Italia, and only that regime, with which he would have to deal before he could assume that he was safe.

Maximus had no interest in which kind of Christian worshipped in which church, but he was no fool, and it was clear to him that Ambrose's successful resistance to the Arian court had given him an opening. Out across the empire went his couriers carrying his call to arms in defence of the true faith and besmirching the name of the dowager empress and her son as heretics who were endangering religion and, through God's inevitable wrath, the very empire itself.

The emperor did not open his mind to his senior advisers before moving forward with his plans. The princes Gadeon, Conan and Erbin knew nothing of any design to take Roma. Nor did Elen, until the day that her husband sent Andragathius south to assemble the troops. When she finally found out what her husband intended, she was appalled. This was all that she had feared. She had no faith in the outcome of this new campaign and, in particular, did not believe her husband's protestations of the likelihood of Theodosius accepting any further aggression. She was distraught, but she could not show it, either in public or in private to her husband, who was breezily preparing to move south to join his *magister militum* and had ordered his train to be packed and ready. She was torn; she could not, she knew, let him go to war in the belief that his wife did not accept what he was doing. She kept her peace.

She resolved, however, to do whatever possible to help her husband. All she could do, she thought, was to pray in the most efficacious place, and that, she believed, was at the feet of the holiest man in the western empire. If she could get the holy Martin to pray for her husband's success, God might listen to his voice.

"I shall pray for your success, my lord," she told her husband. "I shall go to the holy Martin and seek his blessing upon your defence of our true religion."

"My love, that is a perfect idea. You have our authority to travel there, and we shall give you an escort."

"Let me take Peblig," she went on. "Ever since he arrived here, he has been asking when he would receive Martin's blessing. I can see a future for our boy in the kind of life that Martin leads. Were he to prove to be half as holy and revered as Martin, it would redound to the glory of our family."

"Take him, wife, let him also play his part." Maximus kissed his wife, whose good sense was continually astounding him. "You do more than play your part, my love," he went on. "You are our great support and the sane, reasonable voice at our right hand. We shall be together again soon and we shall have such a life as you have not dreamed of. We thank the gods for the day we met. You will have our love, always."

Maximus had never before spoken so effusively to Elen, who was deeply touched. She promised that she and Peblig would pray for the success of his enterprise. "God will grant our pleas," she replied, and was sure that she was right.

*

As Maximus and his palatine troops set out for the south, Elen made preparations for her trip. It would take her carriage over two weeks to reach Martin's monastery, so she and Peblig would have to be away for several months. She intended to bring Ursula with her. Until now, Ursula had been grudgingly acting as one of her maids and had scarcely set foot outside the palace. Elen had gently been leading the girl to her own faith, and meeting the holy Martin was, Elen thought, a perfect way to convince her. For her part, Ursula was itching to escape the court with its cloying protocol and the pointless monotony of her daily tasks.

Despite Elen's own view of her simple needs on the journey, the court thought differently. She was the empress, so she and her son needed protecting by a military escort, as did the gold they carried for the road and the presents for Martin's monastery. When they stopped in places where there were no guest houses, they would have to be housed in marquees, with comfortable bedding and furniture. They would have to be fed by cooks from a ready supply of the foodstuffs carried with them. The empress' raiment had to look imperial; a rich array of different clothes would be needed for different occasions. All had to be transported and kept clean. With them in the convoy would travel Elen's chaplain, who brought his mass equipment; scribes to write her letters and keep their records; military standard-bearers and trumpeters; musicians to play for the empress at night; and a whole host of slaves to administer to the needs of all of these. In all, Elen's expedition to meet the holy Martin involved a cavalcade of several hundred soldiers, officials and slaves.

Word of the empress' expedition was sent to the diocesan and provincial administrations along her route, with the result that her journey this time through northern Gallia was utterly unlike her earlier travels across the country. Delegations met her at each civic boundary. Vicars, governors and city councillors hosted and feted her in every town through which she passed. She did not enjoy this official entertainment, but grew used to it, and was genuinely surprised at how popular she seemed, for it was not just the officials who welcomed her. Crowds of ordinary people thronged the sides of the road and crowded around each palace or *mansio* in which she stopped the night. It became clear to her that her devotion to the holy Martin had already become something of a legend. Very shyly at first, but with growing confidence, she acknowledged the crowds and, when they passed by men and women strewing her way with flowers, she had the curtains of her carriage opened so that she could wave and smile. Never had she felt so exalted, and she thanked God that he had brought the holy Martin into her life.

At last, it dawned on Elen that after what had seemed to her a very long, melancholy time, she was actually beginning to enjoy herself. The road was good, the weather was in a delightful summer phase, the countryside was green and rich. They passed neatly kept villages with well-cut hedges and neat fences. She saw pastures with lush grass where fat cows grazed. Sleek-coated horses galloped up to fences to see the passing cavalcade. The many countryfolk who crowded the road to see her, or who worked in the fields alongside the road, looked well fed and happy, particularly the children, who were given flowers to throw and who sang as they spread them along her way. In the distance, she saw many white-walled villas surrounded by clusters of farm buildings, so extensive in some cases that they looked like substantial villages. It was a dreamy journey, one of a lifetime, and she found that she did not want it to end.

Eventually, of course, it did and the caravan reached the first monastery that Martin had founded near Civitas Turonum; he still preferred to stay there despite having founded a second house. Martin was waiting for her at the gate, leaning on his staff, slightly older and more wizened in the year since she had last seen him. Elen need not have worried that there would be any lingering difficulty over the Priscillian affair. Martin simply smiled in welcome and ushered her, Peblig and Ursula inside the compound. They had expected it to be a simple place, but the courtiers were taken aback by how primitive it was and tried to persuade the empress that it was unfit and that she should stay elsewhere. Elen was having none of it and insisted that she accept Martin's invitation to stay in the old building which he had rescued from dereliction and made his home.

The house had formed the main wing of a rustic villa, really a big farmhouse that had been abandoned some decades before. Martin had patched up the roof and put wooden shutters in the empty window frames. He lived there with one acolyte who looked after his very simple needs. The house had a kitchen and a dining room, a small library and a few bedrooms. The bathhouse was a ruin and the hypocaust no longer functioned, but water still ran through the pipes and drains and the ablutions seemed to work. The old barns and outhouses had been made sound for storing food and fodder for the animals. One had been converted into a chapel. Encircling the house and some distance from it was a series of small mud-walled huts with thatched roofs. These were the individual cells of the monks, which seemed to be the only really new buildings that had been erected, and these had been thrown up in haphazard fashion by each new monk who joined the community. Also new was the wall that enclosed the whole area, which in some places incorporated earlier farm walls and in other places was just an earthen bank, with only one gate opening through it. It was all primitive and very plain, but it stood in open countryside near the river, surrounded by trees and farmland, and Elen fell in love with it as soon as she saw it. Her entourage, on the other hand, hated it and camped sulkily in the pasture outside the enclosure.

Martin took them straight to the tiny chapel to thank God for their safe arrival, then had refreshments brought to them on the ramshackle verandah of his house. "Brother Marcus will take Publicus and Ursula and show them around," he told Elen, "and we can sit here, watch the sun slowly go down over those hills, and you can tell me why you have come."

Peblig gave his hand to the raggedly dressed Brother Marcus and joyfully let himself be taken off to see the barn, the pigsty and the cells where Marcus and his brethren lived. Ursula was not yet convinced by all this holiness and trailed reluctantly behind. "I have never seen my son so elated," Elen told Martin. "We have had a lovely journey here, and the best of it is seeing what you have built for our Lord Jesus. I am so glad to have been able to come."

Martin smiled. He had met and talked with many emperors, empresses, generals and high officials, but this one was different. She had, he thought, a generosity of spirit and a simplicity that must come straight from God. He had been struck by her when he had first set eyes on her in the grand basilica in Augusta. She had shone, not with pomp or earthly glory, but with the golden light of a pure heart. "How long will you stay, my lady?" he asked.

"Just a few days," she replied. "My husband has marched south and I promised to come here and seek your prayers for his safety and for the safety of our family. When I have done that, I must go back to be with my son, Victor, who has been left with responsibility in Augusta."

"So, we have time to pray together and to talk," he said. "Come, let me show you what we have built here."

Over the next few days, Elen unburdened herself to the holy Martin. She told him of all the fears that she had held in her heart since they survived that dreadful time in Moesia.

She told him that she knew that her husband had committed terrible sins, both there and since. She related her efforts to bring him to God and to find forgiveness, but confessed that she suspected that her husband's baptism did not mean that he had found Christ. She told Martin that she feared for his soul and that she was afraid that whatever God might cause to befall him would harm her children.

Martin did his best to comfort the empress with the word of God, which he read to her from the Bible. He also gave her his own counsel. He could predict nothing, he told her, and no man could make promises on God's behalf. God's plan was not something he claimed that he could see, but he did know that God could be swayed by the prayers of the righteous and that it was in his nature to forgive sinners. The prayers of the Lady Elen would reach God, he was sure, and He would not rebuff her purity of heart. He took Elen with him to chapel to spend an hour on their knees together before the altar and did so again on each of the days of her stay.

Peblig and Ursula knew nothing of the empress' anxieties. Despite her initial reservations, Ursula found herself slowly warming to what she saw at the monastery. It was a down-to-earth place where the monks lived an almost impoverished life, one very much like that of the peasants among whom she had grown up. Things did not seem so different here. Both of them felt the love that emanated from the holy Martin and had inspired the community he had built around him. As a result, they both spent a very happy few days with Brother Marcus and his fellows. They joined in the worship, listened to the brethren and helped out in the fields and in the kitchen. Peblig had never enjoyed such freedom. It was natural, therefore, that when Elen gently suggested to both her son and Ursula that the holy Martin might be prepared to baptise them, they both gladly assented. Martin led them down to the riverbank and baptised them both.

When the time came, all too soon it seemed to them all, for them to return to Augusta, Peblig told Martin and his mother that he never wanted to leave. "I have seen what I want to do with my life," he exclaimed. "God has called me through you, holy Martin, and through Brother Marcus and through every stone, every blade of grass here in this holy place." Turning to his mother, he said: "We must bring this way of God's life to our peoples back home. When we go back to our island, I shall one day build my own monastery and copy everything I have seen here."

"That is one prediction I think I can make," said Martin laughing. "You have God within you, Publicus." Elen smiled too. She had seen God in her son long before, but here Peblig virtually shone with the light of the faith. Now, through her son, He had given her an indication of what she should do with her life.

"Yes, my son, you are right, we shall do this. We shall copy what the holy Martin is doing here and we shall bring to our homeland this way of reaching God's love."

The sour look on Ursula's face made it plain that she was aggrieved rather than happy at the end of their visit. "What is it, my child?" asked Martin.

"There are no women here, holy Martin, only men. What about those women who, like the men, want to worship God in this way? You have built nothing for them."

She was right in what she said. Martin and his monks kept everything female as far away as possible. To their minds, women were a terrible temptation, a lure and a distraction.

"We do not allow women in the monastery for the good of all," replied the holy man. "Men are weak."

"Then women must go elsewhere," retorted Ursula. "God wants us to worship him too, just like you do." She stomped off to join the waiting convoy and did not stop to bid her host farewell.

Martin stood at the gate to the monastery compound and waved the empress' cavalcade on its way home. He could not know it, but through Elen and Peblig he had passed on his gospel of love and his inspiration to a future he could not imagine. Nevertheless, he was certain that God had brought this woman and her son to him and that He had great plans for them. He was not so sure about Ursula, but he had a nagging doubt that she was right about the need to allow women to live a godly life. He was rather glad that this was not his problem.

Martin had planted in all of them seeds of the faith that would take root in many soils across the west. Through Elen, Peblig and Ursula, the light of the culture in which Martin had been soldier, bishop and monk would flicker through all the dark days that were to come, and it would not go out.

Chapter Twenty-two

OVER THE ALPES

Before starting on his journey south, Maximus wrote a letter to Valentinian II complaining of his tolerance of Arianism in the empire. This letter, along with several others to Bishop Siricius of Roma, was copied and sent to eminent men and officials across the western empire. In his missive to the bishop, Maximus reminded him of his thirst to establish orthodoxy throughout his domains, a desire, he claimed, that had motivated the execution and exile of members of the Priscillian faction. In this correspondence, he again admitted that this had been an error; he acknowledged that he would not again interfere in church disciplinary matters and he drew the bishop's attention to the fact that, subsequent to the Priscillian case, he had handed a heretical priest over for judgement to a panel of bishops in Augusta. He was determined to get the church onside. Having trumpeted his case to the world, and following in the wake of his couriers, he rode south to join his *magister militum*.

*

Andragathius had based his headquarters at Arelate in the south of Gallia. The city lay near the mouth of the River

Rhodanus and also boasted its own canal to the sea. It was a strategically important spot, close to the Via Julia Augusta, which led along the Ligurian coast into Italia, and similarly close to the Via Domitia that ran east across the easiest pass over the Alpes. Forces assembling in Arelate could march into Italia by at least two routes or move from it by sea.

Constantine was already present at Arelate, having marched his regiment down from Augusta to prepare for the emperor's arrival. Gerontius had found time after the imperial party got back from Britannia to give his friend word that they were about to march south to launch an invasion of Italia, so Constantine had been able to arrange that his unit bring more stores and supplies than normal, giving out only that there would be hard training ahead.

Before the emperor arrived from Augusta, Andragathius spent the time considering their courses of action. The emperor's secret orders were to prepare to invade Italia, but he had given no detailed instructions, and as the general was unable to discuss the invasion yet with his officers, he had been unable to take their advice. By spies and in despatches from Julian, who was relying on what was being fed to him from the court in Mediolanum, he was well informed about the deployment of Arbogast's Army of Italia, its logistics and its state of morale, which was encouragingly bad. He had also started to identify commanders within the opposing forces who would be susceptible to bribes and might defect or stand neutral. There were many of these. The Arian Germans were now severely disaffected and, if secretly promised tolerance, would defect without being paid to do so. Many of the Roman troops were also near mutiny over the court's Arianism and its failure to impose order. These would also be susceptible to corruption.

It was a stroke of luck for the planned invasion that the Italian field army was currently on the move to the east, preparing for campaigns against barbarian incursions in Pannonia and Raetia. Although some of its troops were battle-hardened, having taken part in Bauto's recent campaign, most of its units had not been to war for many years; many of their troops never had been. The Italian army left few garrison units at the western end of the valley of the River Padus and what was there was too weak to hold the mountain passes into Gallia. At sea, ships of the imperial Italian fleets were very weak in number and concentrated at Aquileia on the east coast. On the Italian west coast, there were only a few scouting vessels based at the port of Genua.

Under his command, Andragathius had most, but not all, of the units of the field Army of Gallia, which were being joined shortly by Maximus' own palatine escort army, as well as by elements from the forces in Hispania. He had few ships, mostly lumbering freighters supplied by Julian's agencies, so had given orders for the building of more. Ships would be useful both as troop carriers and to supply troops marching along the coast road. The scouts and secret couriers he had sent out had reported back on the state of the passes. It was not yet even autumn, and winter's snows were a long way off, so none of the lower passes were blocked. Given the emperor's usual luck, the way to Italia seemed open.

*

When Maximus arrived at Arelate, he covered his intentions by giving out that he was on tour. The word went out that he wished to meet the chief dignitaries of the city, to see its famed attractions and to give games. His arrival was accompanied by the usual ceremonies and acclamations, the excitement in the city heightened this time by the news that had been spread before he came that he would sponsor a mammoth event in the arena. The city was sophisticated and rich, a rival to Massilia, which lay further around the coast. It had an amphitheatre that could seat thousands, a campus for chariot racing and a theatre. The Emperor Constantine had himself ordered the building of magnificent baths there. One of the unique features of the city was a massive mill on the river, its sixteen wheels set one above the other with water spilling down over each to drive the next in turn.

The city was beautiful. Its public buildings were immaculately kept, its squares and street corners were filled with statuary and the green spaces of its city parks linked in an arc within the extensive city walls. Maximus genuinely wanted to see it and he intended to enjoy himself there while his troops quietly assembled in the surrounding countryside. As Andragathius' preparations went on apace, the emperor showed himself regularly to the crowds at the games and races with which he entertained them. He was generous with the coinage scattered in his wake as he processed. His popularity soared.

Official business was kept for the evening and the night, so that it was by torchlight that he gave audience in the city basilica to another embassy sent by the government of Valentinian. This time the ambassador was a senator named Domninus, who had been sent to enlist Maximus' help in joint action against the German tribes that were threatening Pannonia. This played nicely into Maximus' hands. He entertained the ambassador and took him about with him in the city, keeping him busy until Andragathius reported that all was in place. At their last interview, Maximus delighted the ambassador by promising to send troops to fight with Valentinian's forces in Pannonia. The emperor went further and took Domninus to see some of the troops who were assembling outside the city, giving him the impression that they were being assembled as reinforcements for Italia. The ambassador was escorted back to Mediolanum by what he thought was the advance party of the troops coming to his own emperor's aid, but which was actually the advance party of the invading army. It was a clever move, but a sad piece of treachery.

In the wake of this party, Maximus gave the order to Andragathius for the army to cross the Alpes by the road the ambassador had taken, giving out that it was coming to the aid of the Army of Italia.

"Strike swiftly and always with deception," were Maximus' last words to Andragathius. "Use whatever gold you need to buy support. We shall get it all back later, and it will prevent rivers of Roman blood, which I have no desire to shed."

*

A few days later, the leading troops marched through the pass at the Mons Matronae, past the, as yet, undefiled temple of Janus, the god whose two faces looked west to Gallia and east to Italia. Descending into the valley of the Padus, they passed the major city of Augusta Taurinorum without any alarm being raised. It was at Novara that anyone in the Army of Italia first realised that the force approaching the city was far from being a reinforcement; for one thing, it was too big. It seemed, indeed, to be most of the field army of Gallia. Novara's small garrison was brave enough to shut the gates in Andragathius' face, so he started to cut off the city, too late, however, to prevent a message being sent to Mediolanum. The delay allowed Maximus himself to catch up with his advance guard. Assessing, correctly, that the garrison was too small to resist an assault, he pushed Andragathius to move on ahead towards Mediolanum, where he hoped to capture the imperial court, and ordered that Novara be assaulted that night. Troops went over the walls in places where the garrison was too weak to defend them and opened the gates. There was widespread slaughter of both the garrison and the civilian population, and the city was looted.

Maximus ordered this deliberately. He wanted an example made of Novara that would show Italia what would happen were he to be resisted. In his campaigns above the Wall and on the German frontier, he had always behaved in this way. In his experience, fear always worked. He had kept the cohort of Segontienses close by him to assist with the massacre. He knew that they, and especially their tribune Pulcher, would willingly do anything he asked of them and that they would enjoy doing so. As he rode up to the city gate, he called Pulcher to him and gave him his instructions.

The tribune of the Army of Italia who had been in command in the city was dragged out into the open ground before the gate. His uniform was stripped from him and his few surviving men, and they were all beheaded. Maximus sat watching this, impassive on horseback at the smouldering ruin of the gate. Then, with the rest of his army, the emperor marched away as Pulcher's troops began to round up those of the city's survivors considered useful enough to be enslaved. Those deemed unfit to be sold were put to the sword or allowed to flee out of the city into the surrounding countryside. Pulcher's troops then started to burn what was left of Novara to the ground.

Gerontius had of necessity been present at the initial sack and the executions, though he had not had to see the final stages of Novara's destruction. He had found it very difficult to watch what his emperor had done. Novara was a city of Roman citizens. He could recall nothing in any history of civil strife in which a Roman commander had ordered the butchery and enslavement of a whole town of the empire's own people.

He was appalled by the fate of the garrison's tribune, who seemed to be the one officer they had met so far in Italia who had done his duty. His execution, and that of his men, was unnecessary. More, thought Gerontius, it was murder. He rode on with his escort around the emperor, very sorry for the day that had called him to the duty that he now very bitterly had to perform.

*

The gold which Andragathius had wisely and liberally disbursed in the imperial capital had done its work and as his cavalry clattered up the road towards the city, the gates of Mediolanum swung open for them. There was no resistance at the palace, for the dowager empress, Valentinian and the *magister militum* Arbogast were not there, having moved to Aquileia on Italia's northeast coast to be ready for the campaign in Pannonia. No one they had left behind was able to coordinate any resistance. Maximus and his entourage moved into the palace while Andragathius drove his troops on further east. The Italian garrison units between them and the coast were all bribed or persuaded to lay down their arms. It was now vital to get to Aquileia before Valentinian's court could escape, but the major part of the Army of Italia was assembling around the town of Opitergium for the forthcoming campaign and were thus between Maximus' troops and Aquileia. To acquire the loyalty or at least the neutrality of these troops took some time. In the event, the suborning of the Army of Italia was a success, but by the time it had been achieved, the imperial quarry had fled.

The *magister militum* Arbogast had begun to get a full picture of what was happening to his army only when Maximus destroyed Novara. The loss of Mediolanum without a fight was a blow that had been followed by the serial submission of the troops along the Padus. Arbogast was a hardened realist. Rightly, he did not believe that the men of the Army of Italia would lay down their lives to fight Maximus, either for Valentinian or for him personally. So, when the dowager empress, who had sought to put some steel into her son's backbone, demanded that they stay and fight, he ignored her command and had her and her son placed on board one of the small fleet of ships that he had kept waiting in Aquileia's naval station. Leaving no word and no orders, he embarked with them that night and ordered the flotilla to head straight down the Mare Adriaticum and around Graecia to Thessalonica, aiming to throw himself and his charges on the mercy of the Emperor Theodosius.

At the flight of the imperial family, all the troops in Italia went over to Maximus, swiftly followed by those in Africa and on the Danubius in Pannonia and Raetia. Maximus was now the *de facto* emperor of all the west.

*

While Maximus regarded his swift and almost bloodless success as a God-given triumph and began to boast to his subordinates of his own impeccable judgment, the means that he had chosen to achieve his victory bore the seeds of his ultimate fate. He had created implacable enemies in three figures whom he had deceived and forced to flee. They would have no choice but to fight him now. The dowager empress and her son, the rightful imperial family, who had been recognised as such by Maximus himself and were still so recognised by Theodosius, were now heading to safety and the protection of the eastern emperor, the only person who could pose a threat to him. Their general, Arbogast, already an enemy, would be itching to avenge his humiliation.

What had Maximus gained by taking Italia? Its troops, now his troops, were not the best in the empire, as he had proved himself. They could not be relied upon. Italia was riven with religious controversies, all of which would now be as thorns in the side of his rule, and which would not only distract him from more vital matters but would ensure that he was almost certain to alienate a large part of his people, whatever he did. He had now brought his capital to Mediolanum, leaving his son, Victor, in Augusta Treverorum. History had taught his predecessors that the best-placed station from which to hold the frontier against the barbarians was at Augusta, not any palace in Italia. There would be more trouble now on the border, that was for sure. Looking at things, as he did, sitting now in the luxury of the imperial palace, he quickly came to realise that the status he had won might have placed him in greater peril than he had been before. If he had thought that Theodosius would not come for him before, he was less sure now. He put the thought aside. Theodosius was his friend.

Anyway, he was now emperor of half the world. He had thrown the dice and he had won. If he were unable to suppress all doubts of his ultimate triumph, he would never show them to the world. It was more than ever important to appear nothing but supremely confident, and he had long practice at doing just that. Reality would be what he made it. The carapace of his self-belief thickened and hardened around him until none could any longer come close enough to save him from himself.

Chapter Twenty-three

NOVARA

This was the season of Maximus' glory, for he was now emperor of all the west. The flight of Valentinian and the collapse of any military opposition in Italia had left all in his hands. The praetorian prefect of Italia and Africa, Flavius Neoterius, had fled with his emperor, and although Maximus hesitated before appointing another, the vicars subordinate to Neoterius in Italia, Noricum, Pannonia, Raetia and Africa all recognised Maximus as emperor. Aside from the massacre in Novara, his coup had been bloodless. The gold that it had taken to bribe the opposing troops could now be recouped, for the imperial treasury in Mediolanum was now in his hands. The north of Italia was rich; it and the rest of the empire gave many opportunities for creaming off a percentage.

The lack of reaction in Constantinopolis remained encouraging. Theodosius issued no statement. He had his hands full with keeping the Gothi quiet, with handling another barbarian incursion into Moesia, and with negotiations for peace with the Persian empire. Maximus had, at least for now, room to breathe.

Taking a firm grip on his new power and seeking to justify his usurpation, Maximus ordered the imperial court to send out despatches to all the civilian and military officials across the west, stating that he had acted to remove a heretical regime and that he had the support in so doing of the eastern emperor, Theodosius. The last part of this statement was a mistake, as not only was it unbelievable to anyone who had any grasp of imperial politics, but it was also certain to enrage Theodosius, who had so far been forced to tolerate Maximus' usurpation.

Until this second seizure of power, Theodosius had been doing what he could to bolster Valentinian's shaky regime without going to war in the west. The eastern emperor had intervened to prevent religious conflict over the basilica which Ambrose had barricaded in Mediolanum. He had nominated trustworthy senior officials from Constantinopolis to western posts, including the praetorian prefects of Italia and Africa. He had sent his senior general, Flavius Bauto, to campaign in Raetia on Valentinian's behalf. To the whole empire, it was clear that he stood as the protector of the young Valentinian's regime. Now the boy and his mother were in flight, somewhere at sea, grievously betrayed with a very underhand trick by a usurper who had promised friendship and military aid. It was humiliating. To any objective observer, it was clear that the Augustus of the east could not let this go without endangering his own throne. Theodosius had to reckon that, based on recent experience, he himself was now under threat from Maximus.

His western counterpart was, however, increasingly suffering from a fatal dose of hubris and would not believe that anything could now overturn his good fortune. In Maximus' view, all his plans had worked out and the world was at his feet. His new God was on his side. Slowly, but inexorably, as his grip on reality began to slide, his oft-vaunted ability to take sensible advice, to plan, to prepare carefully and to avoid dangerous risks, began to evaporate. He had also omitted to think about his wife.

*

Elen and her escort were still on the road, some way behind the army. She had descended the harsh mountain slopes into the broad and prosperous valley of the Padus. She was just beginning to believe that she would like this sunny country, with its well-tilled farmland and rich villa estates, when her party came across what she took at first to be a group of beggars on the side of the road. Following her usual custom, she called a halt and dismounted from her carriage to distribute some small coins. These people were, she found to her horror, not the usual sort of destitute. Some of the older men and women were wearing what had clearly been clothing befitting the rank of substantial people. One or two had ears or even a hand missing, their wounds still bleeding and suppurating. Thinking that they were victims of bandits, Elen asked what had happened to them and whether they needed help. They told her that they were refugees from Novara and they related what had befallen them.

Staggered that the army of her husband had so maltreated its own people, she demanded to be taken there to see for herself. Gerontius had managed to get a message back to the commander of her escort to prevent the empress at all costs from travelling via the sacked city, and the *protector* at first attempted to dissuade Elen from going there. She was having none of that, intending to find out who had done this so that she could report the crime to her husband, who, she was sure, would punish those who had so besmirched his name. For the first time, she issued a direct order to her escort, so they reluctantly turned aside into a new road and came upon what was left of Novara.

From a distance, the first thing Elen noticed was the clouds of smoke billowing up from behind the trees. Then came the smell of burning wood and, worse still, flesh. When they reached what was left of the gate, she stopped, appalled, for inside the walls she could see through the ruined entrance to the city that there was little left standing in it. The entire city was a heap of burned rubble. Here and there a few dazed survivors were combing through the wreckage of their houses, and even as she watched, some of what were clearly her husband's troops were rounding these up, kicking and punching them into some sort of line, which was being joined together by chains and shackles.

"Who is in command here?" she asked her escort, who sent riders into the ruins to find the culprit.

"Do not go further in, my lady, it is not safe," warned her *protector*. It took only a few minutes for the tribune Pulcher to emerge from the gate. He marched up to the empress, saluted and paid his compliments as if he were on a parade ground. She was taken aback by the fact that he seemed so pleased with himself.

"Tell me what has happened here, Pulcher," she said. "Who has done this?"

Pulcher ignored the attempts of the *protector* of the escort to warn him not to speak and carried straight into an account of the assault and sack of the city, an account calculated, so he thought, to show himself in the very best light. Elen listened with disbelief, interrupting only once to question the man. When Pulcher proudly reached the point in the story at which Maximus had especially asked for his unit to carry out the sack, she asked: "It was my husband, the emperor, who gave you the order to do this?"

"Yes, my lady, he sent for us as he knew we'd do a good job."

Elen found herself unable to stomach talking to the man and turned away. She walked to a bush, then retched several times onto the ground. As she walked back to Pulcher and her escort, her face was pale and her expression set hard. "You will stop this now, Pulcher," she ordered. "You have done quite enough to fulfil my husband's order. From now on, no one from this city is to be killed, injured, in any way abused. You are to release all these people then follow me immediately to Mediolanum. Do I make myself clear?"

"Yes, my lady. At once." Still not understanding what had just happened, Pulcher hastened away to comply. Elen looked at her *protector*, who, shamefaced, could not look her in the eye.

"Take me out of here," she said, "and get word to the local authorities to come and help these people."

As the carriage bore her to Mediolanum, she found the numbness in her brain slowly turning to ice. She had seen death and violence before. She was married to a soldier and had lived with him as he served in Africa and Moesia. She had never, though, seen an atrocity such as she had just seen at Novara. Now she knew that it was her husband who had personally ordered this crime, but she had no idea of the reason why. She thought of her journey to the holy Martin to pray with him for her husband's victory. Martin had prayed with her and God had granted their prayer. He had given Maximus the victory, a bloodless victory, and her husband had thrown it back in God's face by committing this work of Satan. There could be no forgiveness, she knew, for betraying the Lord.

The realisation of her husband's unspeakably evil act stripped away the last layer of her affection for him. It seemed to her now that she had always fooled herself that he was redeemable. She had known what he was like when his mistreatment of the Gothi in Moesia had led to their rebellion, but she had trusted herself to be able to bring him to the forgiveness of Christ. Her pride in achieving his baptism had blinded her to the fact that he was using her faith to fool those he needed to achieve power. He had fooled even her. Now she knew better. She did not believe he was redeemable, ever.

That, she was certain, meant that he was doomed. Without the help of the Almighty, the powers of this world would turn on him and destroy him. She could no longer help him. She no longer wanted to. All that she could do now was to save her family. They were all at risk. Theodosius would come for them. She had to think of what to do.

*

Elen had plenty of time to decide on a course of action, for it was some weeks after she entered the imperial palace in Mediolanum that Maximus rode in to sit upon its throne. He had been very happily busy. The frontier in Pannonia, where the German tribes had seen an opportunity to raid, had needed his attention. The border with Illyricum, the nearest area held by Theodosius' troops, had needed to be strengthened. New officials had to be posted throughout the newly acquired dioceses, as the appointees of the court of Valentinian had to be replaced. Maximus now intended to go to Roma to be acclaimed by the senate, a journey that had already begun to involve much planning due to the weight of protocol that precedent required.

His good mood did not last long when he met his wife. She greeted him icily before dismissing the slaves, then looked him straight in the face. He had never seen her like this, and despite his callousness and brutality, he flinched.

She did not mince words. "Why did you destroy Novara?"

He hesitated. "It was necessary, my love. They opposed me. I needed to teach a lesson to prevent further bloodshed."

"No, husband, you did not. These people had the ill fortune to live in a town where the garrison did its sworn duty and closed the gates. The people had no choice in the matter. Yet you ordered their murder, rape and enslavement."

Maximus found himself grasping at excuses. "It was done without my knowledge, wife. I found out too late."

"I met Pulcher."

Maximus knew that he had lost, but this made him angry. "Whatever I did, I did for Roma. It is not for you to judge me. You know nothing of such things. I will not be accused by you. You will know your place, wife, and hold your tongue."

"Yes, my lord, I know my place. We are all poor sinners before our Saviour. I prayed for your victory. I went to the holy Martin and together we prayed to the Almighty. God granted our prayer and because of that you won. He will not forgive you for what you did next. I shall say one thing to you, husband, then I shall for all time hold my tongue. You betrayed the Lord our God. You are doomed in this world and the next."

Elen turned her back on her husband and walked out. Maximus found himself shaking. She had for the first time seen inside his soul, and she had cursed him.

*

As the troops returned from the east to their stations around Mediolanum, Constantine and Gerontius were at last able to meet. They did so in what was now the former's considerable residence in the centre of his regiment's camp. After supper, when the slaves had withdrawn, they reclined in the apse of Constantine's dining room to talk uninterrupted and unheard. Constantine wanted Gerontius to relate to him the details of the sack of Novara. He knew that his friend had the full story and he found himself dismayed by what he related.

"The discontent in the army over this is palpable," mused Constantine. "The Italian army resents what was done to their people, and in particular to the garrison's tribune, who is honoured for being the only officer in Italia to have done his duty. The Christians are up in arms as Pulcher managed to burn down two Christian basilicas while he was pillaging the city. What happened at Novara was such an unnecessary waste of the emperor's good name. All the people had loved him until now. He has taxed them lightly and administered justice impartially. The soldiery has loved his liberality with gold. He had not, until now, been seen to be cruel. Now the empire has glimpsed a dark side that many don't like at all. The men are beginning to wonder what he is capable of."

"I know now what he is capable of," responded Gerontius, "and I am sorry for it, especially for the Lady Elen, who was taken to see the place and actually met the boneheaded Pulcher in the middle of his butchery."

Neither man was a sentimentalist, but both had believed that they followed a clever as well as a lucky man. The gods or God, depending upon which of them was thinking this, did not give luck to those who spurned the good fortune granted them.

"I do not think that this is coming to anything at the moment," went on Constantine. "My officers are keeping a close eye on it and I think this will pass. But if Theodosius moves quickly, it will not help to have a disaffected army to lead against him. He will come, of that I am sure. No one believes that he asked the emperor to enter Italia. He was Valentinian's *de facto* guardian. The place was almost Theodosius' own portion."

"I am glad that I shall not be here to see what occurs," replied Gerontius. "I am being posted, so we shall have to part again, and amongst whatever has happened recently, that makes me the saddest. I am being promoted for my 'good work' commanding the *candidati*. Within two weeks, I leave for Britannia to be *praefectus* in command of the *ala I pannoniorum sabiniana* at Hunnum on the Wall."

"I am glad for you, brother. You deserve the promotion. I am happy that we shall be of equal rank again." This was not quite true, for Constantine was commanding one of the elite regiments of the *scholae*, but there was no doubt that this new promotion meant that Gerontius was still on track to higher things. As he so well deserved, thought his friend.

"I do not think that this posting was meant as a favour, Constantine. The emperor saw the look on my face while he was briefing Pulcher. I think he no longer wants me near him."

"Then you are definitely better off out of what we fear is to come, Gerontius. I, alas, have no chance of leaving my post. I am likely to be in this job for many years before I get the chance to move to other things."

"Then you will see how all this plays out here," replied Gerontius. "I do not envy you that. There is one other issue I need to tell you about before I take my leave, something I have noticed that will add to the difficulties you will face. There are moves afoot by the emperor's brother, Marcellinus, to replace the *magister militum* Andragathius in the emperor's affections. It started back in Augusta, where Marcellinus made himself very thick with the emperor's son and with the praetorian prefect Evodius. He and Evodius both have the same idea of clambering up the greasy pole, and Andragathius stands in their way. You know as well as I do that the *magister militum* is a real soldier. He has guided the emperor with good advice since his time in Moesia. I have never seen him out for himself, unlike Marcellinus, who seems to me a very shifty character. If he succeeds in replacing Andragathius, the emperor will have exchanged a soldier for a fool. Watch that man, brother, he is dangerous. Now I must say goodnight. May your gods preserve you."

"And may your God preserve you, too, my brother."

*

There was much to arrange and a great deal of politicking to be done before Maximus could accomplish his heart's desire of a ceremonial entry to Roma and acclamation in the Roman Senate. He was now openly acting through Julian, whom he had appointed urban prefect in place of Symmachus, whose tour of duty was fortuitously coming to an end. For the first time, it became clear to the senate how important was this man, one whom they had not hitherto thought very significant. Julian had secured the principal position of power in the city, and he immediately began to rake off profits from the import of grain and the sale of offices to recoup his outlays in launching Maximus on his imperial way.

The senate was anxious to please the new emperor and now that Valentinian and the dowager empress had fled, hoped for improved relations with the imperial court. There was certainly no sign of any purge or persecution of any of the old regime's supporters. The senate sent Symmachus up to Mediolanum to use his oratorical skills to acclaim Maximus and to acknowledge that he would be appointed sole consul for the following year. Copying his two predecessors, the new emperor, in his self-appointed role of guardian of Christian orthodoxy, replied to the senate that he would refuse the title and robes of *pontifex maximus*, the state's chief religious official under the old dispensation. To the great disappointment of many, he added that nor would he restore the Altar of Victory.

There was also the business of the marriage of his remaining daughter Magna to arrange. Julian had found a very suitable spouse from a highly aristocratic but comparatively impecunious Roman family, an up-and-coming politician named Flavius Ennodius, whose first wife had just died. The large dowry that Maximus was offering easily overcame the distaste that this man's family felt, but of course did not show in public, for this match with the half-British daughter of a parvenu upstart from the army. Ennodius accompanied Symmachus to Mediolanum for the marriage ceremony. The match was, as were almost all aristocratic marriages, a matter of politics. Elen pitied her daughter but had known that this would come and had prepared her as well as she might. They both endured the brief civil wedding ceremony in the imperial palace, after which Magna returned to Roma with her new husband.

It was not to a happy life that she journeyed. She was to suffer the continuous contempt of her husband and unrelenting harassment from her mother-in-law. Her new household made it clear that they regarded her origins with disdain. Her husband's son by his first marriage, a boy named Flavius Felix, a child only eight years younger than herself, bawled every time he saw her. Except when the family was not there, she was not permitted to speak her native tongue with the maid she had brought with her, her only friend in Roma. Left alone in the evenings, she wept bitter tears.

*

Religious worries had proved unpredictably troublesome to Maximus in Augusta, and he was determined to avoid them as much as possible now that he had absolute power in the west. Aside from inviting Bishop Ambrose to the palace on a single occasion, and that among an immense audience granted to all the new officials, officers and local dignitaries whom he had appointed, Maximus issued him no further invitation to court and refused all his requests for a private audience. When any religious matters came before the throne, he dealt with them in letters written not to Ambrose, but to Bishop Siricius in Roma.

For once, Ambrose suffered this seeming banishment from his emperor's ear without public complaint. Despite the fact that he was in full knowledge of the massacre at Novara and the destruction of its churches, he stayed silent on the subject. When Christians in Roma burned down a synagogue, Maximus condemned the deed as a breach of public order and ordered the punishment of those who had done it. Ambrose seethed, but said nothing in public, confining himself to recording in his writings the hostile reaction of the Roman Christians, some of whom scandalously alleged that Maximus had converted to Judaism and treasonably prophesied his downfall. It seems that Ambrose was uniquely unsure of himself with this new emperor. He had seen Maximus' ruthlessness and his hostility towards him in Augusta, and perhaps he was one person who had taken the lesson of the massacre at Novara to heart. Surprisingly, he gave Maximus no trouble.

*

Plans were soon put into effect to send back to Gallia the elements of the field army which had entered Italia. They were surplus to establishment now but were very much needed where they had come from. Just as the tribes over the border from Pannonia had seen the regime change as an opportunity to raid, so now numbers of Franci in the northern sector of the Rhine frontier did the same, crossing the river and devastating the left bank. Their numbers seemed to threaten Colonia Agrippina and Moguntiacum, although the Franci proved too weak to besiege either, being in any case more interested in taking easy pickings. Maximus' son Victor was at Augusta with the two generals, Nanninus and Quintinus, whom Maximus had appointed to protect his son and Gallia in his absence, just over a hundred miles away from the scene of the incursion. Forces were swiftly assembled at Colonia, and these managed to ambush many of the raiders in the vast *silva carbonaria*, the Charcoal Forest. What was left of them was pursued across the Rhenus, but there the tide turned, and the situation did not stabilise until the troops had returned from Italia.

*

The situation on the Rhenus, especially around the city of Colonia, was a great worry to Elen, as she had learned to her consternation that Ursula was there. The empress had left Ursula with Gratiana in Augusta, fearing that ill might befall them all in Italia and thinking them safest in the palace. This had proved a mistake, but not because of the Franci. Ursula had fallen foul of Victor, who had come upon her one day near Elen's old quarters. Ursula had no time for Victor, whom she regarded as a pompous, spoiled brat, and on this occasion she stared at him, a look of contempt on her face. Victor flew into a rage. "Do not look at the Augustus! I am your sovereign lord," he screamed.

"You are a foolish boy, and no sovereign of mine," Ursula responded, then stalked off leaving Victor shaking in frustrated, helpless fury. That evening, Victor called for the prefect Evodius and told him how he had been disrespected. "I want her out of the palace," he shouted. "Get rid of her." Evodius had been careful over several months to gain Victor's confidence and could not now ignore him, but he also knew that Ursula was important to the empress and that she could not be harmed. So, he had the girl secretly bundled into a carriage and sent under escort to "visit" Severinus, the Bishop of Colonia, who was told to be her host until she could rejoin the court.

Ursula found all this greatly exciting and was glad to escape the palace in Augusta, which she had quickly come to think of as a stiflingly stuffy prison. To Elen, of course, all this was very worrying and added to the anxiety which she felt growing steadily inside her. She was also furious with Victor that he had left Gratiana with no one to care for her; she knew that the boy did not regard Gratiana as his sister and treated her with contempt.

*

Some days after Maximus had settled into Mediolanum, Elen received a letter from Gadeon informing her that her father had died and that he had now succeeded as Prince of the Dumnonii. Eudaf's growing inheritance had, according to custom, been divided by the prince, who had decreed that Conan should be prince of his people in Letavia. Eudaf had lived to extreme old age, having seen his people vastly increase their wealth and their influence. His fleets had won him and his successors power on both sides of the sea. On his death bed, he told his councillors that he died content; he commended to them his two worthy successors.

Elen's letter of both condolence and congratulation to her cousin was accompanied by a more private one, in which she revealed to Gadeon her fears of what might happen in the near future.

"Dearest cousin," she wrote, "I write separately to make you understand the dire change of circumstances that I foresee here, and to warn you of the peril in which we all may be.

"My husband appears blind to the danger that he is in. He believes that the Emperor Theodosius will not act against him. From all that I have seen here, I am sure that he is mistaken, and that Theodosius' coming is only a matter of time. If the emperor of the east does come, I do not have faith in the army to defend us. They are venal and disaffected over religion.

"If we wait until too late, we shall not be able to protect our family. I despair for Victor, who is his father's heir in more ways than one. We can, however, save the others. Please warn your fellow princes to place Owain and Annun out of harm's way. I think that we should move Custennin and Severa out of Eboracum to join their betrotheds, even though they are still not of an age to wed. Please do it now. I am going to send a message to Augusta to have Peblig visit Conan in Darioritum. Conan can send him on to you."

Gadeon was not surprised to receive this letter. He had already thought through the implications of what had befallen in Italia. Maximus' plans, he thought, had been perfectly feasible up until he had won Augusta. Now, he had grown overconfident and his hubris was endangering them all. Gadeon's priority now was to secure his family and the future of his people. There was much to play for. Conan was at risk in Armorica. He was too closely identified with Maximus to easily survive the emperor's fall, and he was not subtle enough to evade retribution without help. He would have to warn Conan. He must work out what to do, and quickly.

Chapter Twenty-four

ROMA

The preparation for Maximus' *adventus*, his ceremonial entry into Roma, took several months to complete. In the capital, the whole event was prepared and managed by Julian, its new urban prefect. Everything cost a very large sum of money, which Julian was, of course, able to ensure was provided. At court in Mediolanum, the emperor's consistory worked with him to get the details right. His entry into the eternal city would be taken as an indication of his fitness to rule. It would, he believed, write his name irrevocably in its history books.

No emperor since the time of Diocletian, almost exactly a century before, had resided in Roma. Yet the city retained its place in the empire's psyche and all emperors who survived long enough to do so found it necessary to visit the eternal city at least once. A protocol for the imperial *adventus* had grown up over the years; the entry of the Emperor Constantius II, some thirty years before, had set a standard of extravagance that would have to be matched or exceeded. Maximus desperately needed the visit and his official recognition by the senate to go well.

Whether Elen liked it or no, she found that she would have to accompany her husband to Roma. Other than on official occasions, she no longer spent time in her husband's company, so the weeks ahead were daunting for her. She was, however, secretly excited by the visit. Aside from the spectacles which she knew the city would offer, she planned to meet the Bishop of Roma, the west's senior Christian prelate. She would have time away from Maximus as the official programme would exclude her from much of it. She was relieved that she would travel in a separate carriage on the road and when they reached the city she would not have to endure too much of her husband's company in public, and very little in private.

As she had vowed to her husband, she now held her tongue before him. In the days when she had held few firm opinions, she had never felt constrained in speaking, although she had been too shy or unconfident to do so. Now, when she was much surer of herself and the words welled up inside her, she vocalised none of them. She felt lonelier than she had ever been. She had felt alone when they had first arrived in Augusta, but it was worse now. She was stranded alone, seemingly forever, by lost love for a husband she now despised.

*

Roma could put on a show like no other city in the world. It housed nearly a million people, whose origins were the most diverse on the planet. In its streets you could hear every tongue spoken in the empire from Syria and Arabia to Africa, Hispania, Gallia and Britannia. The accumulated wealth of the empire was on display here. The city's rulers and plutocrats had endowed public buildings and monuments to their own and the empire's glory over many centuries. Roma's white marble and gilded paintwork shone in the sun as if it were some heavenly vision, a city on not just one hill, but seven. It was a vast, glittering, yet noisome place, reeking of the humanity pressed into the seemingly endless series of flat blocks that housed the poorer classes. It was also a dangerous city, liable to break into tumult over religion or the races, and one where only the rich with their clients and slaves were truly protected from the almost endemic crime. It was the most exciting city on earth.

*

When the day came to set forth from Mediolanum, Maximus set out with a cavalcade that dwarfed the one that had escorted Elen to visit the holy Martin. The train numbered thousands rather than hundreds and stretched over several miles on the road. As a result, it made slow progress south, which suited Maximus, who had ample time to let himself be seen by the people of his new domain. All along the route, crowds gathered to cheer on their emperor and to lay flowers in his path. At Placentia, they were feasted in a civic reception. The whole town turned out onto the Via Aemelia at Ariminum. From here, the Via Flaminia ran straight as a die to Roma, but progress slowed as the size of the caravan grew, provincial and military officers joining it as it passed, all wanting to be part of what was to happen at their destination. It took over two weeks to make the journey.

There was one final stop, two hours outside the walls of the city, where the procession formed up for the parade that would march to the forum. In the early hours of the new day, they started the final leg of the journey, led by a double line of the standards of all Maximus' Italian units, each regiment's symbols and honours embroidered with gold and silver thread, all their trappings of precious metals. Constantine rode behind these with his entire regiment of *scholae*, the metal of their armour and the tack of their steeds shining with burnished gold, the plumes on their parade helmets flashing blood red in the breeze. They guarded the emperor, whose chariot followed immediately behind them, its sides covered with chased gold panels set with precious stones. Maximus stood next to his charioteer, erect, magnificent in his armour, but with head bare, saluting the troops that lined the road and with raised right arm acknowledging the acclaim of the crowds massed behind them. He was clearly vastly enjoying the unfolding spectacle and the Romans loved him for it. They went wild with their cheers and strewed the procession's way with flowers.

Right in front of the emperor's chariot were the *draconarii*, the standard-bearers, carrying aloft the purple dragon emblems of their cohorts. Close in by their emperor marched tight ranks of *candidati*, their uniforms of brilliant white, their shields highly polished, their task to prevent anyone coming close to their imperial master. Making doubly sure that none would spoil the emperor's great day, a second regiment of *scholae* rode behind the chariot, bringing up the rear of this symphony of gold and silver that flashed and dazzled in the morning sun. Horns and trumpets blasted continuously, piercing the roar of the crowds. The noise along the way was deafening. A quarter of the city, some 250,000 people, had spilled out onto the streets to see their emperor.

The Empress Elen followed, riding in a quieter segment of the parade, her carriage open to the crowd and surrounded by her household slaves. With her sat Magna and her new husband, who had joined her outside the city. The fame of Elen's piety had reached Roma and she was genuinely touched by the warmth of the welcome the people showed her. She allowed herself to smile and wave shyly on both sides. Behind her rode a third regiment of *scholae*.

As they came within sight of the Porta Flaminia, the column was confronted by a mass of dignitaries standing before it, behind whom on a many-tiered stand stood the entire senate, all in white togas and purple stripes. The emperor's column reached the gate, where the city's officers, led by Julian as urban prefect, made obeisance then turned to lead the parade into the city. Julian had spent large sums tidying up the streets, ordering the repainting and repair of its civic buildings, cleaning away the accumulated filth, deporting the beggars. All the streets and steps the column passed had been scrubbed spotlessly clean. Everywhere, marble shone white in the sun.

They marched on through streets closely packed with spectators. Fountains ran with wine at each road junction. On platforms erected in the open spaces along the way, choirs of children formed tableaux, and actors and dancers depicted scenes from the city's history. As the tail of the third regiment of *scholae* entered the gate, the mass of senators fell in behind as the column snaked past the tomb of Augustus and the Campus Martius, headed for the forum.

Finally reaching the heart of the city, the procession threaded its way under the triumphal arch of the Emperor Septimius Severus and entered the Forum Romanum. The emperor was led to the Rostra, the platform at the forum's centre, where he and the empress were shown the view of the vast public edifices that spread all around them, each described in turn by city officials anxious to make their name with the new regime. Then, following the lictors, Maximus and Elen were escorted to the Curia Julia, the seat of the senate. Women could not enter here, so instead Elen was brought to the nearby Basilica Julia by a select group of aristocratic wives, who, over sweetmeats and wine, which Elen refused, vainly attempted to engage the empress in polite conversation.

Alone, now, Maximus entered the senate house. This was one of the oldest buildings in the forum, its exterior unlike its surrounds in that it remained uniquely plain, even ugly. Inside, however, the walls, floors and ceiling gleamed in white marble. Stone benches ran in a semicircle around the walls, a space at one end still showing where once had stood the Altar of Victory and the statue of its goddess. By protocol, Maximus should have been seated between the year's two consuls, whose duty was to preside over the session, but there was no consul then in Roma. The Emperor Valentinian had been made consul this year, but he had just fled. His colleague, Eutropius, had just died in post. So, the emperor presided alongside Julian, who as urban prefect conducted the short business of the day. Symmachus, as the most widely esteemed orator of his generation, delivered a long and flowery panegyric extolling Maximus' character and reciting his achievements. At its end, the senate was unanimous in acknowledging Maximus' rule, their scripted cries of acclamation lasting nearly half an hour.

Maximus spent the day elated, floating on this cloud of adulation. No man, he told himself, so deserved to enjoy such good fortune as he. No other could be so honoured. Even Theodosius had experienced nothing like this. Maximus let himself believe in the shallow words of praise that engulfed his senses and he thanked the senate with genuine warmth. With no sense of what that would come to mean, he pledged his life to the service of the empire.

*

When the grandeur of the day was done, Maximus and Elen were led to the imperial palace on the Palatine Hill, a vast, echoing set of buildings that were kept expensively ready for any emperor who passed through the capital. Although none had lived there permanently for over a century, the palace was still so luxuriously appointed that it made the imperial palaces in Augusta and Mediolanum seem but primitive copies. To Elen's relief, she was taken to a completely separate suite of quarters and left to her own devices with her slaves.

The official *adventus* was over, but the city's welcome to their new lord was not. Over the week that followed, the imperial couple followed a carefully managed programme that took them to visit the key sites of the city and to meet the key figures in its administration and senate. Maximus attended circus races and the games, which he paid for himself. There, he won the favour of the crowds by ensuring that the old Roman rules of combat were followed, thus ensuring so much bloodshed that the spectators went wild. Elen was with her husband for the chariot races but refused to enter the staggeringly huge Coliseum, which was a place of horror to her; she knew that so many of her co-religionists had met their gruesome deaths there and she had no wish to see men kill each other. She therefore feigned exhaustion from the heat and left her husband to enjoy the roars of adulation from the vast crowds that packed the stadium. Her husband's delight in the bloodshed he was paying for made her feel physically sick.

Everything Maximus and Elen saw in Roma was bigger, grander and more beautiful than anything they had ever seen before. There was little, it seemed to them, that was not adorned with gold and silver leaf or semi-precious stones.

Their Christian religion was known to their hosts; nevertheless, they were taken to see the key sites of the old state religion. Maximus had no qualms about this, but Elen's heart was as sore as her feet were made by so much sightseeing. Yet, she could not help standing in awe beneath the massive dome of the Pantheon. There was still much of the old religion in evidence in the city. The sacred flame still burned in the Temple of Vesta, tended by its seven virgin priestesses, although the temple was no longer looking quite so opulent as it once had; Gratian had taken away its state subsidy. The massively columned Temple of Jupiter on the Capitol, the greatest shrine in the empire, remained as magnificent as it had always been. Romans called it a wonder of the world; all else, they said, was like earth compared to heaven.

The splendour of the buildings was matched by the elaborate flattery to which they were subjected everywhere, something that Elen could not appreciate, for she was aware that it hid a condescension and an arrogant contempt. She had expected nothing else and did not mind enough to care. With distaste, she watched her husband absorb more and more of the spurious adulation. Being treated almost as a god day after day soon went to his head and he began to take note of anyone who failed to show what was now his expected level of deference. He marked down a few of those; he told himself that he would make regret those whose attitude he interpreted as arrogance. Symmachus was one.

As their time in Roma drew to a close, Maximus gave audience to Julian to thank him for what he had done for him. He was, for once, genuinely grateful. He knew very well that he was in Julian's debt, not just for the tremendous success of the visit, but also, and more importantly, for the entire outcome of his two usurpations. He sat enthroned in the audience room of the palace and gave audience to the man who had been his partner, but who to Maximus was now standing in his proper place at the foot of the throne.

"Julian," the emperor said, "we thank you for all that you have done for us, both in this our visit to the capital and for your help in making our project succeed. You have done well, and we wish to reward you."

"My lord," replied Julian, "it has been my joy to see your great good fortune unfold. I need nothing from you as a reward save for your gracious favour."

"You are, we know, much out of pocket in your work for us, and we wish at least to ensure that this is recompensed. It is in our mind that we make use of the ill-gotten gains amassed by your predecessor, Symmachus, who, it is now clear to me, has spent the years of his various offices exploiting the people. I intend to have Symmachus brought to justice in your court. If he is found as guilty as I know he will be, it is our intention to turn over his estates and wealth to the disposal of the urban prefect."

"A sound plan, my lord. I doubt that Symmachus has many friends here who would object to such a course."

"Next year," the emperor went on, "we shall need new consuls. I shall, of course, be one, and it is our wish that you join me as the second."

Julian was well satisfied and bowed his way backwards from the audience chamber, vowing as he went his continued support for the emperor, come what may. Everything, he thought, had worked out even better than he had hoped.

*

The *adventus* had proved a massive success. As they rode north to Mediolanum, Maximus thanked all the gods he had ever worshipped, among whom the Christian god was but one, for the fortune that they had bestowed upon him.

His wife, however, had no illusions about what her husband had achieved and what was to come. She thought of nothing now but the perils that she was sure the future would hold. Elen sat in her carriage following in her husband's wake, rigid with apprehension, sure now that her husband's pride would be the prelude to his fall. She could not avoid facing the fact that her husband was a ruthless, calculating, cold-blooded killer. He had proved this again in Roma, where he had spent a fortune shedding blood in the Coliseum, all for his own glory. Full in front of her now, too, stood a truth about herself that she could no longer avoid. She hated Maximus.

She saw him again in her mind's eye, standing proud in his chariot. There had been no slave by his side as he paraded through the streets of Roma, no one to puncture his conceit by whispering in his ear of his inevitable fate. Instead, Elen found herself doing so now. She whispered to herself repeatedly the old words, "*memento mori*", "remember you will die".

Chapter Twenty-five

RETRIBUTION

The clouds that Elen had so feared were now swiftly gathering in the east, a rising darkness that threatened to overshadow any joy or confidence that Maximus could delude himself into enjoying. Fear hung like a pall over the court in Mediolanum. There was a hush throughout the palace. People went about their duties as if holding their breath. Maximus could not avoid seeing it now. The Emperor Theodosius was on the move.

Immediately the news of the usurpation in Italia had reached him, Theodosius had left Constantinopolis to meet the western imperial fugitives at Thessalonica. He knew that the confrontation with his boyhood friend and colleague, one that he had long seen coming, was now unavoidable. He had thrown his protective cloak over the young Emperor Valentinian; Maximus had cast it aside and trampled on it. In his cool assessment of Maximus' character, Theodosius knew that if he were not opposed now, it would only be a matter of time before he marched east. The longer the conflict was delayed, the more powerful Maximus would become. He was sure that he had little option but to face the challenge now.

The eastern emperor reached Thessalonica soon after the dowager empress and her son came ashore. They were in a sorry, bedraggled state, much afflicted by the sea sickness that had plagued them during the journey. The dowager empress broke down in tears before Theodosius and his court. After a few days put aside for them to recover and draw breath, they began a series of meetings in which a plan of action was thrashed out. The fugitives naturally clamoured for Theodosius to march immediately to their aid. The Dowager Empress Justina was beginning to suffer from the illness which she suspected would be fatal and which would indeed go on to kill her within the year. She wanted action now. She used every argument to push Theodosius into action, not appreciating that he had already made up his mind to do so; he was a man who always kept his thoughts close to himself before making any irreversible decision and he was not, he had earlier decided, going to reveal his intents to this overemotional woman now.

Justina was desperate enough to dangle her own daughter under his nose. Theodosius had just lost his first wife, Aelia Flacilla. She had given him two sons, Honorius and Arcadius, so the succession to the empire was seemingly secure, but Theodosius was only forty and had plenty of time to have more children. Justina threw Galla, her unmarried teenage daughter, at his feet. She had thoroughly coached the girl, who dutifully wept piteously over their plight and implored the emperor to reinstate her brother. Theodosius had far too cool a head to be persuadable in such fashion, but Galla was of the imperial house, she was attractive and she was young enough to promise him more sons. He put aside his distaste for her mother's behaviour and decided to marry the girl anyway. Marriage to Galla, he knew, would be seen by the empire as a declaration of war on the usurper, so once he had finally made up his mind, he had the ceremony conducted immediately in the city's basilica and sent out word across the empire that it had taken place.

Now it really did seem to Theodosius that God – to whom he prayed fervently morning and night – had so arranged events that he had the opportunity to march west. Peace had just been concluded with the Persians and for once there seemed no sign of barbarian trouble on the Danubius. Relations with the Gothi were stable; taking large numbers of their fighting men off to war would provide a useful way to occupy them safely. He began to gather his forces. At the same time, to make it clear to the world that it was not he who was the aggressor, he sent several fruitless embassies to Italia to demand the restoration of Valentinian.

Maximus' reaction was predictable. He dismissed the envoys without reply and was first to open hostilities by moving his troops up to the border with Illyricum. He garrisoned the strategic frontier city of Aemona in strength. This lay east of the major city of Aquileia and was still just inside Italian territory, guarding the main road to the fortress of Sirmium on the River Sava, the route likely to be taken by any invader from the east.

Once this was done, Maximus seemed to his council to be for once in a quandary as to what to do next. Theodosius' move had shocked him to his core. The new reality, rather than waking him up like a cold douche, seemed to have stunned him. He was not helped by the fact that his consistory was far from in agreement about what course he should take. Instead of a gathering of cool heads, the council meeting called to debate the options available to them turned out to be a fractious, chaotic meeting that broke down in an acrimony that would prove fatal to his cause.

The emperor's right hand, Andragathius, advocated

following their old policy of acting swiftly, secretly and with deception.

"If we merely await the arrival of Theodosius," Andragathius counselled, "and his highly competent commanders – for Flavius Báuto and Arbogast will be with him – we shall leave him the initiative. More than that, it will ensure that we must fight a set-piece defensive battle, which the considerable number of unreliable elements in our army are very likely to choose not to face. We outnumber Theodosius' forces. I counsel disrupting the eastern army's advance by a swift move into Illyricum. Take large amounts of gold to bribe away their troops, and strike hard and fast, my lord!"

"A counsel that would be a huge and unnecessary gamble, my emperor." Marcellinus had a smooth tongue, well-oiled in the practice of flattery. He poured scorn on what he called Andragathius' "contemptible barbarian reliance on corruption and human weakness". In a flourish of empty words, he doomed his brother. "You, my lord, are the emperor in the stronger position. Bribery is beneath you. Everything you do, lord, should be in accordance with your imperial dignity. The empire is watching you now as never before. Let the weak emperor of the east come and founder on the rock of your firm position. Of course, the army is loyal. They will be unbeatable on a ground of your choosing."

The emperor, although he knew nothing of this, was surrounded at the table by the group of officials and officers that his brother had carefully assembled around him over the past few months. In seemingly independent opinions, all these in turn advised the selection of a static defensive position on the Illyricum border where Theodosius could be defeated. To his chagrin, Andragathius saw that no one was going to support him. The argument flowed away from him and at the end Maximus nodded to his brother.

"Marcellinus, you speak much sense, and the opinion of my council is clear. We shall take your advice. We place the campaign in Illyricum in your hands. Prepare for it now."

The council broke up leaving Andragathius distraught. He, the most accomplished soldier in Maximus' council, had been excluded from influence and his advice spurned. He rightly suspected that he would be left out of planning the campaign altogether. The emperor had placed his fortune in the hands of his brother, a man who knew little of war and had never fought a battle. *Without some miracle of the gods*, Andragathius thought, *we are doomed.*

*

Far away on the other side of Gallia, Prince Conan was just returning to Darioritum from a very enjoyable expedition to destroy a band of Saxon raiders who had been working their way south along the coast towards Armorica. He had come upon them while they were ashore, looting one of the small coastal villages near Erbin's settlements. He had taken their almost unguarded ships, killed their remaining crew, emptied them of their loot, and burned them to the waterline. He then landed his men. The Saxons on the shore had been too busy looting and raping the village women to notice what was happening in the bay. When they saw that they were cornered, they fortified themselves in a stone farmhouse on the edge of the settlement.

Conan loved this sort of engagement. His adrenaline flowed in the heat of battle. This was, he could see, going to be an easy fight. He had the roof of the farmhouse set on fire and as the raiders staggered out of the smoke, he had them cut down, all except two who appeared to be the leaders of the band. These he had crucified on the beams of some of the buildings they had destroyed. He left them on the small jetty as a warning to any of their people trying to repeat their brigandage. Returning their few possessions to the surviving villagers, he put to sea. Satisfyingly, he could hear the screams of the two Saxones writhing on their crosses until his ships rounded the headland at the mouth of the bay.

When he reached base, he was very surprised, and not very pleasantly, to find the small figure of Peblig awaiting him on the quayside. Peblig was his least favourite nephew, a boy with whom he had never bothered much. He had no desire to play uncle to the lad, unlike the boy's siblings, whom he regarded as fine young men, and whose company he enjoyed. He had received no warning that the lad was visiting. Save for the few soldiers of his escort, Peblig was alone.

"Why are you here, boy, and where is your mother?" Conan demanded.

Peblig flinched before this giant of a man, whose tunic had yet to be washed and still bore the blood of the Saxon barbarians he had himself despatched. "I don't know, uncle, I was just told to come and stay with you. No one told me why. Mother sent a message. She is in Mediolanum in Italia."

Conan stalked up the hill to the fort with the disconsolate Peblig trailing behind him. It seemed that the boy had no luggage; all he had to wear was what he had on, and, with what he did have on, he had contrived to look like one of the holy Martin's brothers. Conan despised holy men as much as he hated Scoti and Saxones. In his eyes, they were useless parasites, who bleated about a god that wanted men to turn the other cheek, but who sought power and wealth when they could. He hoped that someone would soon come and relieve him of the boy.

The mystery was solved a few days later when a letter arrived from Prince Gadeon, who had not long had Elen's warning and was working out what to do about it.

"My brother," Gadeon wrote. "Our empress has written that she thinks that her husband, Maximus, is overreaching himself and is provoking the Emperor Theodosius to come down upon him, maybe as early as this year. She warns us to take precautions in case Maximus should fall. She is sending you her son Peblig to protect. Keep him with you until any storm has passed over.

"I am taking steps here to put Owain, Annun, Custennin and Severa out of harm's way.

"Our people have come so far under this emperor and I do not intend that we should lose it all. I am working to keep the princes together in whatever befalls and to make the best arrangements for our people. If I appear to betray any faith in doing this, believe me, brother, it is for the good for which we have all fought these last few years.

"As for you, dear brother, I know you will not desert the post that the emperor has put in your trust. Our people now with you in Letavia look to you to keep them safe. If you are replaced as *dux*, which is almost certain if Maximus falls, you will still be the leader of our people there.

"Warn Erbin and take very good care," the letter concluded.

Conan might have had the reputation of being the brawn to Gadeon's brain, but he was shrewd enough to be well aware of the way fortune could lift up a man then pull him down. He had, from his remote fastness in Armorica, watched what was happening in the empire, and from the moment that Maximus made it clear that he was intent on seizing Italia, Conan had realised that this was a very perilous course. *For me, it is of no real consequence*, he thought. *I have no child to follow me. Erbin is my heir. He and my people here in Letavia are those I must now protect.* Yet he did have some fears, for he could not see how, in the worst case, Elen and Victor could be saved. He had to think this through and be ready.

His first course was to warn Erbin. He got a message to him to sail round to Darioritum and, when his brother arrived, he showed him Gadeon's letter. "Brother, we must be ready for the worst. I want to warn you that all we have achieved here may be at risk. We have to make sure it will not be lost. You are my heir as Prince of the Dumnonii here in Letavia, not just in the mini Dumnonia you have built around Aleto, but also here around Darioritum. I think you will be safe. If Theodosius wants a sacrificial victim here, it will be me. I do not think he will attempt to eject our people. We have a treaty issued by the empire. At the worst, he may appoint another prefect to govern our affairs, but you will be able to manage any officer they send, and the real ruler will be you. So, be prepared to look menacing and make them think twice about attacking us. Build more ships and arm more of your men. Make sure your settlements are defensible. More important than all this, hold Roma to you as your friend.

"One last thing. Keep a ship for our sister, the empress, and her daughters. She may need to be spirited away and fast."

Erbin understood and sailed back north, this time taking Peblig with him, much to Conan's relief. The boy had been moping about the fort and seemed to spend all day saying prayers. *May the gods help us all if that is what we have to rely on*, Conan thought to himself. Aleto was a place to which they were unlikely to come looking for him, and, if they did, there was always a ship to take him away.

*

In Londinium, Gadeon gathered the principal princes of the tribes in his private quarters before the next diocesan council meeting. They were almost all there, for Gadeon had warned them there was an issue that they needed to face together, and by now they knew him well enough to trust his warning. The southerners, the nobles of the Atrebates from Calleva, the Cantiaci from Durovernum and the Belgae from Venta came in together. They tended to act as a group; their interests were similar and they often saw things differently from the princes of the west and north. Their links with Gallia gave them a better idea of what was going on in the empire than that of their fellows from the interior. The northerners were not a group in the same way, having little to do with each other in the normal course of life, but they were all here now, the princes or their representatives of Alt Clut, of the Selgovae, the Novantes and the Votadini. Vitalinus of the Cornovii was pre-eminent among all the princes and was by now a firm ally of Gadeon. They had come to value each other's counsel and generally ensured that they sat next to each other when the council met. Also present was the allied Prince of the Silures. The atmosphere in the room was heavy with apprehension.

"My fellow princes," Gadeon commenced. "I have had disturbing news from Gallia and Italia. It seems that the Fates may be about to end the run of good fortune that has favoured us here and across the water. The emperor, whose rise has lifted us with him, and which seemed set fair to elevate us further, is about to fight the eastern emperor, Theodosius, who will not, it seems, accept the seizure of the Italian throne from Valentinian. There is about to be a civil war."

There was an audible intake of breath in the room. Gadeon went on: "If our emperor is victorious, our good fortune will go forward. If he loses, those close to him are likely to go down with him. There is a danger of the reversal of any arrangements he has made across the empire. We need to act to prevent things going backwards, but to do so without raising suspicion or bringing down upon us the wrath of Theodosius."

As Gadeon looked around the room, he saw some very worried faces but also nods of agreement. So far, so good.

"Our object must be severalfold. We must safeguard our peoples and maintain our self-government. We also need to be able to carry on maintaining our own fleets and troops in the service of Roma. Without these things we shall always be at the mercy of whoever is in power. To achieve these things, we need to retain our position on the council and in the running of the affairs of our island. We must make sure that the officials, our own people whom we have been appointing recently, are not purged.

"The difficult thing is to see how to do all this. I do not, alas, see that we can succeed in any open opposition. We do, though, have some cards to play. What we have done so far has in no sense been treasonous. We have acted in the service of Roma. We can offer to continue this service to whomsoever comes out on top. I do not think that Theodosius will have the time or the interest to pick off any or all of us, but if we see any sign of that, it would, in my view, be time to remind him that by continuing the current arrangements he will ensure a peaceful and loyal province. Were he to prefer to overthrow it all, he would be faced with the united opposition of those who are now keeping these provinces safe. If we stick together, and do so loyally, peacefully and reasonably, we can keep our position and, more to the point, keep our heads."

There was much talk after Gadeon had finished. The southerners and Vitalinus felt very exposed. Their neighbours were not going to be of any use to them in any crisis. It was all very well for those whose lands were at the fringes to take a robust line, but the administration was really only interested in what went on in the cities and left the rest to the military. Gadeon agreed. The tribes had to stick together. They could all agree on that, and at the last the room swore unanimously on the course Gadeon had proposed. Gadeon also emphasised to them the need to keep the army on side.

The army command, currently loyal to Maximus, would be facing similar dilemmas. Somehow, the soldiers had to be made to understand that by working together with the tribes, they might just keep the Furies at bay. Gadeon promised to reach out to the two current counts and the duke after the council session.

He was not sure that any of this was going to work. If Theodosius was an old-style emperor prepared to crush an entire world under his boot, they were probably all doomed. If, however, he was as sharp an operator as Gadeon thought he very well might be, and a Christian into whose ear the Bishop of Milan would be whispering, then there might, just might, be a safe way out of this for them all.

Chapter Twenty-six

SISCIA

Once he had made up his mind to act, the eastern emperor Theodosius moved swiftly. His force set out from Thessalonica, moving north into Macedonia in high summer, heading for the great fortress of Sirmium in Pannonia.

Theodosius was well aware that he was taking a huge risk. His army was outnumbered and at the disadvantage of operating far from his home base; Maximus' army was more numerous and on home ground. However, he knew that the Army of Italia was faction-ridden and riven by religious argument. Much of it had never forgiven Maximus for overthrowing Valentinian, who was now rumoured to be returning with Theodosius. Many of its officers resented what had been done at Novara. Others were unreliably venal; Maximus had proved this himself by bribing them to bend with his wind, and winds can blow in many directions. Theodosius took with him all the gold he had.

The Army of the East was not a homogeneous force. The emperor had been forced to leave many of his regular troops to garrison the east, to watch the Danubius and the Persian frontier. What Theodosius did have were thousands of Gothi, warriors still under their own chiefs, tribesmen whom he had fought to a standstill in Thracia. He had won their respect and they would fight for him. He had made sure of their antipathy to Maximus by informing them that it was he who had sold so many of their people into slavery in Moesia. It was he, so the Gothi were told, who had caused so many deaths and so much destruction. They were now out for his blood. Maximus might try to tempt them with gold, but this time he would find that he could not buy the loyalty of those who wanted him dead.

There was little difference in the quality of the two emperors as soldiers. Maximus had spent his life fighting border wars against unsophisticated barbarian enemies. When faced with regular Roman forces he had won his battles by politics and corruption. He had not, even once, fought a pitched battle. Theodosius had spent seven years fighting the Gothi inside the empire in a war of manoeuvre and occasionally in battle, but he had not distinguished himself in the field; he was not made from the same mould as his illustrious father. The Gothi had beaten him several times in battle and had only started to come to terms with him when forces lent to him by Gratian had driven them out of Thracia.

Where the Army of the East held the advantage was in its leading generals. Flavius Bauto was a skilful soldier who had learnt his trade under the old Valentinian and had fought all over the empire, most recently in the area to which they were headed. He held the respect of his soldiers. Arbogast was not much his inferior, and in his case burned with a desire to revenge himself on the man who had ejected him from his command of the Army of Italia. Maximus had a similarly skilful general on his side, as he always had done, but Andragathius was out of favour and for this campaign he had been marginalised. In his place, Maximus was placing reliance upon his brother, a mediocrity with no experience of war. News of this had reached the east, and Theodosius hoped that this would give him a telling advantage.

*

To worsen his brother's prospects even further, Marcellinus had managed by intrigue to engineer a foolish scheme to get his rival Andragathius out of the way completely. Intelligence had been received that the dowager empress, with, they thought wrongly, the young Emperor Valentinian, had embarked and was at sea, heading west from Thessalonica to cross the Adriatic. Despite the clear impossibility of intercepting ships whose location was unknown, and which could land anywhere along the whole coastline of Italia, Marcellinus persuaded the emperor to send Andragathius in the tiny fleet then available at Aquileia, some half a dozen ill-equipped ships, to sail the length of the Adriatic to apprehend the imperial party.

Andragathius fell into despair. He knew that this was a wild goose chase. He obeyed, as he had to, and took the only course that held any chance at all of succeeding, which was to sail to the seas off the port of Brundisium, the most likely point of entry to the foot of Italia, in the hope of intercepting the dowager empress there. He knew enough about Marcellinus to know that he was no match for Theodosius or any of his generals. Andragathius was now more than ever sure that they were all doomed.

*

Within a month, the Army of the East reached Sirmium. On receipt of this news, Maximus was at last stirred to move his forces into Illyricum. He marched his troops as far as the town of Siscia on the River Sava but went no further, instead choosing a strong position there to prevent his opponent crossing the river. Just outside the town, three river systems joined in a convoluted series of bends, loops and lakes, giving cover on three sides to a force defending the crossings. He sited his army to straddle the road to the west. This ran through hilly and wooded territory, making it hard to bypass, or so Maximus thought. It seemed to the emperor that this was as strong a position as he could find. He did not, therefore, move his army any further forward and he failed to deploy scouts deep into eastern territory.

Theodosius was thus left the initiative and he cleverly distracted the western army by dividing his force into three. Two detachments marched up the Sava, one led by himself and the other by his principal general, the *magister militum* Bauto. The other column, under Arbogast, made its way up the River Drava on a more northerly but parallel route. When news of this reached Maximus late in the day, he weakened his strength at Siscia by detaching part of his force to the north, placing it under the command of his brother Marcellinus, who was ordered to hold a position at the town of Poetovio. This was not a position that had been selected for defence, but it was another site, a legionary fortress, that guarded a crossing of a river, this on the main road to the north of Pannonia.

*

On the night of his arrival in Siscia, Maximus slept fitfully and in the small hours of the night the vision that had haunted him in Britannia came to him once again. Only this time it was different. He was back on the same dais, looking at the same sea of faces, but now they stared at him with suspicion or derision. None would meet his eyes. Britannia was there in his dream, he could feel it, but it was a far-off speck on a distant horizon, and at that a pang of homesickness and loss hit him. Elen was not there, and he knew she was the only prize in his life that had been worth winning, but that somewhere he had lost her. He looked for her in the crowd, but she was missing. He was bereft.

What was there was the heavy, turbulent darkness that had threatened him before, only this time it was gushing forth from within him. He tried to close his mouth to hold it in, but the darkness kept spewing out until it enveloped everything. Nothing could hold back its foul torrent. At last, when there was nothing but utter darkness, there was a flash of silver, a sword, and he woke drenched in sweat and fearing for his life.

*

The Army of Italia drew up its positions outside Siscia behind newly constructed banks of earth, topped with wooden ramparts and fronted by a series of ditches and pits containing stakes and fire traps. They covered the main approaches across the Sava and demolished the bridge. Maximus deployed his forces with one of his flanks on the river and another on a swamp that led into it. It seemed to him a very strong position, but its defect was that it was so constricted that it gave little room for manoeuvre so that the cavalry, in reserve in the rear, could not attack from either flank.

Constantine was with his unit close to the centre of the position, in the second line in front of the location where Maximus had placed his standard. He had little faith in their success in the forthcoming engagement. His troops would fight to the death, he was confident, as would the other two regiments of *scholae* who were drawn up in front of his own unit, but he regarded the rest of the army as a disaffected, venal rabble who would be thinking solely of their own advantage in the coming fight. He doubted that they were up to fighting a set-piece battle; they were more likely to make a run for it on first contact. All he could do was to ensure that his regiment prepared their position as best they could, so he spent the few days they had left sharpening his men up and adding to the defences to their front.

*

When Theodosius reached Siscia, he had already had the land reconnoitred and had prepared pontoons and small boats for his men to cross the river. He had no intention of launching his poorly trained and inexperienced force in a frontal assault across it. Instead, in darkness, he marched his troops south to a crossing site that had been left unguarded and foolishly unwatched. Bauto's detachment marched around the north to do the same. They both crossed the river unopposed that night.

Before sunrise the next day, the still of the morning was broken by the sudden roar of the eastern army's artillery opening up across the river against Maximus' centre. Both stones and ballista bolts began to tear into the front ranks, where men began to fall immediately. Across the still dark sky fire darts poured in onto the massed ranks. Tents and other combustible material began to burn, and sparks from these fires ignited the fire pits in front of the lines. Smoke soon enveloped much of the centre, so that it became hard to make out what was happening. Maximus concluded that his enemy was intent on breaking his centre and ordered his men to stand fast, which they did, although they began to take heavy casualties, unable to respond effectively to the fire from the arrows and slingshots coming in from across the river.

As the sun rose upon the confused but still strong position, the terrible sound of bugles from both flanks revealed to

Maximus and his men that the attack on his centre was a feint. To his horror, it soon became clear that his enemy was on his side of the river and in strength. He had placed his least reliable troops on his flanks, and, just as Constantine had predicted, these broke at the first contact, fleeing in terror from the swords and axes of the Gothi who launched themselves against their lines, screaming their war cries, exulted by bloodlust. Within minutes, the Italians on the right flank were in full flight, streaming back towards the centre, heading for the road west, which was the only way of escape. Panic ensued as they spread across the field. As the Gothi turned each unit of the Army of Italia in turn, the troops broke and fled in headlong flight to the rear. The day was already lost and seeing this, the cavalry waited for no further order, galloping off to the rear in disorderly flight and riding down any of their own infantrymen who got in their way.

Only in the centre was the fighting fierce. The three *scholae* regiments wheeled about to face Theodosius' men and stood shield to shield with their backs to the river, forming three sides of a square with their emperor within. Refusing to surrender, they fought bitterly, showered from what was now their rear by missiles from Theodosius' engines and archers on the other bank; any troops who could have replied to this barrage had by now fled. The Gothi came in fast, breaking the front ranks of the *scholae* on the right. They were careless with their lives, drunk with alcohol and seeking to reach the emperor, whose standard they could see behind the lines that were giving way before them. Yet the line was replaced and held, and the few Gothi who were left of the first onrush ran back into the trees.

Constantine, seeing that there was still a little time left to do something before a total disaster ensued, galloped up to the emperor, who was sitting motionless on his horse, saying nothing.

"My lord, we must break out. If we stand here we shall all perish. The enemy has yet to come up on the left. There is still a gap there through which we might withdraw."

The emperor gave no reply. Constantine saw to his horror that he was wasting his breath. He could see that Maximus no longer had any part in what was going on around him. The darkness that had spewed out of his soul had enveloped everything around him. He was utterly unmanned. Of a sudden, without a word to Constantine or any of his staff, the emperor spurred his horse in the direction Constantine had indicated and fled, followed as fast as they could ride by the officers of his staff. To Constantine's dismay, they disappeared, trailed by a cloud of dust that hung briefly between the trees.

With disgust, Constantine acted to save the lives of his regiment. He ordered his men to lay down their arms and surrender, and his action was repeated down the line as the other units of *scholae* realised they had been abandoned and betrayed. Slowly, as word of Maximus' desertion spread and as Theodosius' command to stop further slaughter reached even the Gothi, the fighting stopped.

*

On the next day, at Poetovio, most of the Italian force melted away before Arbogast and his men, who smashed the few who remained loyal to Marcellinus and killed him.

Chapter Twenty-seven

THE ROAD OUTSIDE AQUILEIA

The plan of static defence that Maximus had allowed his brother and his consistory to persuade him to adopt had been a disaster. How he now regretted letting them push Andragathius away. His old comrade was now so far away that he was totally out of reach. He had, in fact, no idea at all where his faithful lieutenant was. All he knew was that he could not recall him to his side.

Maximus found himself alone. He had lost everything. All that was left in him was the fear of capture. Those few staff officers who had stayed with him could see that the shock had paralysed him mentally. His hands had started to shake so violently that he could only with difficulty mount his horse. The fear inside him began to affect those around him and those who could began to make themselves scarce.

The emperor's last and only decision had been to flee and to continue to flee as far away from the battlefield as he could get. With only his small group of *candidati* bodyguards and some staff officers, he had spurred his horse on the road back to Aemona. It was there that he heard that his brother, too, had met with disaster and was dead. Pausing no longer, not stopping to find out whether any of the forces he had placed on the Sava had survived, he rode on as far as Aquileia. Here he shut himself up in the fortress with its few garrison troops. The scent of death was upon him. Slowly, his entourage began to steal away, their only thought now to save themselves from the wreck.

Emperor now in name but little else, Maximus had no idea what to do, save to shut himself up in his quarters. The meagre forces which remained in Aquileia were too few to hold the city, and, seeing their demoralised officers abandoning their posts, the men began to trickle away. In desperation, Maximus sought to fall back on the tactic he had used successfully in the past, to sway men's minds with bribery, but he had precious little gold left to disburse and none of it was in Aquileia. He sent an urgent message to Julian in Roma to send him aid. No reply came.

He would never again get a response from anyone in the capital. The city fathers knew that his luck had left him and with it his power. The city was in a state of panic. It was only a few months since the senate had lavished praise and hospitality upon the man whose cause, it was now clear, was collapsing before the might of the eastern emperor. As soon as the news of the battle at Siscia came in, leading figures began to trim. No one in the capital, it now seemed, was, or ever had been, a supporter of this illegitimate usurper; instead, they had all been waiting loyally for the hoped-for return of their legitimate lord, Valentinian.

Julian, still clinging to his post as urban prefect, was anything but a fool and had seen the way the wind was blowing before the rest, for he had, as usual, received the earliest intelligence. He had so far not been identified as being the financier who had enabled Maximus to take power and he wanted that state of affairs to continue. He was desperate not to be included in what he could see was the downfall to come. He joined those in the senate who now sent messages and sureties of their loyalty to Theodosius. So, when it came, Maximus' plea for gold fell on deaf ears. Julian sent no gold north to Aquileia and instead instructed his firm's agents to have no more dealings with any part of Maximus' regime. They were also instructed to destroy any written records of what they had done. Julian rapidly began to cover his tracks.

*

On the field of battle, Theodosius took the surrender of the surviving troops of the Army of Italia. He had instructed Arbogast to do the same at Poetovio. He wanted as little bloodshed as was necessary to secure power in the west. There was a vital need to preserve Roman military manpower, so he ordered the absorption of the units of his enemy into his own force. He had a soldierly admiration for those who had done their duty and fought, although he took no chances on their loyalty and relieved the senior officers among them of their duties. These men he had brought before him now, disarmed and on their knees in the dust at his feet. In the noisome aftermath of battle, while the air still resounded with the cries of the wounded and dying and the fires still burned across the devastated landscape, the emperor sat before his tent and questioned those who had surrendered, Constantine among them. He replied to Theodosius' questions bravely and honestly and made it plain to the emperor that he had saved both his and Theodosius' men from any more needless bloodshed by ordering a surrender when Maximus fled. Theodosius could not but be impressed at the sight of his civic crown. Although Constantine was relieved of the command of his regiment, the emperor took neither his life nor his rank. He and his fellow officers were asked for their word that they would take no further part in the war, then were placed under arrest in their tents.

The fleeing remnants of the Army of Italia were pursued by Flavius Bauto as far as Aemona. The general had been ordered by Theodosius to capture rather than kill the stragglers that his troops found in his path. His emperor had no wish to further deplete imperial forces by slaughtering prisoners and in any case was actively employing a policy of mercy and reconciliation rather than punishment. Bauto did not have good intelligence of what forces Maximus had left to deploy against him, so decided against taking the obvious route west along the coastal road. Instead, he marched north to the town of Virunum in Noricum, then swung west through the passes of the Alpe Iulia. Although, before he had been sent off to sea, Andragathius had suggested that precautions be taken to guard the passes, no troops had been placed there, so Bauto's troops marched through unopposed. Once clear of the mountains, the road south was open. Bauto led his men down off the mountains and marched through the plain, empty of opposition all the way to Aquileia.

When Theodosius' forces reached the city, Maximus was still holed up inside, in a catatonic state of fear. Had he had any wits left to him at all, he should have long ago headed west to escape and rally his forces, but he had given no orders and made no plans. When it became clear that Bauto was about to besiege the city, what was left of the garrison mutinied and surrendered. To save their skins, their remaining officers thought to hunt down their emperor and hand him over. They broke into the imperial chambers to discover Maximus handing out the remaining gold in the treasury to the Moroccan cavalry, whom he was, all too late, trying to persuade to ride with him to Mediolanum. The Africans, however, could see the way things had turned out; they simply took the gold and left, indicating to the mutineers that they could do as they liked with their erstwhile emperor. Maximus was dragged out into the courtyard, chains were put on his arms and legs, and he was bundled into the back of a farm cart to be driven ignominiously out of the city gate, crowds of people jeering him as he went. He was thrown into a shed in a nearby farm.

*

Theodosius did not arrive for some days, during which Maximus was not ill-treated. The emperor wanted him dealt with publicly and by legal means. Although there were voices in his retinue that were for killing him on the spot, the emperor intended that Maximus be tried according to Roman law and in a fashion that would reverberate across the empire. He took the time to assemble a formal tribunal, for which he had a dais erected on the plain at the third milestone east of Aquileia. It was a place where the whole army could be drawn up to watch the spectacle. A lesson was to be taught to any who might again be tempted to challenge imperial authority.

At the time appointed for the trial, Maximus was brought before the tribunal, shorn of all his robes and marks of office, with the shackles still on his wrists and ankles. His days in captivity had not been good to him. He had shrunk visibly in stature and now looked like an old man. His clothes were dirty and his beard was unshaven. When he stood before the tribunal, he looked around himself wearily, seemingly bereft of hope. A sea of cold, stony faces gazed back at him on three sides, men in their thousands, not only of the regiments of the Army of the East, but also of the Army of Italia, men whom he had abandoned on the battlefield. In front of him was the dais, and at its feet was a line of the officers whom he had left to their fate and whom Theodosius had pardoned. Directly in front of him he saw Constantine. Maximus was cut to the quick in shame and could not look at him.

Theodosius and his young co-Augustus, Valentinian, mounted the dais and sat in the seats of judgement. It was not a very long trial. Evidence was adduced to the fact that Maximus had ordered the killing of the Emperor Gratian, the counts Merobaudes and Vallio, that he had overthrown the lawful Emperor Valentinian, that he had sought to kill that emperor and his mother, and that he had ordered the sack of Novara. Maximus could not refute these charges. There was none there to speak for him or to plead for mercy on his behalf. Given the chance to speak, he could think of little to say.

"What I did, I did to protect the empire," he whispered.

"Speak so that we can hear what you say, Maximus," ordered his chief judge. "You have this last chance to justify what you did."

Maximus rallied slightly and repeated what he had said so that Theodosius could hear him. "I could see," he went on, "the danger that was coming from across the frontier, and I wanted to prevent it." In a last attempt to cause dissension among his judges, he summoned the strength to look directly at Valentinian. "I saw that God wanted me to cleanse our empire of the stain of Arian heresy that had infected its rulers." Valentinian flinched and glanced at his senior colleague, but Theodosius looked straight ahead and said nothing.

All that Maximus had left now was a personal appeal to his boyhood friend. "I acted to avenge your father. Count Theodosius was the best, the most magnificent officer I ever served under. He brought me up in Hispania just as if he were my father. He paid for me to be educated and to be commissioned into the army, just as he did for you. He looked after my career in Britannia and Africa. He found me two wives, both of whom I loved. He was murdered by Gratian and his officers. I wanted revenge, and to honour his name I killed his murderers."

Whether or not this attempt to justify what he had done might have touched Theodosius or even saved Maximus' life was never to become clear, for there was one charge that Maximus still attempted to deny. "I believed that because of your father's murder you would consent to the death of Gratian. I believed that you would support my replacing him. You recognised me as Augustus. That is why I proclaimed that I had your support and why I claim still that you supported me in what I did."

There was a kernel of truth here, a kernel that was uncomfortable for the eastern emperor to acknowledge. For the sake of expediency, Theodosius had indeed been forced to acknowledge Maximus' usurpation. That fact now had an effect the exact opposite of that which Maximus seemed to be hoping, for it had become a matter of honour for Theodosius to make Maximus admit that his proclamation had been lies.

"You were never encouraged by us to murder your lawful sovereign, to usurp his throne or to attempt to overthrow my colleague Valentinian," shouted Theodosius loudly enough that he could be heard across the regiments. "You will admit this."

Maximus shook his head.

"You are guilty of all the charges against you," responded Theodosius. "Your sentence for your murderous treason is death. But if you do not confess that you lied that we supported you in your infamy, we shall have no recourse but to make that death so slow that you will plead to end the agony, and you will confess before you die. It is not our inclination to use torture, but your actions and the false proclamations you made involved the intended death of two emperors, and that means that the law allows us the use of torture. Confess that you lied."

Maximus again shook his head. Theodosius waved his hand at the waiting executioner, who tied Maximus to the post erected behind the place where he stood. He was stripped of his remaining clothes. Theodosius again gave him the chance to admit that he had lied. When Maximus once more refused, he nodded to the soldier standing by with a metal-tipped scourge. The lash fell in regular strokes, each timed to let Maximus begin to appreciate the pain before the next fell. The torture was bloody, the scourge cutting deep cuts into his back and sending gobbets of skin and muscle flying with each stroke.

After five strikes, Theodosius stopped the flogging, and once again asked Maximus to confess his lie. No answer came.

"We shall not ask again until you give a sign that you confess. You will not be allowed to die until you acknowledge that you lied. The length of your death is now in your hands."

The flogging continued until the blood that flowed down Maximus' legs had collected in small red pools in the sand at his feet. The blows came regularly now. Maximus writhed in agony and began to scream at each cut.

The end came when Maximus realised that there was only one way to end his torment. He could no longer speak, instead raised a hand to the tribunal. Theodosius halted the flogging and had water thrown to revive him. "Speak, then, finish this."

Maximus was revived enough to find words through his pain. "I lied," he whispered. "I needed that lie to persuade the army to support me. You did not give me leave to kill Gratian or to come into Italia."

Theodosius looked with contempt at his old comrade and childhood friend. "Your confession of that lie will be promulgated in the empire from east to west," he said. Then he nodded to the executioner, who pulled the bloodied Maximus to his knees in front of the tribunal. He lifted his sword and Maximus' head fell at their feet.

Chapter Twenty-eight

MAGNUS MAXIMUS' DREAM

There was no sign of the ships bringing the Dowager Empress Justina back to Italia. Andragathius spent a frustrating and utterly wasted couple of months at sea sailing back and forth off Brundisium. At last, needing supplies, he ordered his small fleet to put into port, only to learn that Maximus was already dead and that the local governor had pledged loyalty to Valentinian. Andragathius realised that all was lost. He was the man who had murdered the Emperor Gratian. There would be no mercy for him, a barbarian general. He had the small flotilla put out once more to sea, instructed the senior *navarchus* to return to his duties in Aquileia, then tied a weight to his belt and slipped out of history into the sea.

*

Now all that remained to the world was to await whatever settlement Theodosius was going to impose. The senate did not tarry to find out. They passed a decree of *damnatio memoriae* against Maximus, wiping his name from the record, and sent a fawning embassy to Mediolanum to pledge their undying support for the new regime. All the images of Maximus that had been erected in Roma were destroyed. In this, they were only just ahead of the eastern imperial authorities, which shortly thereafter ordered the eradication of all the statues and memorials of Maximus that had been erected across the empire. A new list of key appointments in the west followed.

Julian found himself replaced as urban prefect by an old supporter of Valentinian named Sextus Aurelius Victor. Fearing for his future, but still aware that his part in the conspiracies was unknown, he rapidly removed himself from Roma and disappeared into his estates in Gallia. He was lucky that Theodosius had set his face against launching a purge, so that his connections with Maximus were left unexplored. The emperor chose to forgive men who were even more eminent turncoats than he, the principal of whom was Symmachus, who, at the fall of Maximus, had fled into sanctuary to avoid arrest on a charge of treason. He was surprised to find himself pardoned. His grovelling apology was judged sufficient, partly because he was able to provide evidence that Maximus had initiated an action to prosecute him for corruption. Two years later, totally forgiven, he would even be elevated to the consulship.

It was only those considered beyond official redemption who faced the ultimate sanction. Arbogast was despatched into Gallia to hunt down Maximus' heir, the Augustus Victor. He found him still in the palace at Augusta; the boy was strangled. The emperor had particular contempt for the soldiers who had betrayed Maximus. The Moorish cavalry who had abandoned him in Aquileia had not got far and had run into Theodosius' troops in the cordon around the city; they had been disarmed and imprisoned. The emperor had them all beheaded.

Others were treated with deliberate leniency. Officers who had been in posts that would bring them close to either of the surviving emperors, for instance in the bodyguard or units of the *scholae*, were simply posted out. Constantine had already lost his command, so he felt himself very lucky indeed when he was posted back to Britannia as prefect commanding the *ala secundae asturum*, a cavalry wing at Cilurnum on the Wall. This was a demotion in terms of status, but it had the double compensation of taking him back to Britannia and of bringing him once again close to Gerontius. Their units, he found when he arrived in the north, were near neighbours. He could well consider himself fortunate to have both survived the battle on the Sava and to have come out of the wreck so very much intact.

Theodosius' last piece of business in Aquileia was to send back to Gallia and Britannia the remaining troops which Maximus had brought into Italia. All went home, except, that is, for the Segontienses. He addressed them personally on parade and told them that, for the crimes they had committed in Novara, they would never be allowed home. Instead, they would serve on the Danubius frontier fighting barbarians until the end of their service and then would be allowed to settle there. Pulcher he had brought to his knees before his men and beheaded on the spot.

*

In Mediolanum, the Empress Elen was still in the palace, where she had been left behind by her husband. When he marched east, Maximus had not sought to bid her a private farewell, nor, since then, had he sent her any message. She had to gain what little information there was to hear from the consistory at court. She had no illusions about what was going to happen, and when she was informed of her husband's death, she evinced no emotion, simply put on mourning and waited for Theodosius to arrive.

The emperor reached the city within two weeks of the execution and came to visit her in the palace. He had never met Elen, but word of her piety and simplicity had reached him in the east. He entered her quarters alone and did her the courtesy of bowing.

"Do not get up, lady," he commanded, as Elen began to rise from her couch by the window. He smiled gently. "I would very much like the privilege of talking to one who has known the holy Martin."

Elen could not help showing her surprise. She had resigned herself to this interview and had always imagined the worst. She no longer cared what happened to her, but she was determined to do what she could to ensure the safety of her family. If she had to grovel and plead to achieve this, then grovel and plead she would. Now, though, the man she had feared and whom she was prepared to placate was talking to her of her faith. More than that, he talked of the man she most admired in the whole world.

"He has become the guiding light of my life, Lord Theodosius. He is the most Christian man I have ever met."

"I have met many Christian prelates but none, I think, as truly holy as they tell me that Martin is. Tell me how you came to know him."

So, Elen told the emperor the stories of how Martin had come to Augusta and how she had stayed in his monastery, while Theodosius sat on the couch beside her and watched the light shine from her beautiful eyes. He was deeply touched. As Elen ended her tale, he took her hand. "My lady," he said, "I am sorry for your husband's death. I cannot deny that I ordered it, but I did so with a heavy heart. Maximus and I were once friends. We served together in your homeland. I had not forgotten our comradeship, and I do not forget it now. I intend you and your family no harm. I shall send you and your daughters home."

Elen felt a huge weight lift from her shoulders. She bent her head and wept.

"You have daughters with you here, I am told," went on Theodosius. "I would like them educated in the true faith, so that when they marry, they may spread the Gospel. I have given orders that a sum be set aside to provide for this."

"You are more than generous, lord," Elen replied. "I thank you. I shall take the younger, Gratiana, home to Britannia, but the elder, Magna, has just married the senator Ennodius in Roma."

"No matter, I shall have this done there, too. When you reach Britannia, no harm will come to you, but I must ask that you take no part in any politics when you are there. I seek the peace of the empire and we must have no more dissension."

"You have my word, emperor, I have seen enough politics and bloodshed for a lifetime. What I really want to do is to spread Martin's good news, to bring our faith to our people, who mostly still live in darkness."

"Then we have the same aim, my lady. I intend to make this empire one in God's image. I shall say nothing more of this to you now, but believe me, this is my life's work, and one day you will watch what I shall do. You shall leave tomorrow. I wish you a safe journey home and a good life. I am very glad that we have met, but we shall not meet again."

Theodosius rose, bowed once more and left. He was as good as the word he had given Elen, who was escorted with Gratiana and all her personal goods in a caravan that was to take her to the coast and a ship. Before she left, the emperor prevented Maximus' head being exposed in the city. After her departure, it was stuck on a pole at the gate, and after a few months it was sent around the western provinces until it finally reached Carthago, where it was left to slowly rot away over the next fifty years.

There was much, now, that had fallen to Theodosius to accomplish. Immediately, he proscribed sacrifices and divination. Two years later, he prohibited all pagan worship, even in private. The temples were finally closed.

Earlier emperors had found running the entire empire an impossible task for one man, which is why for a hundred years there had usually been at least two co-emperors reigning jointly. Now, however, Theodosius exercised sole power from Persia to Scotland. Valentinian was still only seventeen, too young to cope with rule, so he was packed off to the town of Vienna, just south of Lugdunum in Gallia, which was now designated the new imperial capital of the west. Augusta Treverorum was reckoned to be too far from the east and too close to the German frontier; never again would it house a legitimate imperial throne. The dowager empress died almost as soon as her son was restored, so to keep Valentinian from creating trouble, Theodosius placed with him the *magister militum* Arbogast. After over a year in Mediolanum, Theodosius finally returned to the east.

His departure tolled the death knell of the teenage Emperor Valentinian II. Within three years of establishing his seat at Vienna, he was dead, murdered by his general Arbogast, whom he had petulantly attempted to dismiss. Arbogast soon regretted his hasty deed. To try to give his act legitimacy, he claimed that the youth had committed suicide. He was forced to set up a puppet emperor named Eugenius, and so became the first barbarian general to grasp that his control of the Roman military might allow him to control the Roman state. It did him no good, for Theodosius came back to the west and killed him too. His evil deed was a sorry precedent for much that was to follow.

*

It came as no surprise to Conan when he learned that a cohort of regular troops was within hours of arriving in Darioritum. He had entertained no illusions about his future when the news of Maximus' failure reached Armorica. He had already made arrangements for Erbin to succeed him and had prepared his people for his demise. A warrior's death had always been what he wanted; there was no way he was going to grow old and feeble like his uncle, Eudaf. He had enjoyed his life immensely and it was now ending. By the time the arrest party arrived at the gates of the fort, he had sent all the people closest to him, including his warband, away by sea. He sat watching the tribune in command detailing off his men to search him out. Pre-empting them, he took his sword and strode out of the gate. So astonished was the tribune that he did nothing until Conan's sword sliced through his throat. Coming to life too late, the troops fell upon the Briton, who took several more of them with him as he succumbed to their blows. So died Conan, the *mare dux*, who would go down to legend as Conan Meriadoc, the first of his line to rule the British in Armorica.

No one in Gallia seemed to think it a good idea to seek the destruction of Erbin, who now succeeded to rule his people from Aleto. Theodosius had never heard of him, and the provincial administration preferred to do nothing to overturn Maximus' dispensation. Why cause trouble, after all? The land had been empty and much of it barren. The British were a people imperially recognised there and they had already proved that they were a good defence against Saxon raiders. So, they and their small colony of Bretona in Galaecia were left in peace, and both the princes Gadeon and Erbin saw to it that the trickle of immigrants continued to cross the sea.

*

In Prince Gadeon's mind there was, however, no point in taking chances with the surviving members of the imperial family. As soon as Elen and her daughter reached Britannia, Gadeon had them swiftly spirited away, firstly to Dumnonia then to the protection of his men still stationed in Segontium. They were joined there by Peblig, who had been smuggled out of Armorica on one of Erbin's ships. Segontium was an unlikely place for anyone to look for an empress, and it was under Gadeon's own control. Were any imperial party intent on their arrest or murder to try to reach it, they would be spotted long before they arrived and their quarry could be whisked away.

In any case, although sensible, the plan was to prove unnecessary. Theodosius' policy of mercy was followed in Britannia. A new vicar was sent to take over from Desiderius, who, though tainted by his association with Maximus, was allowed to retire without penalty. The new man was a Gaul, who was interested only in restoring legitimate imperial authority and not in causing unnecessary trouble, and he desisted from searching for anyone close to Maximus. Wisely, he accepted the increased roles which Maximus had delegated to the princes and their peoples, and he came to rely upon the good counsel of princes Gadeon and Vitalinus.

As a precaution, it seemed to Gadeon that it would be advantageous for the diocese to show signs of its devotion to the legitimate imperial authorities and, in particular, to the Emperor Theodosius. Gadeon had no personal interest in religion, but he was well aware of the emperor's devout orthodox Christianity. Like they were in much of the empire, British Christians were riven by faction and theological argument. What better way to gain Theodosius' favour, as well as to show him that the island was not the backwater the rest of the empire thought it, than the establishment of a Christian college of orthodox theology. This was something of which, to date, there had been in Britannia a total lack. All Christian teaching and the preparation of priests had so far been conducted in small schools run by bishops in the major cities.

The idea of a college had arisen in Gadeon's mind during a conversation with his sister, who was at that point, as usual, both extolling her faith and praising the piety and mercy of the emperor. Gadeon took up the idea and persuaded the council to fund the building and staffing of a college to be named after Theodosius. It was to be situated in the lands of the Silures, near their capital, Venta, a site chosen as it was in the most civilised of the lands under princely control. The college was established and soon teaching staff were appointed from Gallia and Italia. Christians came to study there from all the cities of the diocese. Whether Theodosius was pleased or no, there was no way of knowing, but it could only have helped in ensuring that before he went back to Constantinopolis for a second time, he left Britannia well and truly alone.

*

It seemed that it was only Gadeon who was left with any good fortune after the passing of Maximus' grand schemes. Within two years, Erbin too was dead, slain by Saxon raiders whose ships he had encountered at sea. Erbin, like Conan, had no son, so Gadeon took up the rule of his people on both sides of the water, ruling Armorica under the name Gradlon. He ruled carefully and, whilst never loved, was greatly admired, so much so that he went down in history as Gradlon Mawr, Gradlon the Great.

One of the means by which he secured his place in the legends of his people was an unexpected one. Before he went back to Gallia for a second time, Maximus had entrusted him with guardianship of his money, which he had deposited in the name of the empress in several of the principal temples in Londinium. At the time, Gadeon had no idea just how much gold and silver had been placed there. Immediately on his receipt of the news of Maximus' death, he had withdrawn all of this wealth. He was staggered by how much Maximus had accumulated, but he planned to ensure that Elen and her children would have it. She wanted none of it. When she and the children reached Britannia, she told Gadeon that the money was tainted and abhorrent to her. Adamant that she wished from now on to live as simply as she had as a girl, she gave it all to Gadeon to use for their people. The money made him one of the richest men in Britannia. After he had taken steps behind the scenes to ensure that Elen and all her children had access to enough of it to live on, he used the vast majority of it to buy land, ships and armaments. Ironically, it paid for a good part of the College of Theodosius, and so boosted his standing among his peers, who were thus no longer faced with paying their share of its cost. The money also gave him the means to bribe the new imperial officials to help let sleeping dogs lie and to keep Maximus' family and his political legacy in Britannia safe.

There was also enough money to ensure the comfortable survival of his cousin, Ursula, who was still in the bishop's household in Colonia. She had been kept safe there when the general Arbogast entered the city. He had never heard of her and had his hands full with dealing with the Franci across the river, so she was not hunted down like Victor had been. She was in any case only very small fry. Now that Conan was dead, she had no immediate prospects of marriage, and wanted none. She could devote herself at last to something that she wanted to do, and that was to bring Martin's faith to the frontier, and, which with her was more to the point, to its women.

*

Elen sat on the seawall at Segontium with Peblig, watching the sun setting in the west. She looked back towards the channel between the mainland and the island of Mona, darkening now, the channel that she had journeyed up with her husband those few years before. She was still in some shock after all that had happened to her and her family, and was once again trying to get to grips with her feelings, trying to find what it had all meant. What had been God's purpose in all this momentous change? What had been the point of her husband's megalomaniac dream?

Elen had been trying not to think about her husband and his gruesome fate, but now that she was here, where it had all started, the memory of all that had passed would not leave her alone. She remembered walking up the path with him just behind where she was sitting now. Had he ever loved her? Had he ever loved anyone but himself? She had come, at the end, to believe that he did love her, as much as he was capable of loving anyone, and she was certain that he had loved her more than he loved anyone else. That was, sadly, not really enough.

Had she loved him? She had to confess that, un-Christian as it was, she had come to loathe him before the end. Did she miss him, though? She had long ago missed the feeling that she loved him, and that had left an emptiness that still hadn't gone away. She missed the way that they had built their family together. He did love his boys, though maybe not very much their girls. But no, she did not miss what he had become. His lust for power had nearly doomed them all. His need to fill what she now saw was a gaping hole at the centre of his being could never have been satisfied. His need for ever more of everything – power, adulation, recognition, money – would always have been insatiable. It had nearly sucked them all down with him. It amazed her that they were all, except for poor Victor, safe.

She kept returning to the same question. What had it all meant? There had to have been some purpose in all this bloodshed and tribulation. Did God not have a plan? Maximus, driven by his growing megalomania, had believed that his dream had shown him that there was some heavenly design in what he was attempting. She no longer believed that her husband had genuinely accepted Christ, but despite that, had God touched him through his dream? Was God using Maximus, this godless, broken reed of a man, as his instrument? It was difficult to believe that God could instigate so much destruction, so much evil, for a good purpose; the idea disturbed her greatly. If God was acting so, this was not the holy Martin's God of love, whom she sought, more like Ambrose's avenging, all powerful and vengeful deity. The idea frightened her.

Peblig sat quietly in the growing dusk, watching his mother's anguish. He put his arm around her shoulders. He was nearly fifteen now, but had grown fast in the last few months. Men were saying that he had the second sight, and he intuited Elen's thoughts now.

"Mother, I think you are seeking God's purpose in what has happened to our family and our land. You find it hard to see."

"You are right, Peblig," Elen replied. "I can't help fearing that everything that has happened to us has been for nothing. I cannot bear it that our family has been the cause of so much pain."

"I think," replied Peblig, "that, for our family, God's plan has yet to be made plain to us. You are not old, Mother, and your children are all, save for Victor, still with us, and we are still young. We have time to make futures in Britannia. All your children are bound up with the peoples whose princes and princesses they have married, so they are truly the future of our land. We cannot know what that future will be, but we can see that our family is flourishing now. I believe it will flourish in the future. I think that must be God's purpose."

Peblig paused to look his mother in the eyes. "As for us, I believe that you and I, Mother, know that we have a heavenly mission, one shown to us by the holy Martin in Gallia. Here in Britannia the bishops are breeding only more Ambroses, both in the cities and in uncle Gadeon's theological college. These people are interested in their own positions in the cities where they live. None of them is taking the word of God to our people in the west and north. No one is trying to help those who live in the countryside. There are still so many in this land who dwell in the darkness of the old religions. We need monasteries like Martin's here in Britannia, to spread the true faith. Those alone will turn the old places of darkness, like Mona over there, into places lit by the light of the Gospels.

"I think, Mother, that this, too, is God's plan, and the more important one. It is what you and I must accomplish. That, I think, is the purpose hidden in all that our father did."

Elen was hugely comforted by what Peblig had said. "I hope that you are right, Peblig," she said. "God has shown me his purposes through my beautiful son. We have come here to save our people. And now we must work out how to do it."

Taking him by the hand, Elen walked them back up to the town. She had a purpose now. She was free at last to hope.

The End

DIGEST OF NAMES AND PLACES

Names

Alamanni – Germans of the middle Rhine.

Aurelius Ambrosius – Roman administrator then Bishop of Milan. Saint Ambrose, Doctor of the Church.

Andragathius – Scythian soldier, Magnus Maximus' *magister militum*.

Antonius Donatus – third son of Magnus Maximus. Known as *Annun*. Prince of the Novantae.

Flavius Arbogast – Frankish soldier, Emperor Valentinian II's *magister militum*.

Atrebates – people of Berkshire and Surrey.

Flavius Aurelianus – Prefect of the Twentieth Legion.

Decimius Magnus Ausonius – writer. Tutor to Emperor Gratian, then Praetorian Prefect. Consul.

Belgae – people of Hampshire and Wiltshire.

Brigantes – people of Yorkshire, Lancashire and Durham.

Caledonii – southern Pictish people.

Cantii – people of Kent.

Conan – Prince of the Dumnonii, nephew to Eudaf Hen, *mare dux* under Magnus Maximus, first British ruler of Armorica, known as *Conan Meriadoc*.

Constantine – fourth son of Magnus Maximus. Known as *Custennin*. Prince of the Selgovae.

Constantine – Moesian soldier. Commander of Magnus Maximus' bodyguard then tribune of a regiment of *scholae*. Friend of Gerontius.

Cornovii – people of Cornwall or people of Powys and west Midlands.

Coriosolites – Gallic tribe on north coast of Armorica.

Damnonii – people of Alt Clut, Dumbarton.

Demetae – people of Demetia/Dyfed.

Desai – Scoti (Irish) tribe settled in Dyfed.

Diviacus – druid of the Dumnonii.

Dobunni – people of Gloucestershire and Worcestershire.

Dumnonii – people of Devon.

Dumnonos – god of the Dumnonii.

Durotriges – people of Dorset and Somerset.

Elen – daughter of Eudaf Hen. Second wife of Magnus Maximus. Empress.

Erbin – Prince of the Dumnonii, nephew to Eudaf Hen, half-brother to Conan and brother to Gadeon.

Eudaf ap Caradog – Prince of the Dumnonii. Known as *hen*, "the old".

Eugenius – Magnus Maximus' second son, known as *Owain Finddu*. Prince of the Silures.

Franci – the Franks, Germanic people inhabiting the northern Rhine area.

Gadeon ap Geraint – Prince of the Dumnonii, nephew to Eudaf Hen, half-brother to Conan, known as *Gadeon Mawr*, and in Armorica as *Gradlon*. Father of Guoremor.

Gerontius – British soldier. Bodyguard to Elen. Commander of the *candidati* for Emperor Magnus Maximus. Friend of Constantine.

Gothi – Germanic people from the east of the Danube frontier.

Gratiana – second daughter of the Emperor Magnus Maximus, wife of Prince Tudwal of Dumnonia.

Flavius Gratianus Augustus – Emperor Gratian. Son of Emperor Valentinian I. Ruler of Gallia, Britannia and Hispania. Half-brother of Emperor Valentinian II.

Guitaul ap Guitolin – Vitalis, Prince of the Cornovii, father-in-law of Severa, father of Vortigern.

Guitolin – Vitalinus, Prince of the Cornovii and Dobunni, father of Guitaul.

Guoremor ap Gadeon, Prince of Dumnonia, father of Tudwal.

Hunni – the Huns, marauding peoples of the Central Asian steppe.

Iceni – people of East Anglia.

Sextus Rusticius Julianus – Gallic businessman and politician. Governor of Valentia.

Justina – wife of Emperor Valentinian I. Mother of Emperor Valentinian II. Dowager Empress.

Juthungi – German tribe from Bavaria.

Magna – first daughter of the Emperor Magnus Maximus, wife of Ennodius.

Martin – Pannonian soldier. Bishop and founder of the first monastery in Gallia. Saint Martin of Tours.

Flavius Magnus Maximus – Spanish soldier. *Dux Britanniarum*, then western Emperor. Known as *Macsen Wledig*.

Merobaudes – Frankish soldier. *Comes domesticorum* to Emperor Gratian.

Miathi – southern Picts in Stirling area.

Novantae – people of Galloway and Carrick, southern Scotland.

Ordovices – people of north Wales.

Picti – the Picts, painted people of Scotland.

Publicus – Magnus Maximus' fifth son, known as *Peblig*. Holy man. Saint.

Pulcher – Roman officer, tribune of the *Segontienses*.

Scoti – the Irish.

Selgovae – people of Kirkcudbright, Scotland's southern coast.

Severa – third daughter of Emperor Magnus Maximus, wife of Vortigern.

Silures – people of Gwent and Glamorgan.

Quintus Aurelius Symmachus – Gallic politician, senator and orator. Urban Prefect of Roma under Emperor Valentinian II.

Flavius Theodosius – Spanish soldier. Father of Emperor Theodosius I, *protector* of Magnus Maximus. Under

Emperor Valentinian I, *comes rei militaris per britanniarum*, suppressor of the Great Barbarian Conspiracy, then *magister equitum*. Executed by Emperor Gratian's officials in Africa.

Flavius Theodosius Augustus I – Spanish soldier. Son of Count Theodosius. Emperor Theodosius I.

Tudwal ap Guoremor – Prince of the Dumnonii, husband of Gratiana.

Ursula – Princess of the Dobunni, intended spouse of Conan Meriadoc.

Flavius Valentinianus Augustus II – Emperor Valentinian II, son of Emperor Valentinian I and Empress Justina. Ruler of Italia, Pannonia and Africa.

Venetii – people of southern Armorica/Brittany.

Vortigern/Gwrtheyrn ap Guitaul – Prince of the Cornovii, husband of Severa.

Votadini – people of the eastern Scottish lowlands and Northumberland.

Places

Achaia	Province in western Greece
Adriatica	Adriatic Sea
Aduatuca Tungrorum	Tongeren

DIGEST OF NAMES AND PLACES

Aemona	Ljubljana
Aleto	Aleth
Alpes	Alps
Alpe Iulia	Julian Alps
Alt Clut	Dumbarton
Aquae Sulis	Bath
Aquitania	Aquitaine
Arbeia	South Shields
Arelate	Arles
Argentovaria	Colmar
Ariminum	Rimini
Armorica	Brittany
Augusta Treverorum	Trier
Augusta Taurinorum	Turin
Bonna	Bonn
Bononia	Boulogne
Bremenium	Rochester, Northumberland

Bretona	British area in Hispania, around Foz
Britannia	Britannia
Britannia Prima	First British province
Brundisium	Brindisi
Burdigalia	Bordeaux
Calcaria	Tadcaster
Calleva Atrebatum	Silchester
Carthago	Carthage
Cilurnum	Chesters
Civitas Turonum	Tours
Clota	River Clyde
Colonia Claudia Ara Agrippinensium	Cologne
Condate Redonum	Rennes
Constantinopolis	Constantinople, Istanbul
Coria	Corbridge

DIGEST OF NAMES AND PLACES

Corinium	Cirencester
Danubius	Danube
Darioritum	Vannes
Demetia	Southwest Wales
Deva, Deva Victrix	Chester
Dubris	Dover
Dumnonia	Devon
Durostorum	Silistria
Durovernum Cantiacorum	Canterbury
Eboracum	York
Ennor	Isles of Scilly
Epirus	Province in northwest Greece
Euxeinos Pontos	Black Sea
Fanum Martis	Corseul
Flavia Caesariensis	The Caesarian Province of Flavius, eastern England
Forum Hadriani	Voorburg

Gallaecia	Galicia
Gallia	Gaul
Gallia Belgica	Gallic province in northern Gallia centred on Trier
Gallia Lugdenensis	Gallic province centred on Lyon
Ganganii	Llyn Peninsula
Genua	Genoa
Germania Inferior	Province of Lower Germany
Glevum Colonia	Gloucester
Grannona	Port-en-Bessin
Gratianopolis	Grenoble
Hadrianopolis	Adrianopolis, Edirne
Hibernia	Ireland
Hispania	Spain
Horrea Classis	Carpow
Hunnum	Halton Chesters
Insulae Sillinae	Isles of Scilly

Illyricum	Praetorian prefecture in Dalmatia and the Balkans
Isca Dumnoniorum	Exeter
Isca Augusta	Caerleon
Isurium Brigantum	Aldborough
Italia	Italia
Letavia	Brittany, Llydaw
Lindum Colonia	Lincoln
Londinium	London
Longovicium	Lanchester
Luguvallium	Carlisle
Lugdunum	Lyon
Lugdunum Batavorum	Katwijk
Lusitania	Province in Portugal and western Hispania
Lutetia	Paris
Maenavia	Isle of Man
Majus Monasterium	Marmoutier

Manau Gododdin	Scottish Lowlands astride the Forth estuary
Mare Gallaecum	Bay of Biscay
Mare Germanicum	North Sea
Massilia	Marseilles
Maxima Caesariensis	The Caesarian Province of Maximus, southeast England
Mediolanum	Milan
Moesia	Provinces in the Balkans, south of the River Danube
Moguntiacum	Mainz
Mona	Anglesey
Mons Matronae	Pass of Mont Genêvre
Moridunum	Carmarthen
Mosella	Moselle/Mosel
Nemausus	Nîmes
Nemetes	Speyer
Noricum	Provinces in Austria and Slovenia

DIGEST OF NAMES AND PLACES

Opitergium	Oderzo
Padus	River Po
Pannonia	Provinces in central Europe south of the River Danube
Pictavium	Poitiers
Pinnata Castra	Inchtuthil
Placentia	Piacenza
Poetovio	Ptuj
Raetia	Province between the Danube and Lombardy, including Switzerland
Rhenus	River Rhine
Rhodanus	River Rhone
Roma	Rome
Rotomagus	Rouen
Rutupiae	Richborough
Sabrina	River Severn
Scythia	The steppes north of the Black Sea

Segontium	Caernarfon
Sirmium	Sremska Mitrovica
Siluria	Gwent
Silva Carbonaria	The Charcoal Forest in Wallonia
Sinus Gallaecum	English Channel
Siscia	Sisak
Thracia	Thrace
Toxiandria	Campine
Usa	River Ouse
Valentia	Fifth British Province
Vallum Aelium	Hadrian's Wall
Vectis	Isle of Wight
Venta Belgarum	Winchester
Venta Silurum	Caerwent
Vetera	Xanten
Vienna	Vienne

Viennensis	Province of southern Gallia
Viroconium	Wroxeter
Virunum	Town on Austria's Zollfeld